THE DARK HISS OF MAGIC

THE CAT LADY CHRONICLES
BOOK TWO

HELEN HARPER

COVER DESIGN BY COVERS BY JUAN

CHAPTER
ONE

I eyed Dave, who was bent over in his garden with the pale crack of his arse visible above his drooping jeans. Although I was reasonably certain that my gorgeously grumpy neighbour had never once bothered to plant anything in his scrap of earth, he was clearly determined to scoop up every soggy leaf that had clumped onto the scrubby grass in front of his house.

'I thought it was considered rude to ogle in these supposedly enlightened days,' he grumbled.

'I can assure you that there is no ogling on my part,' I told him as She Without An Ear wound her way around my legs. 'Not even the tiniest bit.'

He continued as if he hadn't heard me. 'This is what happens when you live on your own for too long. You abandon the bounds of propriety and forget what it's like to be part of polite society. As a result, you can't stop yourself from staring at my pert bottom.'

'Pert?'

Dave straightened up and turned to face me, his scowl deep enough to engrave heavy ridges across his forehead. 'Pert,' he said, swivelling to permit me a profile view. 'And very sexy.' He slapped his rump – but he didn't make any attempt to pull up his jeans.

'I only came out to give you these.' I held up the plate of freshly baked scones, still warm from the oven.

'Last time I ate something you baked, I almost lost a tooth.'

'They're a bit chewy,' I admitted. 'But they're mostly edible.'

Although Dave's scowl grew even more pronounced, he ambled over and took them. 'Thanks.'

I curtsied. 'You're welcome.'

He picked one up and bit into it. It was difficult to judge from his expression what he thought, though he chewed far longer than I reckoned was necessary. Finally he swallowed. 'You are many things, Kit McCafferty,' he grunted, 'but you are not a master baker.'

True: I made a great casserole and I was a dab hand at roasts, but baking had never been my forte. 'If you don't try, you don't improve.'

Scepticism flickered across his face, then he glanced over my shoulder and scowled some more. 'Speaking of ogling...' he murmured.

I turned around and followed his gaze. When I saw who was standing at my garden gate, I jerked in surprise. I hadn't seen Thane, the copper-haired werewolf who'd joined me in rescuing Nick MacTire late last year, for several weeks. I started to smile – then realised that Thane's expression was ravaged and there were black shadows beneath his eyes. 'What's wrong?' I asked in alarm.

A deep growl rumbled from his chest and grew in intensity as he stared at me in disgust. 'You know exactly what's wrong.' He jabbed a finger towards me.

Er, no. No, I didn't.

'This is all your fault.'

I folded my arms. I'd been good lately: I'd not killed anyone; I'd eaten all my greens, and I'd been polite to everyone I met. I was practically a saint. 'What's happened?'

'You.' He glowered. '*You* happened.'

Dave leaned in more closely, fascination lightening his dark eyes. Any second now he'd be getting out the popcorn.

I tried – and failed – to think of anything I'd done that might have offended the lone werewolf. He was a redhead and supposedly they were known for their temper so perhaps I'd inadvertently slighted him and he'd taken umbrage, but I was sure I'd neither said nor done anything. Anyway, I hadn't seen him for ages.

'You'll have to help me out here, Thane. I don't know why you're so upset – but I can see that it's serious,' I added to soothe his ruffled feathers. 'If you tell me, perhaps I can help.'

He clenched his fists. 'Do you have any idea – any idea at all – how difficult it is to sleep when a cat decides to smother you in the middle of the night?'

Ah. Suddenly his attitude was making sense. 'Smother?' I asked, trying to be delicate.

'She tried to sleep on top of my face, Kit. I woke up hyperventilating and with a mouthful of fur.'

I raised my eyebrows. 'You're a werewolf so you must be used to fur. Don't you shed during the full moon?'

'No,' Thane snapped. 'And I don't lie around on stairs waiting to trip people up. Or demand to be fed at half-past four every morning. Or curl up asleep on someone's lap at the very moment they need to go and empty their damned bladder!'

I pressed my lips together. Hard.

'Do you know where she is right now?' he demanded. 'She's asleep on top of my laundry. My *clean* laundry!'

A tiny sound escaped my mouth. 'Mmmmph.'

'She does it deliberately, Kit. She knows *exactly* what she's doing. She's a bloody demon.'

That part was certainly true. When a little ginger kitten had appeared after a grim, bloody summoning and claimed Thane as her own, I'd learned that cats hailed from the netherworld and were indeed demons. It made a lot of sense when you thought about it, though it certainly didn't mean I loved them any less.

'When I came downstairs this morning, there was a dead rat in the middle of my kitchen table! The bastard thing was bigger than she is!'

Good for her. 'It was a present.'

'A present?' Thane's voice rose still further.

'She thinks you need help hunting.'

'I do not need any help from her!' He ripped open his jacket and hoisted up his jumper to reveal a section of his flat stomach. 'Look!' he hissed. 'Look at my skin!'

I peered at the impressive crosshatch of tiny scratches across his equally impressive body. Oh dear. 'Alright,' I conceded with a sigh. 'She can stay with me.'

She Without An Ear whipped up her head and narrowed her eyes at me. 'There's enough space here for a kitten,' I said. Hell, there was *always* space for a kitten.

For some reason that pissed off Thane even more. 'What? You're not taking my cat!'

She Without An Ear allowed herself a small purr of satisfaction.

'I thought that's why you were here,' I said, genuinely confused.

'Tiddles is mine.'

Dave, who was looking totally fascinated as he continued to watch us, leaned over the fence. 'Tiddles?'

'That's her name.'

I sighed. 'I've already told you that cats don't choose their names until they're around six months old.' And no cat would choose to call themselves *Tiddles*.

'I have to call her something, and right now her name is Tiddles.' Thane growled and folded his arms. 'And Tiddles is a hell cat who belongs with me.'

Okay-dokey. 'So are you here because you want to complain about her?'

'No. I need your help – I would have thought that was obvious.'

I frowned. 'Lack of sleep makes you very snippy, Thane,' I informed him.

Dave nodded approvingly. 'She ain't wrong.'

Thane was still glowering. 'In which case, give me some tips to make Tiddles sleep through the night.'

'Easy,' Dave said. 'Shut your bedroom door and don't let her in.'

'Not an option. I tried it once but she threw herself against the door for an hour and yowled loudly enough to be mistaken for a ban sith by my next-door neighbour.'

She Without An Ear's furry body vibrated; I could have sworn she was laughing.

'Besides...' Thane lowered his bright-green eyes to the ground, 'I like it when she sleeps next to me.'

Dave started to back away. 'I'm getting away from you two. I hadn't realised that being a cat lady was contagious.' He spun around, marched up his narrow garden path then disappeared into his house and slammed the door.

I stayed where I was, watching Thane with undisguised amusement. 'Yeah, yeah,' he grunted. 'Laugh it up.'

'It's pretty straightforward. Just tire her out before bedtime. She's a kid – play with her. Get her to chase something – a balled-up piece of paper or a piece of string. And give her a high-protein meal right before bedtime. It's not rocket science. Don't give in if she tries to wake you up during the night, train her to wait until you're ready to get up.'

'You make it sound easy.' He sniffed. 'What sort of high-protein meal?'

'Cooked fish. Salmon, perhaps, or mackerel. You can also get some herbal remedies to keep her calm.'

Thane watched me for a long moment. 'I'll buy you a coffee if you come with me to the market and help me buy what she needs.'

I tilted my head. 'A coffee from Black's?'

'Of course.'

It sounded like a fair deal to me. 'Alright, then. Give me a minute to grab my coat.'

ALTHOUGH THE SKY was a nondescript grey and there was a deep chill in the air, it was the first dry day we'd enjoyed since the New Year so I expected the riverside market to be busy. After the excesses of Christmas, which was celebrated in Coldstream as much as it was in the rest of the country, many families would need to penny-pinch until the end of the month; however, this was one of the cheaper places in Coldstream to shop, and plenty of the regular stalls were still holding seasonal sales.

To my surprise, there were very few shoppers and most of the stallholders seemed to have vanished, too. My feet slowed to a halt and Thane also paused. We glanced at each other. 'Something's not right,' I muttered.

Thane nodded. Even when the weather was at its worst the market was busier than this. I frowned at Natasha's empty stall; the troll butcher never normally left it during market hours but she wasn't there now. The row of stalls opposite also lay empty;

even Trilby, the black-market seller who held plenty of secrets, was conspicuous by their absence.

As an elderly witch shuffled towards us, Thane pulled back his shoulders and started marching towards her. If she was in any way alarmed by his approach, she didn't show it. 'Out of my way, wolf!' she shouted.

'My apologies, ma'am.' He doffed an imaginary cap; no longer the grumpy, sleep-deprived man who'd appeared at my door, he was now the epitome of gentleman-like behaviour. 'I'm sorry to bother you but...'

The witch tutted loudly. 'They think someone's in the river,' she said, clearly understanding why Thane had stopped her. 'Everyone's gone down to help get them out.' She shook her head. 'Stupid, if you ask me. Whoever fell in will already be dead.' She stepped around us and continued on her way without a backward glance. 'It's not the first time someone has died in that damned river,' I heard her mutter. 'And it won't be the last.'

The old woman was right: if somebody had fallen into the River Tweed, there was little chance they'd make it out alive. Forget hypothermia or drowning; there were so many river monsters in its fast-flowing depths that anyone who went for a dip would quickly find they'd become supper.

'We should go down and see if we can help,' I said to Thane.

'I doubt there's anything we can do.' His expression was grim. 'Another couple of rubber-neckers won't be any use.'

I knew what he meant but I stood firm. 'This is my community, Thane. I have to try. These are my people.'

He pulled a face but he didn't disagree further. 'Come on then. We'd better run.'

It didn't take long to locate the large crowd of people. Some were shouting suggestions but most were watching the proceedings quietly, their faces dark and their shoulders hunched.

Thane sucked in a breath. 'Look at those witches,' he said. 'They're casting some sort of spell.'

I could feel the thrum of their magic in the air, and I saw their strained faces when I stood on my tiptoes and gazed over the assembled heads. Maybe there was still hope for whoever had fallen into the river.

Trilby was standing on the riverbank, their eponymous hat perched upon their head. If anyone knew exactly what had happened, it would be them. I marched quickly through the crowd with Thane hot on my heels.

'Good afternoon, Kit,' they said without turning around. 'And wolf.'

How did they do that? How did Trilby know who was behind them? 'Afternoon,' I said. 'What's going on?'

'Someone is in the water. Those witches are deploying every magic spell in their arsenal to keep the river creatures back until the victim is recovered.'

'Alive?' It seemed unlikely.

Trilby shrugged. 'Stranger things have happened.'

I lifted my head and scrutinised the straining witches. Sweat was pouring down their faces. Two of them were on their knees in the thick mud on the edge of the river bank.

I stared harder. I didn't recognise any of them but their clothes – particularly their cloaks embroidered with the golden insignia of their coven – looked expensive. There were three people nearby, none of whom appeared to be witches, who were tying ropes around their waists; they were clearly preparing to plunge into the river in a bid to find the poor bastard who'd gone in. Even with the witches' intervention, it was a bold move. Few people messed with this section of the River Tweed.

'Who is the victim?' I asked carefully.

Trilby's mouth crooked up. 'You're becoming more adept at asking the right questions, Kit. It's Quentin Hightower.'

Thane inhaled sharply and my eyes widened. 'The heir to the Hightower coven?'

'The one and the same.'

Damn. I gazed at the swirling depths then back at the desperate, pained faces of the witches; no wonder they were throwing everything they had into the rescue attempt.

There were numerous covens in Coldstream and it was almost impossible to keep track of them all, but some were better known than others. Everyone knew the Hightowers; they were the richest coven and arguably the most powerful – although the three covens that ran the tram network would disagree. I pursed my lips.

'Did he fall or was he pushed?' Thane asked.

'Another good question,' Trilby murmured. 'I am sure that you've noticed that there's been a great deal of rain lately. It's been terrible for business. And,' they waved a hand, 'it's not done much for the river bank either.'

I leaned forward. Several people were standing around a large muddy section, staring. It was as if something had taken a large bite of the land. Erosion, then; the hapless Mr Hightower had tumbled into the Tweed by accident.

'They should have got him by now,' a druid close by whispered.

'Or at least pulled out his body,' said another. 'It's been several minutes. Not even a witch can hold their breath for that long.'

I stared again at the dark, churning water.

'They're using a subduing spell on the river monsters, right?' Thane asked.

Trilby nodded. 'They are, but it won't hold for long. And,'

they added pointedly, 'with all the recent rain, those river currents are strong.' They paused then added, 'Well, Kit?'

I clenched my jaw; I understood what they were alluding to. '*You're* still here,' I pointed out.

'I have no interest in playing hero. You're our local waif saviour. Here.' They reached into their pocket and drew out a small, white-linen bag. 'This might help you.'

My belly tightened as I took it. The decision had already been made.

'Good luck,' Trilby whispered.

Yeah, yeah. My fingers closed around the bag then I turned and started to push my way through the crowd.

TWO

I heard Thane's shout but I didn't bother to turn my head. As soon as I was free from the press of people I started sprinting, following the course of the river away from the market and down towards the Glebe. I made sure to use the footpath rather than stray too close to the water; if one section of the bank could collapse so could others, and I wasn't one for tempting fate.

Initially I tried to avoid the puddles but it was a wasted effort; I gave up and simply ran as quickly as I could. My trousers and coat were soon splattered with mud and so was my face. I didn't bother wiping it away; it would all be washed off soon enough.

'Kit!' Thane's voice was closer. 'Wait! What are you doing?'

I didn't pause; surely he realised that time was of the essence. Instead I ducked my head and passed under the narrow stone bridge that marked the unofficial boundary between Danksville and the Glebe. The warehouses of the construction crews who made their home in this part of the city were ahead but I ignored them in favour of the section of the river that curved to the south. It was deeper here than it was by the market, and the sharp bend meant that the currents were very different.

I made a beeline for an old wooden bench that overlooked the water. I'd already kicked off my shoes and was yanking off my coat when Thane reached me. 'What the fuck?' he demanded.

I didn't answer; I simply turned to the river and examined its dark, oily surface.

'Kit!'

I exhaled suddenly. 'Look.'

'I don't—' Thane's voice faltered. A beat later, the head that had briefly emerged from the water disappeared again. 'Wait,' he said. 'Was that...?'

I nodded as I tugged at the drawstring on the little bag Trilby had given me and sprinkled its dusty contents down my body. Then I braced myself.

'You're not going in, are you?' Thane asked with genuine horror.

I flashed him a tight grin. 'Let's hope that the subduing magic those witches are casting is strong enough to reach this far – I don't want to be eaten.' A beat later, I jumped into the river.

I was expecting it to be cold but nothing can prepare you for the shock of icy water during a Scottish winter. The sudden chill ripped through my body, juddering my bones, and my heart stuttered from the abrupt change in temperature. Time seemed to stand still and the thought that I'd made a lethal mistake flashed through my head.

Then my limbs remembered how to move and I started to kick through the murky depths. I forced my eyes to stay open, although I couldn't see much beyond a foot or two in front of my face. Detritus swirled past me and I felt the currents tug at my body, but at least here their strength had subsided enough for me to swim against them. I stretched my hands in front of me, searching blindly for a body. Quentin Hightower was somewhere around here: I'd seen him.

As I swam deeper, my vision became more obscured. I didn't know exactly what was in the bundle of bespelled herbs that Trilby had given me, but I knew they were giving me time. Although I couldn't breathe underwater, the magic bound up in them was suspending the natural order and allowing me longer to search before I needed to swim up for air. It would have been helpful if Trilby had provided me with a torch at the same time; this was akin to searching for a teardrop in the damned ocean.

The tips of my fingers brushed against something but it was too cold to tell whether it was a branch, a bag or a body. I reached out and tried to grab whatever it was, but despite my best efforts it slipped out of my grasp. My body shuddered, and even with Trilby's concoction my lungs began to burn. I twisted and kicked hard for the surface.

As soon as I broke free, I gasped in air. My eyes stung painfully from whatever crap had been swirling around; more worryingly, shivers were wracking my body. I wasn't made for swimming – I was a cat sith, not a bloody mermaid. Maybe I couldn't do this; maybe I wasn't strong enough to find Hightower.

'There, Kit! Over there!' Thane was on the edge of the riverbank, jumping up and down and pointing.

I forced myself to turn, feeling more sluggish with every second that passed. There was no obvious sign of Quentin Hightower but there was a faint dappling across the surface of the water that looked unnatural.

Ignoring the foul taste in my mouth I swallowed, then swam hard for the spot. I heaved in another breath and dived once more. There. Something was there. *Somebody* was there.

I threw every ounce of energy I had into the swim and

reached out until I grabbed something with my frozen hands. I told my fingers to dig in, to wrap themselves around whatever I'd caught; it was an arm, I was sure of it. I tightened my hold then twisted and headed for the surface again, dragging the heavy weight of the witch's body with me.

Move, Kit, I told myself. Kick harder. Swim, for fuck's sake. I closed my eyes against the murk and gave it everything I had; seconds later, my head emerged from the water - and this time I wasn't alone.

Quentin Hightower lolled against me; at least he wasn't trying to fight me in that instinctive way that drowning people often do. There was no fight left in him. Hell, I wasn't even sure he was alive. I had to get him out of the water as quickly as possible. There was every chance he needed CPR.

'Kit!' Thane shouted. 'Here!' Something whacked the top of my head, sending a burst of pain through my skull. 'Shit. Sorry!'

I shook away the hurt. Thane had thrown a branch, the end of which had smacked into me with agonising force. I hissed and turned my head. It appeared that he wasn't trying to kill me because he was holding the end of the branch and pointing wildly towards it. He wanted to drag me in, to drag both of us in.

I gasped with relief and reached for it with my left hand. 'Pull, Thane! Now!' I'd meant to yell but my voice was little more than a croak. Thane heard me, though, and understood. He hauled hard on the branch while I tried to kick my legs to help, but Quentin Hightower's limp body got in the way. I was forced to stay still until Thane's strength pulled us both to the river bank and his hands reached for me.

'No,' I gasped. 'The witch first.' I pushed Hightower up and Thane grabbed hold of him, his fingers snagging the wet fabric of the witch's shirt. He hauled him onto dry land and turned him onto his back. Hightower's lips were blue and his chest wasn't moving.

'Fuck.' Thane tilted back the witch's head and checked his airway then immediately started pumping his chest, the heel of his hands pressing in a steady rhythm. Push, push, push, push.

I swung one leg out of the water and reached for a clump of long grass to pull myself out. Thane was still performing chest compressions. Push, push, push, push, push. He leaned over the witch's mouth and prepared to give him two rescue breaths, but he'd barely lowered his head when Hightower choked and water dribbled from his lips.

He was alive. He would make it.

My body sagged with relief – and then something sharp and brutally painful sank into my ankle. A heartbeat later, I was being pulled back into the water.

I didn't know what had grabbed hold of me but I did know that I was in serious danger. The water here was neither my natural environment nor my friend. If I were to survive, I had to act quickly.

The river beastie went for the easy option. With its teeth still latched onto my lower leg, it dragged me underneath, clearly hoping for a simple drowning before it could enjoy a tasty, filling meal of foolish cat lady.

I held my breath as I went under then immediately lashed out with my unencumbered foot and kicked as hard as I could. Although the beast's grip on my ankle loosened, it didn't let go. I kicked again, and again. I had to get free.

Thankfully, the third time was the charm.

As soon as the river monster wrenched away its sharp teeth, agonising bolts of pain flashed up my leg. I tensed. Pain was good; pain told me I was still alive. I had enough experience to swallow it down until I could safely attend to the wound.

As I spun in the water and prepared to head for the surface

again, something else grabbed me. I thought at first that the same beastie was back for more, then a watery image of Thane's face swam into view. He gripped my arms and started to tug me upwards.

The idiotic werewolf had jumped into the water to help, but he'd put himself in the same mortal danger that I faced. The aquatic monsters were having a great day: two for the price of one. With the blood pouring from my ankle, there would soon be dozens of the toothy bastards, regardless of the spells those witches were casting upstream.

When we surfaced, Thane offered me a tight grin. 'You tool!' I growled. He obviously hadn't seen the ripples indicating that another creature was almost upon us.

I curled my hand into a fist, lashed out underwater and connected with something hard and slimy. I had no idea what part of this new beast I'd hit but I knew we only had seconds to get out of the Tweed.

'Swim,' I told Thane as a silvery fin advanced from the left. It wouldn't be a shark. Not here. It would be something far scarier. 'Now!'

We reached the bank in record time. Thane pulled himself out easily but my fingers couldn't get a handhold in the mud. With every second that passed, I expected to feel another set of jaws sinking into my flesh.

Thane, who'd rolled clear of the river's edge, pulled me out. Thank fuck for that. I pushed myself away from the water and collapsed on my back, my chest heaving as I gulped in mouthfuls of blessed air. 'Remind me never to try anything like that ever again,' I gasped.

'If I thought you'd listen to my advice, Kit, I'd have told you never to try anything like this in the first place.'

That was fair. 'At least tell me that Quentin Hightower is alright.'

Thane didn't answer and my belly tightened as I heaved myself up into a sitting position. There was no sign of the witch. 'Where is he?'

Thane pointed to the path that led to the market. Somewhat belatedly, I spotted the muddy footprints leading away from us. 'He went that way.'

'Without saying thank you?'

His lip curled. 'Without saying anything.'

THREE

T hane ripped off a section of his shirt to bandage the wound on my ankle. There was a lot of blood; I would need more than the contents of my magical medication cupboard to tend to it properly. Still, the worst of the pain had subsided to a dull throb and I hobbled along the path without Thane's help. We were both dripping wet, however, and I was shivering.

'How did you know?' he asked as we trudged back. 'How did you know he had drifted all the way to that spot?'

That was easy. 'The other witches assumed his powers kicked in the moment he fell in the water and that he'd have used magic to anchor himself in place. They weren't thinking about the shock that you feel when you hit cold water even when you're expecting it. The currents there are strong. While the witches were concentrating on holding back the monsters, Hightower would already have been dragged away by the river.'

Thane frowned. 'But how did you know to go to that spot in particular?'

When I didn't answer immediately his frown deepened, then his expression cleared. 'Oh. I see.'

'I only ever had two assassination contracts in Danksville,' I said quietly. 'I won't tell you who I killed there, so don't ask. The first one was a simple stabbing in the street and her corpse was meant to be discovered. The second one was supposed to disappear without a trace.'

'So you threw him into the Tweed.'

'I killed him first.' My tone of voice was matter of fact rather than proud. 'I made it swift *then* I threw him in the Tweed. I had to ensure his body wouldn't reappear because I couldn't rely on the river monsters – their behaviour was out of my control. First I ran a series of tests on the currents, then I placed a tracker on his corpse to double-check his location.'

'He ended up in the same spot as Quentin Hightower?'

'He did.' I wrapped my arms around myself. I wasn't sure I'd ever feel warm again. 'There wasn't much of him left after the bloodthirsty denizens of the Tweed had done what they were supposed to do. But I had to be sure.'

I waited for the next questions: *Did he deserve to die? Did I feel any guilt about what I'd done? Would I do it again if I had to?* But Thane only nodded and lapsed into silence. I sneaked a glance at his face. He didn't look judgmental; he didn't look anything other than wet and cold.

Normal service hadn't yet resumed at the market, and the stalls were still devoid of vendors and shoppers. Everyone was gathered in the centre while Quentin Hightower stood on a wooden crate and addressed the crowd. Huh.

'I have faced death this day!' he bellowed with all the verve of an evangelical preacher. 'I faced death and,' he paused for dramatic effect, 'I kicked its arse!'

We stopped at the edge of the crowd. 'He's not lost for words now,' I muttered to Thane.

His mouth flattened. 'Apparently not.'

Hightower's dark eyes roved the crowd as if searching for

something – or someone. A vague itch was bothering the back of my mind; there was something odd about him that I couldn't identify, a tension in his voice that didn't appear related to his near-death experience.

'Several of the river monsters came for me with their teeth gnashing and their fins flapping,' the wet witch shouted. 'They were hungry for my blood – they wanted to rip the flesh from my bones.'

His gaze landed on me but his expression didn't alter a jot. 'I was determined they wouldn't touch me. I fought them every inch of the way and I emerged victorious!' He pumped the air with his fist. 'Nobody can match the strength and power of a Hightower witch! Not even a bottom-feeding monster with teeth the size of an ogre's skull can defeat me!'

Thane scratched his chin. 'Interesting,' he muttered. 'He seems to be omitting the part where he had to be rescued by a middle-aged woman covered in cat hair.'

'You took a dip in the River Tweed,' I said. 'And you were covered in cat hair, too.'

He smirked, then drew breath as if he were planning to publicly challenge Quentin Hightower's version of events. 'Don't,' I said in a low voice. 'It's easier for me if people don't know what happened.' I wanted to keep a low profile.

'He's lying, Kit.'

'We know the truth.' I gazed at Hightower. 'And so does he, deep down.'

Thane's expression darkened. My desire to stay under the radar of the folks in Danksville – and as a result allow Hightower to proclaim himself a conquering hero who could fight the depths of the River Tweed in ways that few other people could – clearly didn't sit well with him.

'It's not a problem,' I said firmly. 'Come on. I need to go home and get out of these wet clothes.'

A voice floated towards my ear. 'You'll catch pneumonia long before you get to your street. So will the wolf.'

I turned to Trilby; they were holding out two steaming cups. Bless them. I didn't ask what it was, I simply drained the contents of one of them in three gulps, revelling in the heat as it spread through my body. Thane took the other cup and did the same. 'Thank you,' he said. 'This is delicious.'

Trilby smiled. 'It's my own personal recipe and it's an excellent remedy for hypothermia.' They held out two blankets that were draped over their arm. 'You'll need these, too.'

'You're amazing,' I said gratefully.

'You've known that for a while, Kit,' they said.

True. I handed them the cup. 'It's worth saying aloud.'

Trilby's smile widened. 'Always.'

Quentin Hightower had clambered down from his makeshift pulpit and was making his way through the crowd. People were slapping him on the back and calling out congratulations; it was rare for someone to fall into the Tweed and recover, so they wanted some of his good luck to rub onto them. Either that or they wanted to bask in the glorious gaze of such a heroic and noble figure. Given my past exploits, I was hardly in a position to judge him or them.

As I turned away, I caught sight of four bobbing red hats moving through the stalls. I shivered – and this time it had nothing to do with the cold. 'Somebody called the Redcaps?' I asked.

They were marching towards us with their familiar body-collection wagon between them. They were dressed in uniform: black double-breasted suits and black shirts. Their shiny buttons were black and the long canes they were carrying were black. The only splash of colour on Coldstream's collectors of the dead were their blood-red caps. For some reason, I always found those hats particularly gruesome.

The Redcaps performed a vital service. They removed dead bodies deftly, were professional in their approach and compassionate with shocked family members, but they unnerved me in ways I couldn't explain. Maybe it was because they were the ones who'd cleared up the messes I'd made in my previous line of work. Their job felt too close to mine.

'They were called in before Hightower's death was confirmed?' I asked Trilby.

'Ah.' They took off their hat and bowed their head to acknowledge the undertakers' approach. 'I don't know who called them, but they won't be here for Mr Hightower. They must be here for the other body.'

Thane and I stared at them. 'What other body?'

'Quentin Hightower didn't die in the Tweed today,' Trilby said quietly. 'But unfortunately somebody else did.'

THANE APPEARED to have had enough of brushes with death for one day. He left of his own accord, squelching his way out of the market with his wet clothes moulded to his body and an unappealing tangle of gloopy river weeds trailing behind his left shoe.

I should have done the same; I knew that the sensible thing to do was to go straight home, change my clothes and head for a clinic to get my ankle wound seen to properly. Curiosity got the better of me, however, and instead I limped to the river's edge to watch the Redcaps in action. It felt horribly unfair that Hightower had survived his encounter with the Tweed while another nameless victim had not.

There was no crowd this time, and no concerned onlookers: the victim was already dead and there was no exciting rescue operation to watch. A few morbidly curious people hung around but their interest was detached and without the energy I'd witnessed after Quentin Hightower had fallen in.

The white sheet covering the corpse made identification impossible but I suspected that the victim possessed neither wealth, power nor the minor celebrity of a Hightower witch. Whoever the poor bastard was they were not considered important, but I knew from my own experience that somebody would care about what had happened to them. Somebody would be missing a friend, a family member or a loved one.

Under other circumstances I might have minded my own business but the effort I'd put into rescuing Quentin Hightower while not realising that somebody else was also in the river made me feel that I was already involved. I wasn't ready to plod home and forget about what had happened.

Asking for permission to examine the corpse was asking to be denied, so I straightened my spine, pretended I wasn't wearing river-sodden clothes and an old blanket, and marched towards it. I bent down and pulled back the white sheet, ignoring the astonished stares from the four Redcaps who were preparing the wagon a few metres away.

'Oi!' one of them barked. 'What are you doing?'

I ignored the shout and gazed at the slack face in front of me. It was a man, probably in his late twenties. His wet hair was a dirty-blond colour, although I suspected it would be lighter when it was dry. His dark-brown eyes were open and already had the fixed glaze of death. A thin red line across his chin indicated an old scar.

I didn't recognise him; despite my good memory for faces, I couldn't recall ever seeing this slack face at the market. I peered more closely at the bite marks on the right-hand side of his cheek and the ravaged flesh around his neck. His body was surprisingly intact, suggesting that he'd fallen in not long before Quentin Hightower and had received the same magical protection from the river beasties' sharp teeth.

The Redcap who'd shouted at me stomped forward. 'Who are you?'

I straightened up and gave a professional smile. 'Kit McCafferty.' I extended a hand, only belatedly realising that there was a streak of dark sticky mud that stretched from my ring finger to my elbow. The Redcap declined to shake it.

I dropped my arm. 'Who are *you*?' I asked with a false air of authority to stave off any further questions and encourage him to believe that I was supposed to be here.

'Fitz,' he said. 'Fitz Williams.'

'And you're transporting the body to the Resthaven Mortuary?'

He shook his head. 'Mathers Street.'

That gave me pause. The Mathers Street establishment was some distance away and Resthaven was far closer. 'The victim is from that area?' I asked.

'We don't know where he's from. That's where we've been ordered to take him.' Williams' eyes narrowed suspiciously and he folded his arms. 'Are you with the *Coldstream Courier*?'

'No. I'm not a journalist,' I said pleasantly.

My answer didn't put him at ease. 'Do you know who he is?' He nodded at the body.

I jerked my head in what could have been construed as a nod but Williams wasn't fooled. 'You need to step aside.' He sniffed. 'We've got a job to do and we don't need you getting in our way.'

I stayed where I was. 'Do *you* know who he is?' I countered.

Williams had had enough. His eyes narrowed and he raised a small silver cone that was dangling around his neck to his nose to inhale its contents. It was a nosegay, probably a useful tool of the trade when you were dealing with the dead. I wouldn't know; I'd never stuck around my own crime scenes long enough to worry about malodorous corpses.

'Step aside.' He yanked the white sheet across the poor man's face, then he and his companions lifted the body onto the wagon with practised ease. They turned it in the opposite direction and trundled off.

As I watched them go, I wondered if I should have played it differently and acted less like a professional. Although the Redcaps weren't pushovers, they were experienced at dealing with distraught family members and I might have learned more if I'd put on a display of grief. I wasn't a particularly skilled liar, though, and pretending to be a grieving relative wasn't exactly respectful.

I glanced at the few remaining onlookers. A few looked slightly nauseous but none of them were overly upset. 'Do you know who that was?' I called. They all shook their heads.

'Never seen him before in my life,' a tall druid answered.

'Was he with Quentin Hightower?'

There were a few uncertain shrugs. Hmmm. I pulled Trilby's blanket tighter. If the victim had any identification in one of his pockets, somebody from the Magical Enforcement Team, the MET, would inform his family. Probably.

My shoulders sagged. The poor man was already dead. There was nothing I could to do save him. Not now.

FOUR

'I shouldn't have to tell a woman of your age not to go swimming in the Tweed,' the doctor told me as he cleaned the wound on my ankle. 'You're lucky to have escaped with your life.'

I wondered if I'd ever reach a point where medical professionals stopped lecturing me. Probably not. I felt a glimmer of nostalgia for the days when I used to limp into the EEL doctor's office after I'd completed a contract and be forced to listen to an hour of finger wagging about how I ought to engage in less risky behaviour. That had been easy for her to say when she wasn't an assassin, and she'd never listened when I'd tried to point out that risky behaviour came with the job.

'Quentin Hightower might be capable of surviving a dip in that river,' the well-meaning doctor said. 'But we're not all high-powered witches like him.'

I gazed at him. 'Oh yes,' he said. 'What happened to Mr Hightower is all over the city. He did incredibly well to escape.'

'What about the man who didn't escape?'

The doctor looked at me blankly. 'Huh?'

'Another man fell into the river. He didn't make it.'

'Today?'

I nodded. The doctor shrugged. 'First I've heard of it.' He glowered at me. 'But it's proof that you should avoid the river at all costs. Given half a chance, the beasts in there will eat you alive. And I'll be amazed if this wound isn't infected.'

He handed me a small glass bottle. 'Keep the bandages clean and dry, and take three drops of this every day for the next week. If there's any discolouration around the bite mark or it's not healed by next week, come back to see me.' He affected a fatherly expression that didn't suit him, given he was at least decade younger than me. 'And don't go swimming in that river again!'

Yeah, yeah. I pocketed the medicine and headed out with only a slight limp, making a mental note to look for a different clinic next time I needed professional help. There was only so much finger wagging a grown woman could take.

The sky was growing dim and a few splatters of cold rain were falling; so much for that dry spell. I turned up my collar. I'd gone home, taken a hot shower and changed my clothes before visiting the doctor, but even with my fluffiest jumper and the afterglow of whatever concoction Trilby had given me, I still felt cold. The river's chill had wrapped around my bones and was refusing to let go.

I decided that some chicken broth from the delicatessen on Anstey Crescent would sort me out. The hedge witch who ran the little shop had a way with magical herbs that worked wonders at this time of year. A brisk march would also help me to warm up. Win-win.

There was only a small queue inside the shop. As I waited, I eyed the cold meats and cheeses in the glass cabinet at the counter and tried to remember what food was in my fridge at home.

'I think he's single right now,' the young woman in front of me murmured to her friend.

'Didn't he used to go out with that tram witch? The pretty one from the Dalmeny coven?'

'Yeah, but they split up last year. Ex or not, I bet she's devastated that he almost died.'

'It would take more than a bit of water and a few river beasties to kill Quentin.'

'He's a Hightower. He might be an airhead but he's still got plenty of magic at his fingertips. Maybe next time *I'll* fall into the Tweed when he's nearby and he can rescue me.'

I rolled my eyes as her friend giggled.

'It would be *such* a tragedy if he'd been killed.'

'Thank goodness he wasn't. He might not be the brightest witch in the coven, but that handsome face deserves better.'

There was a loud snicker. 'So does that gorgeous Hightower body.'

I cleared my throat but neither woman turned around. 'You know,' I said in an overly loud voice, 'somebody *was* killed in that river today. Somebody *did* die.'

The first woman glanced over her shoulder. 'Oh really? That's a shame.'

'Yes,' I said. 'A real tragedy.'

She blinked at me earnestly. 'I heard,' she said in a conspiratorial voice, 'that Quentin was actually bitten by a few of those river monsters before he managed to get out, and that he was dragged half a mile down the river. He could have *drowned*.'

I gritted my teeth. 'He's fine. But the other man is dead.'

She clicked her tongue in vague sympathy and turned back to her companion. 'So what are your plans for Saturday?' she asked.

I tried to tune out their chatter. There was no point getting annoyed that Hightower was garnering all the attention; he was the minor celebrity whom everyone had heard of, and it was next to impossible to quench local gossip when mildly famous people were involved.

Nobody knew the name of the other man who'd died. I reminded myself that the body now lying in the Mathers Street mortuary wasn't there because of me. I'd fulfilled my good deed quota by saving Quentin Hightower.

The bell above the door jangled as another customer walked in. 'Ms McCafferty,' a smooth voice murmured. 'This is a pleasant surprise. How are you?'

I turned to see Alexander MacTire, alpha werewolf of the MacTire pack. I managed a smile while the two women in front of me goggled. MacTire was as well known in Coldstream as Quentin Hightower; any second now they'd be asking for his autograph. 'Fine,' I said. Mostly. 'Yourself?'

'Hunky-dory.'

I checked behind him and realised he was alone. 'Out shopping?' I asked. 'Don't you have minions to do that sort of thing for you?'

He grinned easily. 'I like to mix with you mortals on occasion. It helps to keep me grounded. Sometimes I dress myself, too, instead of waiting for my servants to help me into my clothes.' He winked. 'That's the sort of down-to-earth werewolf leader I am.'

I snorted. 'How's Nick?' MacTire's young nephew had stayed with me briefly – very briefly, because he'd been kidnapped after his first few nights. It hadn't been a joyful experience for him or for me.

'Nicholas is good. I'm sure he'd like to see you at some point. Maybe you should come around and say hello.'

'Sure,' I said in that polite manner of someone who would never do such a thing. A tiny smile played around MacTire's mouth as he recognised the very British nature of my response.

He changed the subject. 'I heard what happened at the Danksville river market today. I also heard that you were involved.'

He was disturbingly well-informed. 'Not according to Quentin Hightower.'

'I know what Hightower is like,' MacTire said. 'There were reports of you and Barrow appearing in soaking wet clothes not long after he did.'

There were several responses I could have made but I elected to say nothing. MacTire already knew too much; he didn't need any information from me to fill in the gaps.

'I also heard that there was another victim,' he went on.

The two young women in front of me were now being served, their attention finally pulled away from the werewolf in favour of the delights of the delicatessen. I sighed. 'Not many other people have.'

MacTire quirked an eyebrow. 'Are you surprised? There are plenty of anonymous deaths in Coldstream.' His smile returned. 'You should know that better than anyone.'

Yeah, yeah. Alexander MacTire knew what I used to do for a living because he'd hired me to kill his father.

'It's not fair,' he continued, interpreting my expression correctly. 'But it is the way of things.'

The pale face of the unnamed corpse flashed into my mind again. 'It shouldn't be.' I looked at the front of the queue. What the hell was I doing here, standing in a shop? If I was planning to wait around for other people to change the world, I'd be waiting a long time.

Whoever had died in the Tweed deserved better than an anonymous burial. The least I could do was ensure his name was revealed and his family were informed. It wasn't as if I were still an assassin. It might be fun to play the good guy for a change.

I stepped aside. 'You can have my spot. There's something I need to do.' I nodded at him. 'Thank you, Mr MacTire.'

He grimaced. 'Alexander, please.'

'Alexander.' I raised a hand in farewell and walked out of the shop.

Calculating where the nearest tram stop was located and how I could get to the Mathers Street mortuary with the fewest complications, I turned left. Before I'd taken three steps, the bell on the deli door behind me jangled again.

'Wait,' MacTire said. 'Before you go, Kit, I'd like to ask you out to dinner.'

Say what? I turned my head to stare at the werewolf alpha. 'You've already thanked me for what happened with Nick. It's water under the bridge.'

'That's not why I want to have dinner with you.' He smiled disarmingly. Damn, he was good-looking. 'I'd like to take you out on a date. Hearts, flowers.' He spread out his arms. 'The whole shebang.'

I couldn't have been more surprised if Quentin Hightower had appeared out of nowhere and thanked me for saving his life. 'Uh...'

Amusement danced in the werewolf's eyes. 'I'll have you home by midnight. I promise.'

I crossed my arms over my chest then immediately uncrossed them. Don't be awkward, Kit, I told myself. It doesn't suit you.

'Aren't you supposed to be searching for a mate so you can continue the MacTire line?' I asked.

It wasn't a given that any of Alexander MacTire's progeny would rise to the vaulted position of alpha, but there was still pressure on him to settle down and reproduce. One of his own werewolves had tried to spike his coffee with magical Viagra to encourage his – er – inner lust.

He didn't attempt to deny it. 'I am.'

'I'm not a werewolf.'

'I am aware of that fact.' He showed me his teeth. 'I've decided to extend my search beyond my lupine kinsfolk.'

'I'm a committed cat lady, Mr MacTire.'

'I've already told you to call me Alexander,' he said. 'And I like cats.'

'I don't want kids. Even if I did, by this point I'd be considered a geriatric mother.'

He laughed. 'I'm only asking you out to dinner. Let's not get ahead of ourselves.'

I gave him a long look.

'Let's say for argument's sake that we hit it off. You know the worst things about me, Kit, and I know the worst things about you.' He took a step towards me. 'And there's a frisson of attraction between us.'

Was there? He *was* good looking, but I still wasn't convinced.

'I'm not a spring chicken myself,' MacTire continued. 'If I settle down with a life partner, my pack will stop complaining and in a year or two I can name Nicholas as my heir. Anything that happens after that is up to him, but at least the baying hounds will be silenced.'

He'd put a lot more thought into this than I'd expected.

'But,' he added, 'as I said, all I'm doing right now is asking you out for dinner. Let's have a bit of fun and see where it takes us.' His eyes glinted again; I had the feeling it was something he practised. 'You might enjoy yourself.'

Stranger things had happened and I couldn't think of a decent reason to say no. I pursed my lips; I had nothing to lose and, if nothing else, it would be an interesting evening. 'Alright,' I said slowly.

'Friday night? I can pick you up.'

'In that monstrous car of yours? No thanks. I'll meet you.'

MacTire didn't look offended; if anything, he was even more amused. 'Fine. Do you like Italian food?'

Who didn't? 'Sure.'

'Vallese, then? Eight o'clock?'

I stared. 'Don't you have to book that place months in advance?'

'Kit,' he said, 'I'm Alexander MacTire.'

I sniffed. 'It must be nice to be important.'

He grinned. 'Sometimes it definitely is. Are we on?'

What the hell. 'Friday night, eight o'clock, Vallese. I'll be there.'

'I'm looking forward to it already,' he murmured. He half-bowed and went back inside the deli, leaving me on the street wondering what on earth I'd agreed to.

FIVE

As I'd said to Alexander MacTire, sometimes it was nice to be important. It was now my mission to make the anonymous victim of the River Tweed important enough to be dealt with appropriately, and I wouldn't allow anyone to get in my way, not even the prim, bespectacled receptionist at the Mathers Street mortuary.

'We only permit family members to enter the mortuary and view bodies,' she said, tapping her pen against her desk in an incredibly irritating fashion.

I held my ground. 'Unless anything has changed in the last two hours, this body doesn't have a name and nobody knows who his family are,' I said. 'So your point is moot.'

'As is yours,' she replied. 'Because it means that you're not his family either.'

I leaned in closer and lowered my voice. 'How much? How much will it take for you to let me in?'

Her brown eyes narrowed. 'Are you seriously trying to bribe a Coldstream council employee?'

I considered my answer – and the receptionist's well-worn clothes. There was an expensive-looking silk scarf around her neck and a delicate silver bracelet around her wrist, but the rest of her clothes, while clean, were definitely threadbare in several places. 'Yes.'

Her lipsticked mouth tightened as her narrow gaze swept me up and down; I had the sense that even her ash-blonde up-do was quivering with hearty disapproval. Then she blinked and gave me a one-word response. 'Hundred.'

My wallet was out before she could change her mind. Unlike the rest of the country, Coldstream was mostly a cash-based society and I had enough notes on me to cover the bribe. I hastily passed over five twenties. 'Third room on the left,' she said.

I didn't bother thanking her; the money had done that for me.

I walked briskly down the hallway past several framed certificates and commendations. I couldn't fathom why they were displayed so proudly on the walls because the dead wouldn't care and their families wouldn't notice. Then again, EEL had given me a titanium-coated curved dagger when I'd successfully completed my first twenty contracts and I still loved it. Perhaps a gilt-framed piece of paper counted for the same when you worked in this sort of environment – and it was better than pictures of dead bodies.

I located the correct door and went inside without knocking. The sterile room was exactly what I'd expected. The floor was tiled, with a drain in one corner for easy cleaning. The far wall was taken up with aluminium lockers, which contained all the bodies currently in residence. There was a small desk with an empty clipboard resting on top and, in the centre of the room, there was a gurney with a body that had been covered with a white sheet. Next to it was a trolley containing the gleaming, albeit somewhat gruesome, implements of the pathologist's trade.

Another clipboard was hanging on a hook on the wall and I peered at it, noting the names, signatures and time stamps next to each one. It was some sort of sign-in sheet, and it didn't help me. My John Doe hadn't been here long enough and nobody knew who he was.

I turned away from the clipboard, moved to the gurney and pulled back the sheet – only to be greeted by the heavy, grey features of a deceased troll. From the white hairs around the ears and on top of the flat skull, this particular one had died at a ripe old age; it was good to be reminded that even in Coldstream such a thing was possible.

I returned the sheet to its original position and headed for the lockers, shivering slightly. I'd only just started to feel warm again and now I was walking around in what was essentially a giant fridge. At least it would encourage me to complete my investigations quickly.

The first locker was empty. The second one contained a middle-aged female druid who didn't look much older than me, so I closed the door quickly. There was another troll inside the third locker, although this poor guy was far younger than the larger one on the gurney.

'Sorry,' I whispered to his slack face and drooping moustache. 'I know it's not fair this has happened to you.'

I was reaching for the fourth locker when the door opened and a thin man walked in. His blue facial tattoos identified him as a druid and his white coat told me he was supposed to be there even though he looked far too young to be a trained pathologist. Perhaps he was an assistant, or perhaps I was now of an age where everyone looked young. Both were equally possible.

I stopped and waited for him to notice me. When he did, his reaction was more resigned than surprised. 'Who are you?' he asked. He sounded neither challenging nor outraged, which concerned me even more than the receptionist's stern façade had done.

Figuring I had nothing to lose, I opted for the truth. 'My name is Kit McCafferty.' Usually I wouldn't have volunteered any more information than what was requested, but I sensed that a more detailed explanation might help. 'I'm here because of the John Doe who was brought in earlier today. He died in the River Tweed close to where I live. I have the feeling that nobody will take the time to find out who he really is if I don't. Nobody deserves to die like that. I want to find his identity and let his family know what happened to him.'

The young druid gazed at me for so long that I started to feel uncomfortable. When he spoke again, his voice was so quiet I had to strain to hear him. 'Kit would have sufficed.'

So much for all that extra detail.

His face had softened and his expression suggested that, despite his words, he wanted to ask me more. 'You were at the Tweed today? You saw him die?'

'No, I didn't witness it. By the time I arrived he was already dead, but I still feel involved somehow. I still want to help.' I shrugged to indicate that I knew my reaction was inexplicable – but it was the right thing to do.

The druid sighed then moved past me to the desk, opened a drawer and took out two brown manila files. He examined the first one for a moment before holding it out to me. 'Here. We're, um, backed up and short-staffed. His post-mortem won't be conducted until later in the week but these notes were made when his body was brought in.'

I didn't move and he waved the folder. 'Do you want it or not?'

I scurried forward and took it. 'You won't kick me out?' I asked. 'Call the MET and have me arrested?'

'The MET have better things to do with their time. You're

not here to steal or desecrate any bodies.' He looked down at the floor. 'You're here because you're trying to do a good thing. I can get behind that.'

It wasn't what I'd been expecting but I'd take it. I looked at him more closely and checked his name badge. 'Thank you, Dr...' I stared at the small, printed letters then at his face: his *Caucasian* face. '...Singh,' I finished. It wasn't beyond the realms of possibility that was his name, though it seemed unlikely. The row of framed certificates along the corridor wall flashed back into my head. The white druid in front of me didn't look like a Doctor Varchan Singh.

He looked at me and I looked at him until eventually he shrugged. 'Of course there might be another reason why I'm not raising the alarm,' he admitted. He tried to smile but it didn't quite reach his eyes. His body was tense now, and I half-expected him to push me aside and run. I was right; I wasn't the only person who didn't belong in this mortuary.

I didn't believe in coincidences; what were the chances that two people would sneak into the same mortuary for different reasons? He had to be there for the same body as I was. I needed to keep him talking, to find out what was going on. 'The coat?' I asked admiringly, hoping I could appeal to his ego.

'It was hanging behind the staffroom door.' He grimaced. 'I sneaked in through the window and grabbed it. How did you get in here?'

'I bribed the receptionist. A hundred quid.'

He raised his eyebrows. 'It was cheaper to sneak in through the back.'

I was clearly off my game. In my defence, I'd had a trying day and it was my first time at this mortuary. I'd expected the perimeter security to be tighter – and I certainly hadn't expected to come across another interloper.

I eyed the druid; I had absolutely no idea what would

happen next. Would he try to attack me? He'd get a shock if he did. Finally I dropped my gaze to the manila file I was holding. Maybe he would relax if he thought I wasn't watching his every move. I was skilled enough at holding a target in my peripheral vision not to need to gaze directly at them.

I scanned the contents. It wasn't a preliminary post-mortem report but an order for coffee supplies. Smart: whoever this guy was, he could certainly improvise. 'Impressive,' I said. 'Although you'd have been scuppered if I'd read this as soon as you gave it to me.'

He managed an awkward half-smile, but he didn't move or speak. When the silence had stretched longer than was comfortable I decided on a direct approach. 'I told you *my* reasons for coming here. Why are *you* here?'

I don't know what he'd have told me because at that moment footsteps echoed down the corridor. A figure appeared in the doorway and peered at us. Uh-oh. 'What's going on here? Who are you two?' He frowned at the druid. 'Is that my lab coat?'

Apparently the time for talking was over. The young druid leapt forward in full flight mode and slammed into the real Dr Singh. The pathologist staggered backwards, then the druid was away, sprinting down the corridor and doubtless out of the window by which he'd come in.

I made an effort to go after him but with a downed patholo-gist in my path and the considerable age gap between us, I knew it was probably a wasted effort. By the time I'd followed his trail through the mortuary and darted to the window, the druid had vanished. There were any number of directions in which he could have run. I hissed through my teeth. Then, because these days I was a good citizen, I returned to Dr Singh.

The grouchy receptionist had heard the commotion and was helping him to his feet. As soon as she saw me, her gaze hardened. She clearly thought that I had attacked him. 'I've called the MET on you!' she said angrily.

I doubted that she had because there hadn't been enough time to make a phone call. Besides, she wouldn't want to explain to the small organisation that dealt with most of the minor crime in Coldstream how I'd managed to stroll in through the mortuary's front door.

'Relax, Cindy,' Dr Singh grunted. He pushed back his hair and blinked at me.

Cindy? I couldn't have invented a less suitable name for the woman if I'd tried. She was an Evelyn or a Priscilla, a snippy Wilhelmina at best. She certainly wasn't a Cindy.

Dr Singh continued. 'She's not the one who knocked me over – and I'm fine. Truly.'

Like the mysterious young man who'd temporarily stolen his identity, the pathologist was a druid, but that was the only similarity. This version of Dr Singh was from a different age group, ethnicity and, by the sound of his cultured accent and the look of his expensive clothes, income bracket.

'I don't believe he wanted to hurt you,' I said, wondering why I was defending the escaped druid. 'I think he was just trying to get away.'

Dr Singh nodded. 'He certainly didn't hang around.' He offered me a rueful smile. 'The people I deal with aren't usually so energetic. The dead tend to be far more obliging.'

Cindy sniffed. 'Why don't you sit in the staffroom, doctor?' she suggested fawningly. 'I'll make you a cup of sweet tea to help you get over the shock. While I do that, this woman can leave.'

I grinned. Poor Cindy was desperate for me to go before Dr Singh started asking why she'd let me in. Unfortunately for her, I wasn't going anywhere. 'Actually,' I said quickly, 'I need to ask

Dr Singh a few questions first. It might help us find out who that man was and why he was here.'

Cindy opened her mouth to protest but thankfully Dr Singh got in first. 'That's fine,' he said. 'Let's sit down next door.' He smiled at Cindy. 'But you can still put the kettle on.'

I tried hard not to smirk. 'No sugar in my tea, thanks, Cindy,' I said. 'A small splash of milk is fine.'

She started to scowl but Dr Singh was already leading me to the staffroom. This was better than I could have hoped for. If I hadn't been so well-behaved, I'd have punched the air with delight.

CHAPTER
SIX

Dr Singh closed the staffroom door to ensure we couldn't be overheard. He didn't offer me a chair, which spoke volumes. 'So,' he said, folding his arms. 'Why don't you tell me who you are and what you're doing here?'

The avuncular twinkle in his eyes had gone. The pathologist wasn't a gullible pushover after all; he'd simply wanted to ensure that Cindy was safely out of the way in case I posed a threat, despite my harmless cat-lady facade. He went up a notch in my estimation – several notches, in fact. He obviously didn't judge people on their appearances and he cared about his colleague's well-being.

I'd obliged the identity thief with the truth so the least I could do was provide the real Dr Singh with the same thing. I met his sharp brown eyes, indicating as best as I could that I was prepared to be honest.

'My name is Kit McCafferty. I'm here because a body was brought in earlier today. A man died in the River Tweed but nobody knows who he was or what happened to him. I believe that if I don't try to find out, he'll end up in an unmarked grave and his family – whoever they are – will never know the truth. I have some...' I searched for the right word, '...skills, and I thought I could put them to good use.'

Dr Singh's expression didn't alter. 'By helping a corpse?'

'He might be a corpse but that doesn't mean he's not important,' I countered. 'The dead deserve respect. It's possible he could have been rescued. Unfortunately he was not.'

'You feel guilty, then, that he's died?'

Perhaps I did, but not for the reasons that Dr Singh assumed. I doubted there was any therapist anywhere in the world who could sort out my tangled thoughts and feelings about the dead. 'Maybe,' I hedged.

'What about the druid? The one who stole my lab coat?'

At least that question was easier to answer. 'Initially I thought he worked here. I don't know who he is or why he broke in.'

Dr Singh raised an eyebrow. 'You broke in, too.'

I pulled a face. 'Not really – I simply persuaded Cindy to let me in. I didn't sneak in through a window.'

'You *persuaded* Cindy?'

'There might have been a financial inducement,' I conceded.

Irritation flashed across his face. 'No wonder she was so keen to get rid of you. How do I know you're not some kind of grubby necromancer?'

From his tone, the mortuary had experienced troubles with their kind before now. I knew of only three necromancers in Coldstream, and they were all cold bastards who were in it for the money. It didn't surprise me that they might have finagled their way into a place like this, or that Dr Singh despised them.

I held up my hands. 'Check my fingernails.'

He flicked a glance at them then looked at my face. 'You know that necromancy stains your fingers black?'

'When you look into the abyss it looks back into you,' I said quietly. 'Nothing comes without a price.' The price which necromancy demanded was high indeed, probably far higher than Dr Singh realised.

His mouth tightened and he sat down. 'You know more about it than most.'

'As I said, I have skills.'

'Do you have any idea, Ms McCafferty, how many John and Jane Does we get in here each year?' He sounded weary, which suggested his attitude was softening.

It might have been a rhetorical question but I answered it anyway. 'Around twenty, I imagine.' Before I'd retired, I would have been responsible for at least three or four of them in any twelve-month period.

'More like fifty,' he said, surprising me. 'People in Coldstream fall through the gaps all the time. Why are you so interested in this one?'

'Because I was by the river when he died.' I drew in a breath. 'I saved one person who fell in but I didn't know about this one until it was too late. The person I saved is well known and people cared what was happening to him, even people who didn't know him personally. Nobody cared about this man. I want to redress that balance.'

Dr Singh considered my words for several seconds then he nodded. 'Very well,' he said. 'I'll do what I can to help you.'

THE PATHOLOGIST TOOK me into a different room lined with filing cabinets. He produced a key from his pocket and unlocked the nearest one. It made a lot more sense that sensitive information about bodies was locked away rather than lying about where anyone could access it.

As he rifled through the cabinet, Cindy reappeared. She was

carrying only one mug of tea and looked unimpressed that I was still there. 'Your tea, Dr Singh,' she said overly loudly.

'Thank you, Cindy,' he told her. 'You can leave it on the desk.'

She harrumphed and did as he asked. I considered reminding her that I'd asked for a cup of tea as well but decided not to push my luck; I didn't want to find myself drinking spittle. I smiled at her instead, but Cindy only tutted and left the room. I shrugged; I'd tried.

'I came on shift half an hour ago,' Dr Singh explained. 'So it was one of my colleagues who took the body in this morning. They'll have done little more than a cursory examination. If a post-mortem is to be held, it will be later on in the week – maybe next week, depending on what we have in.' He paused. 'Unless there are extenuating circumstances, which mean that any forensic investigation into the cause of death needs to be completed more quickly.'

I imagined those extenuating circumstances would be if there was a distraught family member hovering in the background, or if the MET or a similar organisation requested the post-mortem be fast-tracked. For obvious reasons, that wouldn't happen in this case.

'Here we go.' He pulled out a folder triumphantly. 'It must have been Dr Biswick who took possession of the body. Her filing is haphazard.' He flipped it open to read the contents.

I started forward to peer over his shoulder, but he held up a finger and shook his head; apparently there were limits as to how much trust Dr Singh was willing to place in me. Fair enough. I wouldn't trust me either.

'Male witch, judging from the initial examination,' he said. 'Approximately late twenties. Reported cause of death is drowning, though Dr Biswick seems to think that's not actually the case.'

Drowning was difficult to prove or disprove because evidence of foul play was often washed away – and in the Tweed you were likely to be killed by the river beasties long before you actually drowned. Any pathologist worth their salt would take their time before making a definitive diagnosis. However, that didn't imply that my John Doe had been murdered; he could have fallen into the river like Quentin Hightower, but that wouldn't be confirmed until a full post-mortem was carried out.

I still didn't know whether John Doe had gone into the Tweed before, after or at the same time as Hightower, although I was sure that the timing had been close.

'Hmmm.' Dr Singh's frown deepened. 'There was some old netting wrapped around one of his legs. It seems to have been tangled up with both his body and some items on the river bed.' That would explain why he'd not been dragged away by the river currents to the same spot as Hightower.

'But the netting wouldn't account for the wounds on his torso,' Dr Singh went on.

'It was the Tweed,' I said softly. 'The section by the market is where lots of the river monsters congregate. I saw the bite marks before the Redcaps took him away.'

Dr Singh's frown didn't clear. 'Hmmm,' he said again. He snapped the folder shut and marched out of the room. Because I'd not been told otherwise, I followed him.

We returned to the room with the refrigerated body lockers. He took the clipboard from the wall and flipped through the pages of paper. 'You have to sign your name,' he said.

I smiled disarmingly. 'I'd rather not.'

'It's procedure.'

'I bribed your receptionist to get in here,' I said. 'I don't think we need to worry too much about your procedure.'

Dr Singh stood his ground. 'Sign it,' he said. 'Please.'

I didn't want any official record of my visit, but complaining wouldn't endear me to the pathologist and I needed him on my side. As I scanned the sheet, I realised it was the form for John Doe; there was a different page for each body. It appeared that even the dead couldn't escape mindless bureaucracy.

Pursing my lips, I scrawled my name, making sure that my writing was virtually illegible.

'Thank you,' Dr Singh said and returned the clipboard to its place. He glanced at the troll who was still shrouded on the gurney, then at the lockers, then at me. 'Have you seen a dead body up close before, Ms McCafferty?'

There was only one answer to that. 'Yes.' Dozens upon dozens. And I had been responsible for most of them.

'Because, if you're going to faint or vomit or do anything that will cause problems...'

'I'll be fine, Dr Singh.' I smiled faintly. 'I promise.'

Apparently he believed me. 'Very well.' He pulled on a pair of gloves then opened the fourth locker along; annoyingly, it was the one I'd been about to open before I'd been interrupted.

The pathologist slid out the long tray until John Doe's body was fully displayed. His eyes were still wide open but his clothing had been removed and I could see the marks where the netting had snagged his legs. I grimaced at the red welts on his pale, dead skin although Dr Singh barely looked at them. His focus was on the wounds closer to John Doe's head, around his neckline, his torso and on his cheek.

'The last time we had a body pulled from the Tweed, it was virtually unrecognisable,' he said. 'This is quite extraordinary. In comparison, this man is in pristine condition.'

'There were lots of witches present who used spells to keep the monsters at bay while they tried to rescue the other man,' I said.

'They did a good job. There are only a few bite marks that

seem to come from those creatures.' He pointed them out. 'Here. And here. But this wound,' he motioned towards a smaller and neater mark, 'is not from any river beast.'

It was only a few inches wide, on the edge of John Doe's ribs. It hadn't been visible when he'd still been clothed in his wet shirt, but it was clear enough now.

'A straight-edged sword did this,' I breathed. I shook my head. 'The blade was thin but it must be very long because it's been angled upwards. Some sort of rapier, perhaps.'

I stepped to the side to get a better view. 'It could well have reached far enough through his ribcage to pierce his heart. There aren't many places in Coldstream where you can get something like that. They're not for self-defence – they're purely for murder.' I continued gazing at the wound then realised abruptly that Dr Singh was staring at me. I coughed and stepped back.

'Who are you really, Ms McCafferty?' he asked. He tilted his head. 'Actually, don't answer that. I don't want to know.'

He returned the body to the locker and closed the door. 'I think we both know that John Doe didn't accidentally fall into the river and drown. He was murdered. His killer probably imagined that the river creatures would make short work of his body but hadn't reckoned on a bunch of witches casting spells to hold the hungry monsters back. I think John Doe's post-mortem has just been brought forward.'

'Today?'

'Hopefully.' He looked at the shrouded troll. 'Tomorrow morning at the latest.'

'What about his personal effects?' I asked.

Dr Singh hesitated. The confirmation that John Doe had been murdered rather than killed in a freak accident meant that my presence and my questions should be treated with greater caution. 'They'll be locked away in the room opposite,' he said quietly. 'I have no objection to showing them to you, but this is now a murder investigation. I have to consider the chain of evidence and inform the MET and the witches' council, who might want to take over the matter.'

The witches' council would care if this was Quentin High-tower's body, but I wasn't convinced they'd care about John Doe even if he was a witch. I nodded anyway; perhaps we'd get lucky and somebody with more resources and ability than me would take up his cause. I certainly hoped so.

'Will you be here tomorrow morning?' I asked. 'I can come back when you've found out who is looking into his murder. If the MET or the witches' council are investigating, then John Doe doesn't need me.'

Dr Singh nodded sombrely.

'Meanwhile,' I continued, 'perhaps I can try to find out more about the druid who broke in and stole your lab coat. Quid pro quo.' I wanted to find out who he was because he was linked somehow to my John Doe. He had to be. Find the druid and there was a very good chance I'd learn John Doe's identity.

The pathologist looked sceptical. 'You really don't know who he is?'

'No.' I met his eyes. 'I haven't lied to you, Dr Singh. Not once.'

His dubious expression didn't clear, though he inclined his head. 'Thank you.'

'Save that gratitude until I've learned more. And maybe keep your windows shut from now on.'

'And discourage Cindy from taking bribes,' he muttered.

I thought again about her clothes and her grumpy attitude. Despite that pretty scarf and bracelet, Cindy was struggling to make ends meet. 'Public-facing roles are more stressful than people realise,' I said. 'Raise her salary and she won't do it again.' Probably. Only Cindy herself could guarantee that for sure.

Dr Singh looked more surprised than horrified. 'Reward her for taking a bribe?'

'Don't think of it that way.' I smiled. 'Think of it as making sure she's paid a decent living wage. It's obvious she admires you, Dr Singh. She likes you and she respects you – and she rushed in the second it sounded like there was trouble. Cindy risked herself without knowing what might happen if she got involved. That means her problem isn't with her job, per se, but with her salary.' I shrugged. 'And then you can sack her if there's a next time.'

There was goodwill and second chances – and there was being taken a fool. Sometimes there was a fine line between the two.

CHAPTER
SEVEN

First I headed home. John Doe was already dead, I had no immediate lead on the mysterious druid and I had other priorities – most of which involved fish. Given the urgent miaowing from my furry family as soon as I walked through the door, I'd made the correct decision.

Every meal time was the same. All five of them would act as if they'd been starved for days rather than hours, and woe betide me if I was late. Thane had already given ideas to She Without An Ear about to how to enact revenge on me, and I had no desire for her to put those ideas into action. I liked my sleep to be uninterrupted.

I put out five food bowls, replenished their water then checked the corner of the front garden where I'd left out food for the nearby stray and feral cats. All was good.

Back in the house, I ventured into the back room, my all-purpose dumping ground. Sometimes it contained a hissing feral cat recovering from an injury but most of the time it was where I tossed the stuff I didn't want to throw out but didn't know where to keep. I cleaned out the room regularly but somehow it quickly filled up again. I didn't actively wander around buying tat but somehow tat found me – much in the same way as hungry cats did.

I manoeuvred around a cardboard box containing a selection of different-sized glass jars that I'd been collecting on the off-chance I decided to make some jam to go with my scones, then headed to the back of the room and the small wooden chest in the corner.

In this light it looked innocuous enough, but when it was dark a faint glow emanated from the burnished wood. The glow had nothing to do with my dusting and polishing skills and everything to do with the magic bound up into it. It was a miniature version of a witchery store and it held all manner of dried herbs and pre-made concoctions that I'd collected over the years for situations like this one.

The chest was magicked to safely contain the items' power and keep them fresh. I had enough magic of my own to stir the spells into life, but sadly I didn't have enough power to create the spells myself; that was why I bought them ready-made from local witchery stores and kept them here.

I ran my finger across the neatly arranged packets, searching for the one I needed. Not a barrier spell or an enchanted caffeinated teabag to help keep someone awake – and definitely *not* the glamour concoction designed to make the user more attractive. The one time I'd tried that was when I'd been hunting down a target in my old job and had needed to gatecrash a posh party. It had caused far more problems than it had solved. I shuddered faintly at the memory and moved on.

There was a small nudge on my elbow. He Who Crunches Bird Bones was waiting by my side. 'Finished your dinner already?' I asked. 'That was fast.'

I paused my search to scratch behind his ears. His rumbling purrs told me I'd hit the perfect spot. 'I have to find an errant druid,' I told him. 'I don't know his name or where he lives. In fact, I don't know anything about him other than what he looks like. But he's important and I need to find out what he knows.'

He Who Crunches Bird Bones chirruped and padded towards the chest. He sniffed at it delicately then pawed at the contents. 'Hey!' I protested. 'Don't mess up my system!' The white cat ignored me and thrust his head inside. 'There's no bloody catnip in there,' I said. 'Stop it.'

He pulled his head out and blinked at me. I sighed then glanced at the box. One of the white-paper sachets was sticking out. Frowning, I reached for it and gazed at my handwriting on the label. I stared at the cat. 'You,' I whispered, 'are extraordinary.'

He Who Crunches Bird Bones purred again and twitched his ears.

'Yeah,' I said. 'Alright. I'll give you an extra after-dinner treat, though you know it means that everyone has to have one.' I palmed the paper sachet, tidied the box's contents and closed the lid, 'Come on, then.'

As soon as I'd handed out crunchy salmon-flavoured titbits to each of the delighted moggies, I took a sheet of paper from the stack in the corner and sat down at the kitchen table. He Who Must Sleep jumped up and eyed me. 'No,' I said. 'I'm not staying long. If you try to have a snooze on my lap, it will be short-lived.'

He sniffed in thinly veiled feline derision but he backed away and settled on a corner of the table, earning himself several full body strokes. Finally I returned my attention to the paper, smoothed it out and patted down the curled-up corners.

'Don't bother me for a few minutes,' I told the cats. 'I need to concentrate.'

As I stared at the blank piece of paper, I conjured up an image of the nameless druid in my mind. Eyewitnesses were notoriously unreliable and memory could cheat the unwary, but I'd spent half a lifetime practising the art of facial recognition. I didn't have a photographic memory, not even close, but I'd trained myself to pay attention to what people looked like. From my first day as an assassin I'd vowed not to be the idiot who killed the wrong person simply because they resembled somebody or wore similar clothes. I had never broken that vow.

With the druid's face firmly in my mind, I kept my eyes on the paper and reached for the sachet, blindly tearing it open and scattering its contents. From somewhere behind me, there was a miaowed squawk of surprise; it sounded like He Who Roams Wide but I didn't turn around to check. I simply stared at the paper and focused intently until an image presented itself.

The tattoos came first, swirling into position before settling into the paper. A long, pointed nose appeared and gave a little wiggle as if it were sniffing out this new environment. The druid's mouth came into focus, thin and wry, followed by cheekbones and jowls. His curly hair appeared first by his right ear then swept across his skull until it curved down towards the left-hand side of his face. Finally, his eyes emerged, wide at first and with the vestiges of the panic that I'd seen him in before he'd run away. Then they settled into a more amused expression, like the druid had when I'd first encountered him.

I held my breath until I was sure the image was established, exhaling only when the magic faded and the portrait became static on the paper. He Who Must Sleep heaved himself onto all fours and gingerly walked towards it. He lifted a curious paw to pat the druid's hair.

'I wouldn't,' I murmured. 'This is old magic and it can be temperamental.'

He Who Must Sleep withdrew.

I held the portrait at arm's length and examined it. It was a decent approximation; the old spell had held up better than I'd expected. Pleased with my achievement, I made a mental note to thank the witch who'd sold it to me, then I remembered she'd retired three years ago and absconded to Spain for a warmer lifestyle. Oh well. I might find another witchery store that offered similar enchantments. It would be worth keeping more versions of this spell in stock.

I tilted my head at the magicked portrait. 'Hi there,' I said softly. 'It's good to see you again. Now I have a chance of finding out who you really are.'

I STARTED CLOSE TO HOME; there was no point in having a druid as a neighbour if I didn't make use of him. Dave wasn't exactly a social butterfly, and there were at least two generations between him and Cosplayer, as I had decided to christen the young druid: Cos for short. Still, my neighbour had spent some years in prison and he still had contacts from those days. If Cos was part of a criminal druid network, there was a chance Dave would know of him.

He scowled at me from his doorstep. 'What do you want now?'

My smile was bright as I held up Cos's portrait. 'Do you know this man?'

Dave didn't glance at the picture. 'What? No chewy scones?'

'I'm afraid not.' I waved the paper at him. 'Just this.'

He huffed at the injustice of my lack of dodgy baked goods then squinted at the portrait. 'You think I know every fucking druid in town?'

'No,' I said pleasantly. 'But I'm hoping that you might know this one.'

He glared. 'I don't.'

It had always been a long shot. I thanked him, earning

myself a deeper scowl, and turned away. There were plenty more avenues to explore.

'Get that stupid ginger werewolf to help you!' Dave called after me. 'You cat people ought to stick together.'

Yeah, yeah. I waved a hand at him as I walked off, but then I considered the suggestion. Thane moved around a lot, as if he were afraid of what might happen if he spent more than a month in the same location. His current pad wasn't far off Crackendon Square and I was heading in that direction, so it wouldn't take me long to drop by and ask him if he wanted to tag along. Two minds made short work, yadda yadda, and it would look less suspicious if I was part of a couple when I wandered around asking questions.

Besides, I liked it when we spent time together. I didn't have to pretend to be someone else with Thane, and that was rare for me indeed.

'I CAN'T BELIEVE that you've been running around Coldstream conducting an investigation while I went home and put my feet up,' Thane growled after I'd filled him in on the rest of my day. We were walking towards Hirsel Street and its bustling nightlife.

It was close to the old town area on the other side of Crackendon Square and was no less vibrant as a result. Even at this early hour I could hear off-tune karaoke pumping out from competing bars.

Although the very different patrons of Hirsel Street usually behaved themselves and didn't allow a fun night out to descend into fisticuffs – or worse – unless it was absolutely necessary, there were enough establishments packed into the area that the effect could be a real assault on the senses. My days of enjoying loud thumping music and sweaty crowds were behind me; after all, I was an unassuming little cat lady, not a wild party animal.

At least January was one of the quieter months, and a cold, drizzly Tuesday night all but guaranteed that even Hirsel Street would be half-dead. Even so, I was hopeful that there would be some people about and one of them would know who Cos was.

'I guess this unknown dead witch has got under my skin.'

Thane's response was surprisingly gentle. 'You said nobody cared about him – but *you* care.'

I flashed him a quick grin. 'And now I'm forcing you to care, too. But right now we won't think about our John Doe. We'll find Cos instead.'

'He sounds like a leafy green salad vegetable.'

'All the more reason to learn his real name,' I said.

Thane nodded gravely. 'I accept the mission,' he intoned. 'We shall not fail and no lettuce shall remain unturned.'

I wasn't quite so optimistic but I liked his attitude.

'Thank you, Kit,' he said after another beat.

'For what?'

'For giving me an excuse to escape Tiddles' claws for an evening.'

I snorted.

'But mostly for inviting me to join you. For trusting me to help.'

I glanced up and our eyes met. 'You're welcome.' There was a surprising – and pleasing – warmth in my belly. I pulled my gaze away and pointed towards a small, quaint pub on our right. 'Druids often frequent this place. Let's try in here first.'

Thane bowed. 'As my lady commands.'

'Keep that up,' I told him, 'and you're in the running to earn a permanent place as my sidekick.'

'Loner by day, Cat Boy by night,' Thane said, then pulled a face. 'Maybe not.'

'We'd have to get you more kittens first.' And Thane wasn't a boy. He was all man.

He shuddered. 'Please, no.' Then he paused. 'Would Tiddles like a friend? *Should* I get another kitten?'

I smirked. 'Maybe leave it a while yet.'

As we ducked into the pub Thane exhaled loudly; it might have been from relief or it might have been from disappointment.

Unlike many of the other venues along Hirsel Street, the music here was muted enough for the punters to hold conversations. I swept my gaze around the room on the off-chance that Cos was in here having a pint, but that would have been too good to be true. Although the pub was busy there was no sign of him and, frustratingly, the clientele appeared to be mostly older druids rather than a young crowd. It was unlikely any of them would know Cos but we had to start somewhere.

In a vague bid to fit in to the druidic crowd of drinkers, Thane and I went to the bar and ordered two pints of frothy beer. While the bartender filled the glasses, I held up my magic portrait. 'Seen this guy around?' I asked.

The bartender didn't look at it. 'Nope.'

'Please take a closer look,' Thane said, his voice friendly. He knew instinctively that playing the hard man wouldn't work here.

The bartender topped off the pints and put them on the counter. 'Nope.' I drew a breath but he didn't let me speak. 'I don't care who you're looking for. You're not druids and you're not regulars. That means you're trouble.' His smile didn't reach his eyes. 'Enjoy your drinks.'

I cursed inwardly. He'd spoken loudly and the drawback of being in a bar where you could hear conversations was that you could *hear conversations*. Every customer was watching us with narrowed eyes. Less than thirty seconds in and we'd already managed to turn them all against us. Perhaps there were reasons why I'd ended up as an assassin instead of as a private investigator. Neither did it help that Thane was a lone wolf; I doubted either of us possessed the charm and charisma that would encourage these people to speak to us. But I didn't intend to give up.

Thane paid for the beers while I found a small table between a group of bearded druids who looked to be good friends and a couple who were holding hands and gazing dewy-eyed at each other. A roundabout approach might be more productive. I leaned towards the beardy boys.

'Fucking board,' the nearest one was complaining. 'How can they do that? How can they ban us from visiting Myrddin's grave?'

'Control,' one of his friends muttered. 'They want to control us. I told you when this lot were voted in that they'd cause trouble. They're power-hungry bastards.'

There was nothing quite like political debate to get a party started. It didn't matter which Preternatural group you hailed from, there was always someone in power you wanted to complain about – especially over several beers.

'Evening,' I said brightly. 'Do you—?'

'No.' Everyone in the group frowned at me and the druid who'd spoken first pointedly turned his back. Their discussion stopped and they sat in stiff, unyielding silence.

Thane, who had ambled over from the bar, had witnessed the exchange. He sat down next to me, took a sip from his pint and tried the loving couple. 'Braw night.' They ignored him. He persisted. 'Bit chilly out, but not bad for this time of year.'

The female druid glanced at him. 'Fuck off.' She immediately returned her gaze to her partner. I rolled my eyes. Well, this was going just swimmingly.

'The weather?' I muttered. 'Couldn't you think of anything else to start a conversation?'

'At least I managed to complete a sentence,' he returned, tipping his head at the other table.

I couldn't disagree so, for want of a snappy response, I tried the beer. It was bitter and not particularly pleasant.

While I admired persistence and it often produced results, it was important to recognise when a situation was untenable. We wouldn't learn anything here, even if someone knew Cos. It was time to retreat. 'Somewhere else?' I asked.

Thane nodded. Without another word, we stood up and headed for the door, our barely touched pints resting on the small table where we'd left them.

'I'll choose the place this time,' Thane said, turning his collar up against the cold. 'The people in that pub were the wrong generation.'

We couldn't do any worse. 'On you go.'

He walked decisively towards another bar while I followed. There was a collection of people hovering outside sucking on bowl pipes of magicked tobacco and shivering. They appeared to be of a similar age to Cos. There was only one druid amongst them, but maybe a mixed crowd would be more willing to answer questions.

I pasted on a smile. 'Hey! We're looking for a friend of ours. He's gone missing and we're really worried about him.' I held up the picture to draw attention away from my obvious lie. 'Have you seen him around?'

At least this time they looked at the paper but I didn't need to hear their answers; their blank expressions told me they didn't know him.

'Thanks anyway,' Thane said, reaching past them for the door. As it opened, we were blasted with a wave of music. It wasn't disco or heart-thumping dance beats; this was pure country.

The counter was empty and vacant stools lined its length. Nobody was buying drinks and the lone bartender, a troll, was looking bored as he polished a glass. There were plenty of people, but they were dancing rather than drinking and chatting. Line dancing.

'We're still in Scotland, right?' Thane asked.

I gazed at the rows of cowboy boots and tasselled shirts. 'Last time I checked we were,' I said. 'But we're here now. Let's give this place a try.'

I walked up to the first line of jiggling, bobbing people and raised the picture. 'Seen this guy around?'

'Yeeeeeeee-ha!' They all turned away in unison, legs flicking upwards.

I moved around and tried again. As soon as I did, the line of dancers spun for a second time. I looked at Thane and shrugged helplessly. He pursed his lips and leaned into my ear. 'Maybe not here.'

I jumped back as a waving arm was thrust in my direction. Yeah, maybe not.

'What's wrong with young people these days?' he asked as we walked towards yet another pub. 'Why aren't they getting drunk and having a good time instead of...'

'Dancing and having a good time?' I asked.

'The tassels, Kit. All those tassels.'

I smirked. 'I think you'd make a great cowboy.' Especially if he wore tassels.

Thane spun on the spot. 'Howdy partner!' he shouted. 'Let's have ourselves some rooting-tooting fun!'

Oh no. 'I take that back. You'd be a terrible cowboy.'

'Come on, dahlin',' he drawled with a wink. 'We've still got ourselves a varmint to find!'

I raised my eyes heavenward. This was going to be a very long evening.

W e tried an Irish pub, which I was reasonably certain didn't contain a single person from Ireland. Thane got drawn into a long-winded conversation with a female werewolf who recognised him and seemed determined to debate the merits of living within or outside a wolf pack. It sounded to me as if she were trying to recruit him, which was definitely a new experience for Thane.

We both downed two pints of heavy Irish stout but we didn't find anyone who knew of Cos. Thane politely declined the werewolf's offer of a third pint.

'When was the last time you had a proper night out in Hirsel Street?' he asked me, as we wove towards a karaoke bar.

'Probably my retirement party,' I admitted. 'More than three years ago.' A speculative expression crossed his face but he didn't say anything. 'What?' I asked.

'Nothing.'

I pulled a face. It wasn't nothing, not with that look on his face. 'Spit it out, Thane.'

'Alright. Why aren't you dead?'

My steps faltered. 'Pardon?'

He grimaced. 'That came out wrong. It's just that you have a lot of old secrets inside that head of yours. You did a lot of ... stuff ... for EEL, and they let you retire to Danksville with a party – and what? A golden handshake?'

'Pretty much. It's not like the movies or the books. Real assassins don't end up in a pine box because their employer is afraid of what they know or what they might do. If EEL killed off their ex-employees, they'd never recruit any new ones. They trust me to keep my mouth closed and I trust them to leave me in peace.'

'Fair enough,' he grunted.

Inside the karaoke bar, I sang 'Killing Me Softly' while the audience winced. Thane found a tall witch who initially thought he recognised Cos, but we soon realised that he'd mistaken my drawing for a leprechaun he used to know.

'His skin isn't green,' I said.

'Barry the leprechaun's skin is definitely green,' the witch told us. 'And that's Barry.'

It was *not* Barry. We abandoned the karaoke bar.

'Your turn,' I said, once we were outside. I'd drunk enough alcohol that I was no longer feeling the cold. 'When was the last time *you* had a night out on Hirsel Street?'

'Ten years ago.' Thane squinted. 'No. Eleven.'

'That long?'

He grimaced. 'I was out on a date with a dryad from Leet Forest. We walked into a pub full of Barrow wolves. It didn't end well.'

Ah. Thane had been part of the Barrow pack before he'd been thrown out for killing his uncle, the Barrow beta. I didn't know what had made him kill his uncle and I'd not tried to find out. If Thane wanted me to know, he would tell me.

'I spent three weeks recovering in hospital,' he said. 'I never heard from the dryad again.'

'I'm sorry.'

He shrugged awkwardly but there was a lot of pain behind the gesture. 'It seemed wise to stay away from Hirsel Street after that. I'm pretty capable, but I can't win against a dozen drunk and angry werewolves who are out for my blood.'

I bit my lip. 'You don't have to do this with me, Thane. You don't have to be here.'

'I know, but I don't think they'd come at me again like they did last time. A lot has changed since those days. Besides,' he gave me an arch grin to try and mask his true feelings, 'this time I'm with you. You'll keep me safe.'

'I'll stab anyone who comes after you,' I said, and I meant it. Thane was a good guy. Whatever had happened with his uncle all those years ago, I knew he was someone I could trust. I also genuinely liked him and enjoyed his company – and he wasn't even a cat.

Speaking of which... 'I'm sure Tiddles would also happily go after anyone who tried to jump you,' I added.

'That cat would win against any number of werewolves.'

I smiled serenely. 'Any cat would.'

In the Mexican bar we paid for a round of tequila shots for every customer but none of them volunteered anything useful about Cos. In the speakeasy, hidden behind a fake grocer's shop, we were stone walled by the three customers who were willing to pay over the odds for brightly coloured cocktails that tasted of sugary fruit juice. In the whisky bar, nobody could speak without slurring their words, let alone focus on Cos's picture.

After more than four hours, we decided to give up. I was far drunker than I wanted to be and I didn't want to pay for it with a hangover the following morning, so I steered a swaying Thane away from the alcoholic vibes of Hirsel Street towards a well-lit coffee shop called Pork Pies, which was closer to Crackendon Square.

Sadly, I couldn't see any actual pork pies on the menu. I chose not to complain about false advertising and ordered us both very large, very strong black coffees with greasy bacon rolls on the side. One day a powerful witch would develop a potion that successfully prevented hangovers. It hadn't happened yet, but when it did their coven would be the richest in the world. Guaranteed.

I placed the magicked portrait face down on the table and chewed happily on the roll. It wasn't a balanced healthy meal and would likely play havoc with my cholesterol levels, but damn, it tasted good.

'There was a time in my youth,' Thane mused, 'when there were very few people who could drink me under the table, but those days are long gone now. And it appears the less liquor I can hold, the worse my hangovers are.'

I raised my coffee cup. 'To a misspent youth that was hangover free.'

He grinned lopsidedly and reached for his cup. Unfortunately he misjudged and knocked the white cup flying across the table, sending dark splatters of coffee in all directions like blood gushing from an arterial wound. The paper with our only picture of Cos was immediately soaked.

'Shit.' I grabbed it, shook off the worst of the liquid and dabbed at it ineffectively with a napkin. It was too late. Alas, enchanted pictures and black coffee were not a good combination.

Thane looked aghast. 'Oh no. You've got more copies, right?'

I grimaced as I shook coffee droplets off my fingers. 'That was the only one.'

His face drooped. 'I'm sorry, Kit.'

I reached for my napkin and did my best to clean up the

mess. A young waiter with a bright expression that was far too cheery for someone doing the night shift bustled over with a cloth.

'It's alright,' I told Thane. 'It wasn't getting us any results anyway.' I sighed. 'I'm going to the washroom.' I gave him a tired smile, thanked the waiter profusely and turned to the door marked *Toilets*.

Next to it was a bulletin board displaying upcoming events. I glanced at it as I passed. Then I froze and slowly turned my head to look at it again. 'Thane,' I called.

He was trying to help the waiter clean up the mess on the table, though it looked like he was making it worse. I repeated his name more loudly. '*Thane*. Come and have a look at this.'

He frowned, his emerald-green eyes squinting against the harsh fluorescent strip lighting, then he joined me. 'Wait,' he said. 'Is that—?'

'The Blue Tattoos,' the waiter said helpfully. 'They're a terrible band but they're cheap and my boss likes them.'

There were three of them, all druids and all with the unsmiling, scowly expressions of young people trying to be cool. One held a guitar, one clasped a microphone and the third had raised a pair of cymbals as he prepared to crash them together in front of his face – the same face which had confronted me in the Mathers Street mortuary.

'Cos,' I whispered.

'Nah, that's not his name,' the waiter said. 'The drummer,' he said. 'That's who you're looking at, right? He's Knox Thunderstick.'

Knox Thunderstick wasn't his real name any more than Cosplayer, but it was a hell of a lot more than we'd known two minutes ago.

'What's his real name?' Thane asked, his previously alcohol-glazed eyes now clear and focused.

The waiter smirked. 'That *is* his real name. He changed it by deed poll.' He shrugged. 'Well, that's what he tells everyone.'

'Do you know where he lives?'

The waiter's previously bright expression dimmed slightly and he looked warily from me to Thane and back again. 'No.'

I glanced again at the poster. 'The Blue Tattoos,' I said. 'They play here every Wednesday afternoon?'

'Two till six. Every week.' He tilted his head, his suspicion obvious. 'Why are you so interested?'

Uh...

'We're getting married next month,' Thane said. 'We've been looking for ages for a band to play at the wedding reception. Druid rock is my favourite.'

'The Blue Tattoos have more of a folksy vibe,' the waiter said.

Thane grinned. 'Even better. Right, darling?'

I tried to look enthusiastic at the terrible lie. 'Right.'

'Congratulations.' The waiter appeared to relax. 'I could tell you were both deeply in love the moment you walked in here.' He tapped his forehead. 'It's my sixth sense.'

He might want to work on that. I couldn't complain, though; it was partly thanks to the gullibility of the general public that I'd never once been outed as an assassin.

Thane took my hand and stroked it, then draped an arm around my waist and planted a sloppy kiss on my cheek. I was immediately enveloped in a heady cloud of vetiver scent. 'You're a clever fellow,' he declared to the waiter and kissed me again. 'We are very much in love.'

If you can't beat 'em, join 'em; frankly, it was either that or garrotte Thane right there in the middle of the café. The waiter, although annoying, didn't deserve to have to clean up that sort of bloody mess.

I leaned into Thane's hard body and wrapped my arm

around him, dropping my hand to graze it against his thigh. 'How could anyone not be in love with you, Pooky Bear?' I cooed.

He tilted his head towards mine. 'I only have eyes for you, my sweet wifey-to-be.'

I tried not to grit my teeth: Thane was better at this than I was. I pushed myself onto my tiptoes and kissed him on the lips. 'My snuggle-butt.'

Thane returned the kiss. 'My love muffin.'

Good grief. I barely managed to avoid rolling my eyes. I turned until I was facing him properly, pressed myself against him and kissed him again. This time I didn't pull back – and neither did Thane. He deepened the kiss and his arm tightened. A thrill rippled through me and there was a familiar tightening in my groin. Thane's signature scent was making my senses swim.

The harsh strip lighting, the faint aroma of grease and coffee and the cold tiled floor of the café faded into the background. It had been a long time since I'd experienced a kiss as sensual as this.

The waiter coughed awkwardly. 'I'll leave you to it,' he said. 'It's sweet to see older folks like you still getting it on.'

Thane and I broke apart immediately at his words, while the waiter strolled away without a care in the world. I didn't turn around to look at him; instead I stared at Thane and he stared back at me. There were two points of colour high on his cheekbones and I knew I was similarly flushed.

The café door jangled, announcing the arrival of a new customer. The loud chatter of the three women who tottered in was more than enough to break the last dregs of the metaphorical spell.

'I should have another coffee,' Thane muttered. 'I've had far too much to drink tonight.'

'Uh-huh.' Feeling more awkward than I had in years, I put my hands in my pockets. This was ridiculous; I was a middle-aged woman, not a teenager playing games. 'I should go home. I've got to return to the mortuary tomorrow morning.'

Thane eyed me. 'Shall I meet you there?'

I shook my head. 'Another person will likely only confuse the situation. I'll be more successful on my own. But tomorrow is Wednesday – why don't I meet you here at half-past one? We can grab Knox Thunderstick before his Blue Tattoos set begins. Between the two of us we should be able to encourage him to talk to us.'

Thane glanced at the poster. 'Cos suits him better. Who the hell calls themselves Thunderstick? Even the sort of druid who breaks into mortuaries for kicks should have more style than that.'

I smiled faintly. 'At least we'll find out who Mr Thunderstick really is tomorrow – and hopefully John Doe, too.' I nodded at Thane and raised my hand in brief, albeit clumsy, farewell.

Once I was outside and walking away from the café, I touched my still-burning cheeks and my lips. Damn.

CHAPTER
NINE

For reasons known only to himself, He Who Roams Wide chose to accompany me on my return visit to the mortuary. It was in a central location that I knew the sleek black cat visited of his own accord, so perhaps he wanted to ensure my safety. Or perhaps he was merely bored and wanted something to do. Either way, I was glad of the company and I knew that his presence wouldn't provoke anyone in the way that the unfamiliar figure of Thane Barrow might.

I hoped rather than expected that a Fetch from the witches' council would be in attendance. It wouldn't be easy to persuade a council official to tell me any relevant information, but their presence would ensure that John Doe's death was being taken seriously.

That was all I wanted to happen, and I had dressed accordingly in smart black trousers and a crisp white shirt instead of my fuzzy, cat-lady attire. Witches who rose to the lofty heights of the council approved of businesslike, transactional relationships with important and serious people. They weren't likely to offer time or information to someone who wandered in off the street in a colourful old jumper covered in cat hair.

I'd even brushed my purple hair and smoothed it down with an anti-frizz potion that had been lurking in the back of my bathroom cabinet for months. I didn't bother doing anything about the dark circles under my eyes. I'd had a restless night of tossing and turning and my disturbed sleep showed on my face, even though I knew I had enough grim enthusiasm and dark energy to attack the day.

There was a glimmer of sunlight when we set out, but once He Who Roams Wide and I arrived at Mathers Street it had been subsumed by grey skies and a morose drizzle. Such was the way of a dreary Scottish winter. It didn't affect the cat, who darted through the streets and leapt across puddles; he was having the time of his life. His attitude rubbed off on me and by the time I pushed open the mortuary doors, hastily stepping out of the path of two Redcaps who were just leaving, I was buoyed by my sense of purpose. I was sure that I'd learn John Doe's real identity by the end of the day.

Cindy was sitting behind the front desk in exactly the same position and with the same dour expression she'd displayed the previous day. If nothing else, I admired her consistency. I was also pleased that she didn't look surprised when I appeared; Dr Singh must have warned her that I was planning to return.

'I preferred what you were wearing yesterday,' she grunted.

I didn't take offence; I preferred my comfy cat-lady clothes, too. I gave her my most disarming smile. 'It was an impromptu visit yesterday. I thought that I ought to be more respectful today.'

'The dead don't care.'

My smile didn't dim. 'Nobody actually wears black for the dead, they wear it for the living. It's a way of saying that a life might be over but that life still mattered.'

She gave a long-suffering sigh. 'I hear a lot of pop

psychology when I'm behind this desk. I don't know why I thought you'd be different.' She peered down. 'Is that a *cat*?'

I expected her to launch into a long lecture about why animals were forbidden from the mortuary hallways, but instead she jumped up and launched herself towards He Who Roams Wide. 'My goodness, you're a handsome boy!'

I blinked in surprise, but the cat took her admiration as his due. He butted his head against her leg and miaowed, charming her into immediate submission. I should have brought him along yesterday; I'd have saved myself some money.

Cindy cooed over him for several moments until eventually I cleared my throat. 'Is Dr Singh here?' I asked. 'Can I go through?'

She didn't look up. 'Yes, yes, on you go. He's in his office. Third door on the right. How about a treat?'

'I'm still waiting for yesterday's cup of tea,' I told her.

'Not you,' she snapped. She tickled He Who Roams Wide under his chin. 'Would *you* like a treat? Maybe some chicken?' She angled her head up to me. 'I made chicken salad for my lunch today. I can pick out some bits for him. Is that alright? I don't want to upset his wee tummy or anything.'

'You'll upset him if he doesn't get any chicken now he's got it into his head that a feast is coming,' I told her.

'He deserves it,' Cindy said. 'Don't you, my lovely? You deserve some chicken for being so very handsome.'

Uh-huh. I gazed at the pair of them then shrugged and left them to it.

The door to Dr Singh's office was already ajar but I knocked anyway and waited. I needed to keep the pathologist on my side, so observing the professional niceties was wise. Besides, I could hear the murmur of voices and I had no desire to intrude if he was talking to a family member about their loved one.

When he opened the door, smiled and beckoned me inside,

however, I realised that his companion had to be a Fetch from the witches' council. It wasn't the air of sniffy self-importance that confirmed it – although that was impressive – but the tall, pointed black hat that the council members wore without any sense of irony that gave it away.

'Ms McCafferty,' Dr Singh exclaimed with unexpected warmth.

The witch took off his silly hat and placed it on the desk, then peeled off his black leather gloves. I eyed the embroidered insignia on the cuffs: DJ. Maybe the Fetch was a big R'n'B fan.

'It's good to see you again.' Dr Singh gestured towards the witch. 'This is Fetch Jackson.'

'Please, call me Daniel.' The Fetch smiled and the welcoming twinkle in his eyes left me faintly nonplussed. 'Fetch always feels so formal.' He gave a small, embarrassed laugh. 'Every time I hear it, I feel a surge of imposter syndrome even though I've been with the council for more than eight years.' He held out his hand. 'Dr Singh told me about your concern for the poor John Doe who was pulled from the river yesterday. I understand that you were there when it happened.'

I'd not expected any of this. The fact that the Fetch was there in person was surprising, even more so that he was being friendly towards me and appeared grateful for my intrusion. I shook his hand and matched his smile with one of my own. 'Yes,' I said. 'I was there.'

Daniel nodded. 'I also know,' he said quietly, 'that you saved Quentin.' He touched his chest and bowed his head. 'We are all very grateful for your intervention.'

Now I was even more surprised. The Fetch had done his homework. Hightower wasn't part of the witches' council so he must have gone to some lengths to find out about me. Doubly so given that Hightower had been unwilling to admit that he'd been rescued. Doubtless Dr Singh had played matters by the book and told the council of my involvement when he'd informed them of the unknown witch's murder.

'I wish I could have done more and saved John Doe as well,' I said.

'What happened is a tragedy. Did he say anything to you?'

'Uh, no. He was already dead when I came across him.'

Daniel's eyes widened. 'Oh no, I mean Quentin. Did *he* say anything to you?'

I shook my head. 'No.' But why would the Fetch care what Quentin Hightower might have said?

His eyes grew sharper. 'Are you sure?'

I felt an odd tension ripple through my veins and a deepening pressure in my temples. Interesting. 'He didn't say a word,' I replied truthfully.

The Fetch nodded again. 'Well, on his behalf, thank you for what you did.'

I stepped back to put some space between us. 'You're welcome.'

Dr Singh clapped his hands, apparently relieved that we were all getting along. No doubt he'd had more than enough conflict after yesterday's shenanigans. 'Fetch Jackson,' he said, determined to use the witch's official title, 'and I have been discussing John Doe. Although it is unorthodox, he is perfectly happy to include you in the investigation.'

Unorthodox? It was *unheard of* for the witches' council to be so accommodating even to their own kind without considerable persuasion. 'That's ... good,' I said cautiously.

I eyed Daniel Jackson more closely. He didn't look like a maverick council member. He was in his mid-thirties, on the young side for someone in his position, but his smooth clear skin and carefully manicured fingernails suggested he came from wealth as most of them did. His brown hair was short and neat, and there was no visible evidence of anything that the witches' council would frown upon – no jewellery, no tattoos, no overpowering cologne.

'You are clearly a public-spirited woman who can offer a fresh perspective on matters and who cares about her community.' Jackson splayed his hands to indicate he had nothing to hide. 'The least we can do is work together so that this poor man's family is located and informed of his tragic demise.'

Dr Singh clapped his hands together again, which seemed somewhat inappropriate given our reasons for being there. 'Excellent, excellent. I completed the post-mortem last night. If neither of you is averse to the idea, I shall take you through to the main room and show you my findings.'

If the thought of seeing a dead body made Fetch Daniel Jackson feel queasy then he didn't show it. He nodded and picked up his briefcase. 'Yes, that would be good,' he said.

As we trooped through to the examination and storage room I'd been in the day before, Daniel Jackson started babbling. 'It's so sad to think that people might die without anyone knowing who they really were. Thankfully all my family members are accounted for and I have never had to experience the trauma of not knowing what might have happened to them. I had an old schoolfriend whose uncle vanished and it was terrible for his family. Simply terrible. To this day they've never found out what happened to him.' He turned to me. 'Is that why you are so keen to help us identify this man, Ms McCafferty? Have you experienced something similar?'

It felt like an intrusive question given that we'd only just met, but I decided that I would allow it. During my tossing and turning the night before, and in between my agonising mental re-runs of my kiss with Thane, I had wondered why I was so bothered by John Doe's death. The real answer was that I'd never felt enthusiasm for assassination contracts that required the victim's body to disappear because it felt like the terminal punishment was being extended to others. Maybe just this once I could make a difference to a victim's family. Not that I could tell Jackson any of that.

'No,' I said. 'I've never experienced anyone close to me disappearing without explanation, so I can't begin to imagine how awful it must be.' I shrugged helplessly. 'He died at my local market, in my community. I feel a need to help out in any way I can.'

Jackson reached across and patted my arm. 'You are a good woman.'

He wouldn't have said that if he'd known the truth. I smiled anyway and thanked him.

As soon as we entered the room, Dr Singh unhooked the clipboard from the wall. 'You'll have to sign to indicate you have viewed the body,' he said.

'Is that necessary?' Fetch Jackson frowned.

Dr Singh nodded. 'Oh yes. It's procedure. Anyone outwith the mortuary staff who views a body has to sign in.'

I watched the Fetch, curious at his reluctance. He must have felt my eyes on him and he hastily wrote his name before handing the clipboard to me. My scrawled signature was already there from the previous day. 'I've already signed,' I said.

'You have to do it again, Ms McCafferty,' Dr Singh said politely.

I sighed. 'Why?'

'It's procedure.'

For fuck's sake. I signed the damned thing and handed it back; I didn't want to delay this any longer.

The body of the deceased troll had gone and a different shrouded corpse was in his place: John Doe laid out in preparation for our macabre perusal. Dr Singh glanced at both of us. He was already aware that I wouldn't vomit or faint away onto the tiled floor, and the Fetch was also made of sterner stuff than he might have expected. Jackson's jaw was clenched and he had gone rather pale but there was no other indication that the dead body bothered him.

'I can offer you something to allay any nausea or unpleasant sensations,' Dr Singh offered.

Fetch Jackson shook his head. 'I'll be fine,' he said.

The pathologist cleared his throat. When he spoke again, he explained his findings in a practised, professional tone. 'I conducted a full post-mortem. I can confirm that this is the body of a male in his late twenties. Caucasian skin, brown eyes, dark blond hair, with one scar along his chin and two on his upper right thigh that suggest old injuries. From the stains on his fingertips and the preliminary blood tests, he is a witch in origin – the lab work will confirm that within three to five working days. The contents of his stomach suggest that he had been drinking alcohol in the hours before his death and he had eaten some sort of meat sandwich. Again, the laboratory will be able to confirm that in more detail.'

Daniel Jackson swallowed hard. I nodded.

'There is no fluid in his lungs so I am of the opinion that he was dead before he entered the water. There are some external injuries and abrasions on his skin that suggest that his body was carried down the river for a short distance before it was found.'

He didn't fall into the Tweed at the same point as Quentin Hightower then, which suggested that the two incidents weren't immediately connected.

Jackson straightened. 'Interesting. It appears that he's not from your community at all, Ms McCafferty – he's not a Danksville resident.'

'Perhaps not.' I tried to sound non-committal; I'd already made up my mind about this investigation: I wouldn't back away even if John Doe turned out to be from Timbuktu.

Dr Singh continued. 'Cause of death is a single stab wound to the heart.' He raised his eyebrows at me. 'The blade, which must have been a foot in length but only three or four millimetres in width, entered his body lower down and was thrust upwards. Whoever stabbed him intended to kill him. Death would have been very swift.'

He lifted one corner of the white sheet, gestured to the wound on John Doe's side and demonstrated how the murder weapon had been used.

I gazed again at the small incision. It had been made by a professional weapon wielded by a professional hand. It didn't take a hardened assassin to surmise that whoever had killed John Doe had either killed before or had zero compunction about ending another's life. Not that I thought for a moment that it was any of my ex-colleagues' work. None of them would wander around with such an identifiable sword because it could easily be traced if it were found and it would be difficult to carry around unobtrusively.

I glanced at Jackson. His eyes weren't on John Doe's body but on his face. I sucked in a breath. 'You know who he is?'

Jackson licked his lips. 'I believe so.' He raised his head, clicked his tongue and nodded sadly, then went to the table in the far corner of the room and opened his briefcase. He rummaged inside for a moment before extracting a slim folder. He frowned at its contents then stared again at John Doe's face.

'Yes,' he said. 'I know who this is. I'll conduct a trace spell on his blood to be certain, but there's little doubt. Our John Doe is actually a witch called Rory Taggert.'

CHAPTER
TEN

When we returned to Dr Singh's office, Fetch Jackson spread out the contents of the folder on the pathologist's wooden desk. I watched as he moved his hat and gloves out of the way then arranged the sheets of paper so we could all see them. Once he'd finished, I stared at him pointedly.

'I brought the files of all the witches who've been reported missing to us in the last three months,' he explained.

Well, now wasn't that handy?

'It's as well that I did,' he continued. 'John Doe – or rather Rory Taggert – is one of them.'

Keeping my expression blank, I reached for the first piece of paper. 'He was reported missing by his parents?'

'Yes.' Jackson nodded soberly. 'Only three days ago. He doesn't—' he coughed and amended his words '—*didn't* live with them but he checked in regularly. When he didn't make his usual Sunday visit, his father went to his flat and discovered it was empty. He reported his son missing shortly afterwards.' He tapped another sheet of paper. 'Taggert Senior was upset at his son's disappearance but not surprised.'

Dr Singh picked up another piece of paper. 'Drug use. Numerous accounts of petty crime.' He let out a low whistle. 'He was regularly in trouble with the MET.'

'May I see?' I asked. He handed me the sheet and I scanned it. Rory Taggert had a checkered history, from larceny to mugging and opportunistic thieving. Judging by the number of times he'd been arrested, he hadn't been a particularly successful criminal.

'I expect Mr Taggert tried to steal from the wrong person and was stabbed for his efforts,' Dr Singh said quietly.

Jackson pursed his lips disapprovingly. 'From his history, it was only a matter of time.' He gathered up the papers before I could examine them all. 'I will visit his parents and inform them of his passing. When they are able, they can identify his body.' He tutted. 'It's a sad state of affairs, especially for Mr and Mrs Taggert.'

'Can I make a copy of that file?' I asked. I hadn't been able to glimpse an address either for Rory Taggert or for his parents.

'That wouldn't be appropriate, Ms McCafferty. You're not part of the formal investigation and now that we know who he is ...' The Fetch's voice trailed away. 'It's best if we deal with this officially from now on.'

Damn. 'Of course.' I bowed my head. 'I'm simply glad that we know who he is and that his parents will receive some sort of closure.'

The witch offered a sad smile. 'You have done good work here. Coldstream could do with more citizens like you.' He turned to Dr Singh. 'Could I have his personal possessions? His parents will want them.'

The pathologist nodded. 'I shall retrieve them for you now.' He went out of the room.

I looked at Fetch Jackson and he looked at me. There were a thousand questions burning in my head but I chose to hold my tongue. It seemed the wisest option; I didn't yet understand the rules of this particular game and, until I did, I needed to play my cards close to my chest.

Jackson misinterpreted my expression. 'I wouldn't feel too bad, Ms McCafferty. There are lots of young men like Rory Taggert in Coldstream. Some manage to change their ways, some fall foul of their own misdeeds. I won't say that he deserved what happened to him but he wasn't a good person. He wasn't like you.'

It was getting harder to stay quiet. 'Mmm.'

He patted my hand just as Dr Singh returned with faintly reddened cheeks. 'Er, there's no easy way to say this,' he began, 'but I'm afraid that Rory Taggert's effects are no longer here.'

Jackson stiffened. 'What do you mean?'

'His clothes would have been removed from his body when he was brought in, and bagged and tagged together with anything else that was found on him. We keep all such items in a special storage room towards the back of the building.'

'You put them there yourself?'

'No. I wasn't here when Mr Taggert was brought in. It would have been my colleague, Dr Biswick.'

Dr Biswick whose filing was haphazard. 'Is there any chance that she put the items in the wrong place?' I asked.

Singh shook his head. 'No. I'll double-check with her, but I don't see where else she *could* have put them.'

'He was in the Tweed – his clothes would have been soaking wet,' I pointed out. 'Could they have been hung out to dry or laundered?'

'No. We've learned over the years not to second-guess what families want to retrieve and how they wish to retrieve it. Not everyone wants items to be restored and cleaned. The guide-lines are very specific – we wait to hear the next-of-kin's wishes before we do anything. Plus,' he added uncomfortably, 'as soon as we learned that his death was deliberate, there would have been more reason not to tamper with his effects.'

Jackson shifted his weight from foot to foot; he looked extremely upset. 'What about an inventory?' he barked. 'What has actually gone missing?'

The pathologist ran a frustrated hand through his hair. 'Not a lot,' he admitted. 'There was no wallet, watch or jewellery. All he had were his clothes – a blue shirt, dark trousers and a heavy belt with a gold buckle.' He flicked a look at me. 'You don't suppose that man yesterday stole them, do you?'

Jackson's head whipped towards me. 'What man?'

I winced inwardly; I'd been hoping that the matter of Knox Thunderstick wouldn't come up. 'When I visited the mortuary yesterday, I spoke to a man who I thought was Dr Singh.'

'He was wearing my lab coat,' the pathologist interjected. 'He'd obviously broken in here and was snooping around. He jumped out of the staffroom window before we could stop him. He knocked me down and Ms McCafferty—'

I interrupted. 'He was a young man and I'm a middle-aged woman who's not as fit as she used to be.' At least both of those things were true. 'I went after him, but once he'd left the building I knew I couldn't catch him up.'

'You don't know who he was?' Jackson demanded. 'You'd never seen him before?'

I felt the same tension and pressure in my temples as I had earlier. 'Not until yesterday, when I mistook him for Dr Singh.' Again I was telling the truth – but omitting what I'd learned more recently.

'Was he a witch?'

'A druid, I believe,' Singh answered.

A tiny, inarticulate noise escaped Jackson's mouth.

'At least the missing items are only clothes,' I said, watching the Fetch carefully.

His jaw clenched then he forced himself to relax. 'Yes. Only clothes. They're not important.'

'I hope his parents won't be too upset at their loss.'

For a brief moment his expression clouded as if he'd entirely forgotten that Rory Taggert's parents existed. 'I will explain to them and offer the mortuary's sincere apologies on your behalf.'

Dr Singh blanched. 'Please do.'

Jackson looked at me. 'Thank you again for your concern, Ms McCafferty. It has been a pleasure to meet you.' He was clearly dismissing me. He started walking towards the door, manoeuvring in such a way as to usher me out.

I considered my options then obliged. 'Thank you for allowing me to join this meeting,' I said. 'I appreciate that the witches' council has been kind enough to put my worries to rest by including me.'

'We are here to serve the entire community, not only witches.' Jackson smiled, baring his teeth. 'But you are welcome. Let's walk out together.'

As I looked over my shoulder, my eyes met Dr Singh's; he was still looking troubled by the loss of Rory Taggert's clothes. 'Thank you,' I said again.

'Of course.' The pathologist nodded, then Fetch Daniel Jackson took my elbow and all-but marched me down the hallway.

Ignoring his raised eyebrows and flash of amusement, I retrieved a reluctant He Who Roams Wide from Cindy's lap. She sniffed her disappointment that my cat wasn't staying, but, with a Fetch in attendance, she chose to keep her mouth shut.

While he shrugged on his coat and adjusted his cuffs, I slipped out of the front door with He Who Roams Wide by my heels and headed down the street without looking back. I only turned to the cat when I was a good distance away and nobody could overhear me. 'Well,' I said, 'that was interesting.'

He Who Roams Wide flicked the tip of his tail and angled his head up to me.

'That man was a Fetch from the witches' council,' I told him.

There was a small miaow.

'Yep. *That* witches' council. The bureaucratic nightmare that serves only witches, and keeps its doors tightly closed against all others. They sent a Fetch to investigate my John Doe, even though he was neither rich nor famous nor powerful – in fact, it appears he was nothing more than a petty criminal. Even more bizarrely, Fetch Jackson let me join in so I could discover that information. That's quite out of character for someone from the witches' council, wouldn't you say?'

He Who Roams Wide miaowed louder.

'In fact,' I continued, 'I'd go so far as to say that he wanted me to learn John Doe's real name so that I'd stop asking questions and return to my cat-lady cave without so much as a follow-up whimper.'

The cat butted my leg with his head.

I reached up, touched my temples and grimaced. 'He used a truth spell on me. Twice.' I sniffed, irritated by the mental intrusion that I obviously hadn't been expected to notice. 'And the possessions brought in with the body have mysteriously vanished. Knox Thunderstick didn't steal them. He wasn't carrying anything with him when he ran off.'

He Who Roams Wide's ears twitched.

'If Fetch Jackson was telling the truth and I can believe that missing persons' file, John Doe is Rory Taggert. But my questions haven't been answered. In fact,' I mused, 'now I have more.' A lot more.

THE CROWD of people in the middle of Coldstream wasn't He Who Roams Wide's idea of a good time, so he abandoned me long before I reached Crackendon Square in favour of quieter streets. I didn't worry about him; he'd find his way home once he was hungry.

I started to cross the square, hurrying to avoid an oncoming tram, its purple sparks lighting up the dull day. A group of tourists, doubtless from one of Britain's non-magical cities, were standing in my path with their phones poised to take photos of anything weird and supposedly unnatural that took their fancy.

I tried to veer around them but one of their number, a young woman who was wearing what looked like cheap fancy dress bought from the internet for her outing, spotted me. 'Are you a Preternatural?' she breathed, her eyes wide with the wonders of Coldstream.

I wasn't in the mood for inane questions. 'What do you think?'

Somebody came up beside me and the young woman's attention turned to her. 'What about you? Are *you* a Preternatural?'

'No,' came the rejoinder in a surprisingly friendly tone of voice. 'I'm a squib.'

The young woman gasped. 'So am I!'

Not exactly: squibs possessed no magic or special powers, yet chose to live in Coldstream; people without magic who lived elsewhere were just people.

I glanced at the real squib and realised that it was Mallory, the slightly odd woman who lived nearby and who worked as a broker. She wasn't a pawnbroker or a stockbroker: Mallory brokered secrets and favours, and consequently she fascinated me. I didn't understand how her business worked but it intrigued me enough that I wanted to know.

What didn't surprise me was that the young tourist had assumed Mallory was magical. Her appearance was ... interesting. She was as dishevelled as she'd been the first time I'd met her, as if she'd just tumbled out of bed. Her brown corkscrew curls sprang off in all directions and she was wearing a long dress of colourful patchwork. I had no doubt that Mallory really was a squib because I couldn't sense the faintest whisper of magic emanating from her, but she certainly looked as if she possessed unusual powers – and she seemed to be very much at home in Coldstream.

The young woman moved away, her attention caught by a group of druids who looked as unimpressed at her approach as I had been. Then a top-hatted leprechaun on a penny-farthing cycled past and she gave a squeal of delight and jogged after him, her camera phone raised.

I focused on Mallory, this time with a genuine smile. 'Hey, good to see you again.'

Mallory gave me a dazzling smile. 'Kit, right?' she asked. 'Thane's friend?'

I nodded. 'How's Bert?' I asked, referring to the cat she'd been looking after when I'd first met her.

'He's returned to his original home and all is well with the world. I have to confess that I miss having him around. Cats are good company.'

I could only agree.

'How is Thane?' she asked.

There was no reason for me to feel awkward about the question because Thane had introduced me to Mallory, but an unfamiliar twitchiness ran through me nonetheless. 'Good,' I said. 'He's good.'

Mallory's eyes twinkled and I sensed that she could see

right through me. I shifted uncomfortably as I searched for a way to change the subject. 'Actually, I'm glad I bumped into you.'

She raised an eyebrow. 'Oh yes?'

'I'm fascinated by your work, but I don't really understand what it is that you do.'

She laughed. 'Few people do but it's quite simple. I'm a trader but instead of physical goods, I trade in secrets and favours.'

My brow furrowed. 'I know that part but I don't see how it works in practice. People pay you for secrets?'

'Oh no. No money changes hands. I don't need money when I can get all I need through favours.' She smiled at my baffled expression. 'I'll give you an example. Let's say Person A wants to attend a particular event but they're not on the guest list. I'll help them get an invitation, and in return they will give me a high-grade secret about someone or something that very few people know about it. Person B will benefit from knowing that secret so I'll pass it to them if they agree to supply me with whatever I need at that moment in time. It can get more complicated, but essentially that's what I do.'

I wasn't much clearer on how it all fitted together but it made a sort of sense.

Mallory's eyes remained warm. 'Is there some information, some secret perhaps, that you're looking for, Kit?'

It was time to tread cautiously. 'Maybe,' I hedged.

'If you tell me what you're searching for, we can negotiate terms.'

I drew in a breath. I didn't really know Mallory, but it was clear that Thane trusted her and I sensed that she was honourable. Of course, I'd been mistaken about people in the past – and so had Thane, for that matter.

I chose my next words carefully. I didn't want to give too

much away but I needed to provide Mallory with enough information for her skills to be useful to me. 'I want to know what is top of the agenda for the witches' council this week.'

Mallory's eyebrows rose. 'Only members of the witches' council are privy to that sort of information.'

I should have known it was too much to ask. 'Never mind.'

She grinned. 'Hold your horses. If you give me thirty-six hours, I can find out what they're currently focussing on. I have … ways and means. I wouldn't be much of a secrets' trader if I didn't.'

From the delight on her face, Mallory obviously enjoyed her work. Good for her.

'What would you require in return?' I knew plenty of secrets but I'd taken a vow not to reveal any of the work I'd done for EEL; that vow was unbreakable, regardless of the circumstances. There were also limits as to how far I was prepared to go for Rory Taggert; after all, it was far too late to save him.

She tapped her mouth thoughtfully. 'I sense that you know many valuable things that would equal the information you require from me, but I don't think you'd be willing to part with any of that knowledge.'

I watched her warily. Squib or not, her instincts were spot on and I was starting to suspect that she was more capable than I'd first realised.

She swept her gaze up and down my body, then nodded. 'A favour then,' she said decisively. 'One favour, twelve months' limit. If I do not request the favour from you within the next year, you are absolved of your obligation.'

I appreciated the time limit but unspecified favours were dangerous: *very* dangerous. I sucked in a breath and considered. 'I won't physically harm anyone I care about.'

'Interesting,' Mallory murmured. 'In most negotiations of this sort, people say that they won't physically harm *anyone*.'

Oops: I'd already managed to give away more information than I'd intended with that little slip. 'I can see that there might be circumstances when harm is unavoidable,' I parried.

'Indeed.' She looked amused. 'I accept those terms. I shall have a contract drawn up. I have an occasional assistant who will find you when it's ready so you can sign on the dotted line.'

'A blood contract?'

Mallory smirked. 'Is there any other kind?' She checked her watch. 'Let's meet here on Friday night and I'll give you the information you need. Say eight o'clock?'

Alexander MacTire's face flashed into my mind. I grimaced. 'Actually, I have a dinner date then. How about seven o'clock instead?'

'I already have an appointment. I'll come and find you at the restaurant. I won't take up much of your time.'

That would make my life easier. 'Okay. I'll be at Vallese.'

'Vallese? My, my.'

'It wasn't my choice of venue.'

'Now I'm even more intrigued,' Mallory murmured.

I couldn't begin to imagine what Alexander MacTire would make of Mallory but it didn't matter; none of this was any of his business. 'Until then,' I said.

She raised a hand in farewell. 'Adieu.' She paused and her expression altered subtly. 'Do give Thane my best.' Then, before I could say anything else, Mallory melted away into the crowds.

CHAPTER
ELEVEN

P ork Pies café was busier than I'd expected, but I caught sight of Thane at one of the Formica-covered tables and headed straight for him. A small temporary stage had been set up in front of him, complete with a microphone and basic sound system.

There wasn't any sign of Knox Thunderstick or the Blue Tattoos as I wended my way between the people who were waiting for the band to appear. Despite what the waiter had said last night, the group was surprisingly popular and at least two of the customers were sporting Blue Tattoos' t-shirts.

Thane looked up as I approached and flashed a relieved grin as if he hadn't been sure that I'd show up. 'Hey.'

I pulled up a chair and sat next to him, leaning in slightly to catch a whiff of his vetiver scent. 'How's your head?'

'Better than I deserve. You look tired, Kit.' Then he winced. 'Sorry. I didn't mean to criticise. You look good. Just a bit...'

I raised my hands to forestall any further awkwardness. I wasn't remotely offended; I did look tired and there was no point pretending otherwise. The last thing I needed was a false compliment.

'I had a restless night but I'm fine. Truly.' I eyed him as I wondered if he'd say anything about what had happened between us. Should *I* say something? I frowned; I didn't know how I felt, let alone what I should say. Kit McCafferty: trained killer, scared of nothing – apart from feelings. So much for being the Big Bad.

Thane chose to stick to business. 'How did it go at the mortuary?'

I exhaled; that was a much safer topic. I told him everything that had happened, including my suspicions that Fetch Daniel Jackson had been playing me. Thane listened, interjecting with a few questions but saying little else until I'd finished.

'If I were playing Devil's Advocate, Kit, I'd say that you've accomplished what you set out to do. John Doe has been identified, the witches' council sat up and took notice, and his family will be informed.'

'Job done, then? Go home and forget any of this happened?' I nodded towards the door. 'Feel free.'

Thane leaned back in his chair and grinned. 'Not a chance. I don't know about you but I don't want a quiet mid-life before I slip into retirement and fade away. I'm fully invested in Rory Taggert and Knox Thunderstick. I'm going nowhere.'

I met his eyes. 'There's far more going on here than we realise.'

'Whatever it is, it's big,' he agreed.

'We can't back out.'

'Not a chance.'

'We still don't know who killed Taggert.'

'Or why.'

'We don't know how Knox Thunderstick is involved.'

'But we will soon.'

'And the witches' council is acting very strangely.'

Thane nodded his copper-haired head. 'Very strangely indeed.'

We smiled at each other resolutely.

'I might know a few people who can sniff around the council and find out what's going on in their inner sanctum,' Thane suggested.

'Actually, I've got that covered. I bumped into Mallory on the way here and she's working on it for me.'

'You've employed Mallory? You realise there'll be a cost.'

I sighed. 'Yes. I don't exactly know what yet.'

'I hope it's worth it.'

'Me too. She'll let me know what she finds out on Friday night.'

'You're meeting at her place?'

'No,' I said absently as a long-haired druid whom I recognised from the poster as the Blue Tattoos' singer appeared and started fiddling with the equipment on the tiny stage. 'She'll meet me at Vallese. I'm having dinner there on Friday with Alexander MacTire.'

Thane didn't say anything; he was watching me with hooded green eyes. 'A date?'

Oh. I shrugged helplessly. 'I guess. It doesn't mean anything. It's only dinner.'

'He might be a pack alpha but he's a good man.' Thane pursed his lips. 'Mostly.'

'Thane—'

'Your private life is your own affair, Kit.'

Before I could say anything more, a second member of the Blue Tattoos walked past us, a deep scowl on his face. 'He's still not fucking here,' he muttered to his bandmate.

Thane and I exchanged glances. I leaned forward to continue eavesdropping, although I kept my head turned away to avoid looking too obvious. I needn't have worried; neither of the musicians paid me any attention and they made no attempt to lower their voices.

'Where the fuck is he?' the singer hissed. 'First the rehearsal yesterday, and now this?'

'I dunno, man,' came the rejoinder. 'He doesn't usually let us down. And you know that yesterday wasn't his fault. Maybe he's not well.'

'It's not as if he lives far away – he could stumble out of bed and let us know. And he's got a phone. He could call the land-line here and leave a message.'

The young druid pursed his lips. 'Maybe he already has.' He lifted his head and beckoned a waitress. 'Can you check to see if Knox has called?'

'I could,' she answered. 'But the phone's not working. We're waiting on an engineer.'

She'd be waiting a while. If the café was having a magical problem, they could find any number of people who would solve it at a moment's notice but more mundane technology was a different matter. It was far harder to find someone in Coldstream who could fix a phone line or resolve an electrical fault, and engineers often had to be brought in from outside. That took time – and a lot of money.

Obviously annoyed, the singer hissed, 'He still owes us money for the last gig. If this is his way of avoiding paying us...' He bared his teeth. 'We should never have let him take charge of the accounting.'

I pulled back while the two druids continued to mutter angrily.

'Do you think something untoward might have happened to Mr Thunderstick?' Thane whispered.

I grimaced. 'It's a likely scenario. We need to find out where he lives and head there as soon as possible.'

'I doubt those two will tell us, but if he's in charge of the band's finances the café might have some invoices lying around with his address on them.'

Thane had read my mind. 'Time to go snooping,' I agreed. I nodded surreptitiously towards the closed door marked *Staff Only*. 'Shall I create a diversion, or do you want to do it?'

'You're better at sneaking than I am.' He grinned. 'I'll take care of it.'

He stood up and started pushing his way through the crowd. 'I'd like to speak to the manager!' he declared loudly to the poor waitress who'd been speaking to the Blue Tattoos.

She blinked at him, startled. 'Is there a problem, sir?'

'Yes!' he snapped. 'I just had a cup of coffee and it was absolutely disgusting! I want to make a formal complaint!'

I was already on my feet and nearing the staffroom door.

'We have complaint forms...' she began.

Thane interrupted her. 'No, I want to speak to the manager. They will be responsible for buying the pathetic excuse for fresh coffee beans that you advertise. I want to go to the top!' To add emphasis to his complaint, he thumped the counter.

His attitude was far above the waitress's pay grade. 'Wait here, sir,' she said. 'I'll fetch the owner.' She turned and disappeared through the door in front of me.

Customers were staring at Thane, obviously annoyed with him. 'Fucking werewolves,' a dryad said. 'They're always so loud and obnoxious.'

'Hey!' protested a female werewolf wearing the insignia of a pack I didn't recognise. 'Not all werewolves!'

'Tell that to the waitress,' the dryad snapped.

The female werewolf scowled then got to her feet and strode towards Thane. 'What are you doing? You're giving the rest of us a bad name. And there's nothing wrong with the damned coffee!'

I had the awful sensation that Thane's attempt at a diversion was about to descend into a bloody brawl. Fortunately, at that moment the staff door opened again and the waitress and a pretty brown-haired woman, presumably the Pork Pies owner, walked out.

At the same time, the singer of the Blue Tattoos tapped his microphone. 'I'm sorry, folks,' he said. 'But we have to cancel today's performance.'

A groan rippled through the waiting crowd.

'We're short of one member,' he said, 'and—'

I didn't wait to hear the end of the sentence before I slipped through the door into the staff area.

Anyone who's not worked in the service industry could be forgiven for thinking that delightful mysteries lie behind doors marked 'staff only', but I'd been in enough of them when I was working on various assassination contracts to know they hid nothing delightful. The only mystery was why every staff-only space, whether it was a magical premises in Coldstream or a fast-food joint in London, smelled faintly of boiled cabbage. At least this particular area was small so I didn't think it would take long to find the paperwork I needed.

There was a narrow hallway with two doors leading off it, both wide open, suggesting that either the café staff were too trusting and overly complacent, or that there was a secret security system in place. This might only be a café, but it was a café in Coldstream.

Thane would only be able to keep the café manager occupied for so long so I had to move quickly – but that didn't mean I would be stupid. Speed and stealth in equal measures would win the day.

In the first room there were some chairs, a kettle and a sad-looking jar of broken cookies. The second room was more promising, with a row of filing cabinets, a desk and a stacked in-tray. Bingo.

The room seemed to be empty; it was a small space and, although the open door meant that I could only see half of it, I was experienced enough at sneaking around to tell if somewhere was occupied. But something felt off; there was a prickling on the back of my neck and I had the sensation that danger lay ahead.

I had to trust my gut. I crouched down and carefully examined the door frame and carpet. Wards or booby traps seemed unlikely: the door was open and café staff probably came in and out far too regularly to make a magical barrier worthwhile. I checked the door frame and the carpet but found nothing untoward.

The door was a fraction too small for its frame with an inch shaved off the bottom perhaps to accommodate the carpet, which was no longer as fluffy as it had been when it was first laid. I lay flat on the floor and squinted underneath it to glimpse the corner of the room that was hidden from my sight. The floor was bare; nothing – and nobody – was there.

I heaved myself up to my feet, wondering if it was my bones creaking or the floor. Raised voices were coming from the café; I needed to stop delaying and get moving. I stepped across the threshold of the office.

Nothing happened: no alarm sounded, no magical shriek rent the air. So much for those trusty gut instincts.

I moved towards the desk, but as soon as I looked at the wall that had been concealed by the door and saw the portrait, my heart sank. Oh.

I looked at the painting and it looked at me – or rather *she* looked at me. Judging by her dress, she was from the eighteenth century, which made sense because almost all Cursed Portraits were from that period. She was wearing a ridiculously large wig that could have comfortably housed several small birds and their nesting broods, and her silver dress had been painted in such a way that it reflected the light. She was holding an open book in one hand and a drooping rose in the other – but I knew better than to assume she was a bookish, simpering miss.

This wasn't my first rodeo with a Cursed Portrait and I hated the damned things. They were never an accurate portrayal of the sitter because the painter imbued too much of their own personality into the work. It seemed to me that the pictures took on both the worst aspects of the artist and the worst aspects of whoever they were painting. And they were unpredictable.

Cursed Portraits were usually locked away in large houses, part and parcel of complicated inheritance laws, so finding one in the back room of a small, modern café was very unusual.

'Good afternoon,' I said formally, hoping that would be more to the portrait's liking than a cheery 'hiya'.

She blinked at me, and for one optimistic moment I thought I might have stumbled across a mute portrait. No such luck. After a few seconds her nose wrinkled and she sighed. It wasn't a delicate melancholy sound, it was bitter, angst-filled and annoyed.

'You are an intruder,' the Cursed Portrait said in cut-glass tones. 'You do not belong here.'

I had little choice but to brazen it out. I moved behind the desk and responded with an imperious toss of my head, 'Of course I belong here.' I picked up a sheaf of paper and began to flick through it, searching for a Blue Tattoos' invoice. Maybe if I ignored the portrait, I'd find what I needed and make my escape before she started screeching an alarm.

'You are a dirty wretched thief, aren't you? You've come here to steal me away from my home. Well, I can tell you that I will not stand for it.'

I looked up. From the anger in her tone, ignoring her

wouldn't work. 'You look like you've been standing there for the better part of three hundred years,' I said.

Outraged, the portrait gasped, 'I'm barely two hundred!'

I raised a sceptical eyebrow. Maybe keeping her busy was a better idea. 'Hardly,' I scoffed. 'In fact you're closer to four hundred years old. You're certainly looking rather faded and cracked.'

'You lying, thieving strumpet!'

'I am neither lying nor thieving.' I paused and grinned. 'But I'll take strumpet.'

'Ugh!'

'What's your name?' I asked. 'Wait, don't tell me. You're ... Betty.'

'Betty? *Betty?* I am not some common trollop!'

'Oh?' I dropped my gaze, flicking through the papers in my hand at high speed, wanting to get out as quickly as possible. So far, all I'd seen were bills for food and electricity. There was nothing related to the Blue Tattoos or any other bands.

'My name is Lady Augusta De Marcy,' the Cursed Portrait said huffily. 'You may address me as Your Ladyship.'

'Hereditary titles are terribly passé, don't you think? I'll call you Oggy.'

'You will *not!*'

I abandoned the papers on the desk and reached for a drawer.

'You won't find anything of interest in there, you harlot! Get your mucky fingers out of my drawers!'

'Who's the harlot now?' I murmured. 'I have no interest in your drawers.'

Unfortunately I had no interest in the café owner's drawers either; they contained nothing more than a half-eaten packet of mint humbugs and some chewed pencils. I turned towards the filing cabinets, desperately hoping that the woman who ran the café alphabetised her papers.

'I have had enough of this!' Lady Augusta shrieked. 'Harriet! Harriet! Get in here!'

I winced. 'Shush! Harriet is busy!'

'I am in charge of this establishment! If I want Harriet, Harriet will come!'

Goddamnit. Any second now she'd scream the whole building down. I yanked the nearest cabinet drawer.

'I'd have thought,' I said in desperation, 'that running a café would be beneath a lady of your standing.'

'Despite my efforts, my family has fallen on difficult times,' she sneered. 'But I am not afraid of hard work. I will work these delicate fingers to the bone if it means that the De Marcys can be returned to their rightful position in society.'

'I have told you that the De Marcys are gone, Your Ladyship,' said a new voice. 'They haven't existed for three generations. There's nobody left and no rightful position to reclaim.'

I turned my head and my eyes met those of the brown-haired café owner. Then my gaze dropped to the large kitchen knife she was clutching in her hands. Uh-oh.

A half second later, Lady Augusta started to cackle.

CHAPTER
TWELVE

Harriet – because presumably that was the café owner's name – looked fierce enough to use the sharp knife she was brandishing, but my old assassin's instincts had stirred into life and I'd already established three different ways I could use the weapon against her. It would take very little effort to bring her down because she wasn't a professional; neither was she a witch or a druid, so it was unlikely she'd be throwing any spells my way.

It seemed unfair to hurt her, though, when she was only defending what was hers. She hadn't done anything wrong – and I still didn't have the information I needed. I took charge of the situation before she panicked and did something we'd all regret.

'My name is Kit,' I said quickly. 'I'm not here to hurt anyone or to steal from you. All I'm trying to find is a teeny-tiny piece of information about a member of the Blue Tattoos.'

It might have been my imagination but it seemed that Harriet relaxed slightly. 'Two of them are out there.' She jerked her head towards the café. 'You could have asked them.'

'I could have,' I agreed pleasantly. 'But they wouldn't have told me, not without some persuasion. And I'm trying to avoid hurting people unnecessarily these days.'

'Kill her, Harriet!' Lady Augusta shouted. 'Stab her in the heart! Now!'

Harriet lowered the knife. 'Are you succeeding?' she enquired, ignoring the painting.

'At not hurting people?' I considered. 'Mostly. Apart from when they really deserve it.'

Lady Augusta wasn't finished, and she didn't appear to care that Harriet was paying her no attention. 'Claw her eyes out!'

'She's quite bloodthirsty, isn't she?' I commented.

Harriet rolled her eyes. 'You haven't heard the half of it.' She took another step into the room and closed the door behind her.

'Slit her throat!'

'Hush,' Harriet said to Lady Augusta, then gazed at me. 'The werewolf. He's with you?'

There was no point in lying; we'd been sitting together for twenty minutes before Thane had started his coffee-complaint diversion. 'Yes.'

'I've thrown him out,' she said casually. 'And I've told him he has a lifetime ban. He can never come back here. I don't appreciate false complaints with underhand motives.'

Fair enough, though it was a shame for Thane. The bacon rolls here were good. 'Okay.'

'What do you want with the Blue Tattoos?' Harriet asked.

'I want to talk to the drummer. I've got some questions for Knox Thunderstick.'

Her face tightened. 'What sort of questions?'

'They're for Knox,' I said gently. 'Not for you.'

'I'm the one holding the knife.'

'Trust me,' I said. 'When I say that if I wanted to change that situation, I could.'

'That's a threat!' Lady Augusta shrieked. 'That was definitely a threat!'

Something sparked in Harriet's eyes. 'Enough, Augusta!'

'You are unworthy of the De Marcy name!'

'I am *not* a De Marcy. We've been through this. Many times.' She returned her attention to me. 'Do you wish to harm Knox?'

'No.'

'Do you know why he's not shown up today?'

'No.' I paused. 'But there's a chance he's gotten himself into some serious trouble.'

Something tightened around Harriet's eyes. 'What sort of trouble?'

I sighed. 'I don't know exactly – and what I do know is complicated. Does the name Rory Taggert mean anything to you?'

Harriet shook her head. 'I've never heard of him. Who is he? What does he have to do with this?'

'I don't know,' I said. 'Yet.'

'Your brother is always creating conflict,' Lady Augusta hissed.

I blinked. 'Brother? But you're not a druid.'

Harriet shot the Cursed Portrait a dagger-laden look. 'Foster brother. We were both in the system and we grew up together. And, no, before you ask my last name isn't Thunderstick. It's Hemworth.'

Suddenly a lot of things made sense. Her admission explained why the Blue Tattoos played here every week, not to mention her concern and why Knox had changed his surname to something ridiculous. He wasn't beholden to any family name.

I watched her expression then I made up my mind and told her the truth – the whole truth. Now I knew who Harriet was, I had nothing to lose and everything to gain. 'I'm looking into a murder.'

She stiffened. 'Rory Taggert?'

I nodded. 'A witch, by all accounts.'

'I've never heard of him, and I've never heard Knox mention anyone called Rory.'

'When I went to the mortuary where Taggert's body was being kept, Knox showed up pretending to be a pathologist. He ran off before I could talk to him, but I'm assuming he was there for the same body. I don't know what's going on, only that I *will* find out. The witches' council is also getting in on the act. There's a lot more to this than meets the eye and I think Knox could well be involved.'

Harriet sighed heavily, her expression anxious. 'He's always involved in something, mostly ridiculous get-rich quick schemes.' She gestured to Lady Augusta. 'That's how I ended up with her. But he's not a bad person, not really.'

'I'm sure you're right,' I said.

She narrowed her gaze and I instantly realised my mistake. 'You're a Truth Seeker,' I breathed.

Harriet started to lift the knife and her fingers tightened around its hilt.

'That's why you relaxed when I told you why I was here,' I went on. 'That's why your questions have been so specific, and that's why this place is called Pork Pies. It's not because of the menu, it's Cockney rhyming slang – pork pies means lies. You can tell every single time when someone is lying.'

Harriet's face was white and there was fear in her eyes. Truth Seekers were rare – and coveted; there were plenty of powerful people in Coldstream who would try to use Harriet for their own ends if they knew what she was capable of. She wouldn't be left in peace to run her little café, that was for sure.

'I won't tell anyone,' I said quickly. 'I won't breathe a word to a soul. I give you my word.' In Coldstream, that was practically sacrosanct; only a true fool would break such a freely given vow.

Her shoulders dropped. 'It's not as much fun being a Truth Seeker as you might think,' she whispered. 'People often lie for the most ridiculous of reasons. Knox knows what I can do and he still lies to me all the time.'

'*I* do not lie!' Lady Agatha declared.

Neither Harriet nor I glanced at her. 'I suppose you'll find him sooner or later.' She sighed. 'He's never missed a gig before. If I give you his address, will you check on him and make sure he's alright?'

I nodded and she shot me an impatient look. 'Yes,' I said, realising I had to speak aloud for her tainted gift to work.

'Will you hurt him?'

That was harder. 'I won't hurt him unless it's by accident or in self-defence. And I won't let anyone who's with me hurt him unnecessarily,' I added, thinking of Thane. 'That's the best I can do. I don't know Knox. I don't know how he'll react when I track him down.'

Harriet seemed to accept this. 'Sometimes he's his own worst enemy, but he is a good guy at heart and I do love him.' I believed her. 'Thirty-two Glade Cross,' she told me. 'That's where he lives.'

'Thank you.'

'I hope I won't regret telling you.'

I met her eyes again. 'You won't.'

I found Thane not too far from the Pork Pies' entrance, kicking his heels against a wall. He looked none the worse for being thrown out of the café but three werewolves, including the woman who'd called him out for his ridiculous complaint, were hovering nearby and watching him with narrowed eyes.

'Making friends and winning hearts all over the place, Thane?'

He grinned. 'It's all in the name of your murder investigation, Kit.'

'*Our* murder investigation,' I said lightly. I wanted him to stick around so I might as well admit it aloud. That didn't mean I'd tell him about Harriet; I could still keep a secret when I had to.

'Was it worth it?' he asked. 'Did you get an address for Knox Thunderstick?'

'I did and we're in luck. He lives only a few streets away.' I pointed left. 'It's this way.'

We set off immediately and trotted in the direction of Knox's home. I kept an eye on the three werewolves, but thankfully none of them chose to follow us. Not all wolves were that smart; in my experience far too many of them acted first and thought later. And if they'd been aware of Thane's identity, we might have had even more of a problem. Thane Barrow's name had been mud amongst werewolves for many years, although recently that appeared to be changing.

'That woman,' he said. 'The café owner. She knew immediately that my complaint wasn't genuine.'

'Uh-huh.'

'She seemed more concerned about the Blue Tattoos than my tastebuds.'

'Uh-huh.'

'She went into the back. Unless the building's far bigger than it looks, she must have seen you.'

'Uh-huh.'

'But you won't give me any of the details, will you?'

I smiled. 'Nope. She's a nice lady.'

'She's banned me.'

I shrugged. 'Sucks to be you, Cat Boy.'

He jabbed my arm. 'Watch it, Cat Lady.'

I gave him what I thought was an impressive feline hiss and he laughed. We lapsed into a comfortable silence. That was what I liked about him – one of the many things I liked about him: he didn't feel the pressing need to fill every quiet pause with unnecessary words. It was a surprisingly unusual trait.

We reached Glade Cross within fifteen minutes. It was a narrow street with tightly packed stone buildings on both sides of the road. No gardens were visible – and there certainly weren't any glades – but there was a stone Celtic cross laid into the cobbles that doubtless held some significance.

Pleasingly, many of the houses had potted plants and hanging baskets outside laden with a sprinkling of minor magic to keep the flowers blooming all year. I laid a bet with myself that number thirty-two would be flower free. Nothing that I knew about Knox Thunderstick suggested that he was the type of person who cared for floral arrangements, but when we reached his house I was surprised to see that it boasted the most elaborate baskets of all.

Even with magic it was unusual to see so many delicate and colourful blooms in January. I bent to admire a potted arrangement by his doorstep: spiky dahlias, tiny golden buttercups and ostentatious orchids had been deftly planted. They weren't flowers that I'd expect to look good together but somehow this gardener had managed it.

'Beautiful, right?'

We turned to see a troll standing by the front door of the house opposite with his keys in his hand. 'They really are,' Thane said.

'He's not a hedge witch,' the troll said. 'He's a druid. And,' he lowered his voice as if he didn't want to be overheard, 'a drummer.' The troll liked flowers but he clearly wasn't much of a music fan.

'Knox Thunderstick created this?' I asked. I knew I was allowing my prejudices to get in the way but I couldn't help it. The man who'd impersonated a pathologist in a mortuary and caused his foster sister so much upset still didn't seem likely to possess a gentle gardener's touch.

'Oh yes.' The troll swept out his arm. 'He's done the whole street. Knox is amazing.'

And that, Kit, I told myself, is why you shouldn't pre-judge people.

'Have you seen him today?' Thane asked. 'Is he home?'

As the troll frowned, the heavy folds of skin across his forehead bunched up. 'Wednesday, innit? He always plays at Pork Pies on Wednesdays.'

Thane and I exchanged glances. 'Thanks,' I said.

The troll raised a hand, put the key in his lock, turned it and stepped into his home. 'You're welcome.' He closed the door.

I squinted through Knox's windows. It was dark inside so I couldn't make out much beyond the shapes and shadows of a few sticks of furniture. When Thane knocked on the door, the sound was sharp and loud. If anyone was inside, they would definitely have heard it.

We waited a few beats then Thane raised his hand to knock again. Before his fist made contact with the wood, however, there was a sharp retort from inside.

'Was that—?'

My mouth flattened. 'A gunshot? Yes.'

THIRTEEN

T he time for pussyfooting around was over. Thane rattled the doorknob as he tried to gain access to the house the easy way. When it became clear that the door was locked, I stepped to the window. These old buildings were doubtless under a conservation order, so the windows were single glazed: bad for insulation; good for me.

I angled my elbow and smashed it forward, aiming for the corner of the pane where the glass would be weakest. The trick was to be fast and to fight the urge to pull back at the last second – or at least that was what I'd been told during my training at EEL. But I'd never approached a job where I didn't have an alternative entry point or a glass-breaking tool if I needed it, and I hadn't undertaken any contract without knowing exactly what I was walking into. Those were the days.

Pain juddered through my arm making me clench my teeth hard, but it was worth it. The glass had cracked and there was now a spider's web of delicate fissures across the pane. Thane nudged me gently aside while I rubbed my elbow, raised his leg and booted the cracks hard enough for splinters of glass to fall inside the room. He kicked away the remaining shards and hopped into Knox's house.

I followed hot on his heels, pausing only long enough to pick up one of the longer glass shards and hand it to him. He grunted his thanks while I reached around and plucked out the curved dagger that I'd strapped to my back before leaving home that morning. I might not have prepared to the point where I carried all the tools of my old trade, but I wasn't completely witless.

Glass crunched beneath our feet as we moved quickly through the room and into the hallway. Thane turned left towards the stairs that led up to the next floor; I went right, checked inside a large cupboard, then stormed into the kitchen with my trusty knife held high.

Nobody was there. The place was immaculate, with neatly labelled jars and a row of perfectly aligned cookbooks. Yet again, I was forced to rethink the image of Knox Thunderstick I'd been holding in my head.

There was no back door and the windows were secure. A narrow alleyway lay outside but there was no direct access to it from the house, which was clearly a traditional two-up and two-down affair. I nodded grimly. Less space to cover. That was good.

Hearing heavy thumps from overhead, I spun on my heel and darted after Thane. I took the stairs two at a time until I joined him on the first-floor landing where he was shoving his shoulder against a closed door. The second door was open, revealing an empty bathroom.

'Barricaded,' he said between shoulder slams.

That figured. 'Magic?' I asked.

He shook his head. 'I don't think so. Something's in the way – a heavy wardrobe, maybe.' He shoved the door again and it gave an inch.

'Knox!' I called. 'Knox Thunderstick! Are you in there? Are you alright?' There was no answer.

Thane rammed the door again and it yielded another fraction. 'I can smell blood,' he said. 'A lot of blood.'

I grimaced then joined in Thane's efforts. Knox might still be breathing – stranger things had happened. 'Ready?' I said.

He nodded. 'On a count of three. One. Two. Three.'

We both threw ourselves at the door. It didn't exactly spring open, but our combined efforts did what was needed and there was a gap large enough for me to squeeze through.

I elbowed Thane aside. It would be tight but I'd manage. Expelling all the air from my lungs, I pushed my way in. When the room was revealed to me, I gave a tiny gasp. Damn.

Even with all my years' experience of death, this was something else. I'd seen a lot of blood in my time but the scene in Thunderstick's bedroom felt mockingly gratuitous. Knox lay spreadeagled on the bed, his wrists and ankles tied to the bedposts. The sheets beneath his body might once have been white but were now bright red, and his eyes were wide and staring.

I knew he was dead but I checked anyway, edging up to his body and pressing my fingers against his sticky neck. No pulse. His body was still warm to the touch so he'd not been dead for long; the gunshot we'd heard only moments earlier had probably killed him, though there was no obvious sign of a bullet wound. Unfortunately, though, his hadn't been a quick death.

The window by the bed was wide open. I cleaned my fingers of Knox's blood and peered out, but the murderer appeared to have fled in the same manner that Knox had successfully fled the mortuary. The heavy barricade had been a simple but effective trick. I hissed under my breath, genuinely angry.

There was a loud thud as Thane, too large to slip through

the gap, shoved at the wardrobe. 'Kit!' he yelled. 'What's going on?'

I grabbed the sides of the wardrobe and tugged, gaining enough purchase to slide it far enough for Thane to come in. He staggered through, took one look at Knox's body and paled. 'Oh.'

I motioned towards the window. 'Whoever did this is gone,' I bit out.

Thane's expression hardened. 'No. Not with the amount of blood that's in here. I'm a fucking werewolf, Kit. I can track them down.'

I bared my teeth in an angry smile. 'That's exactly what I was hoping you'd say. But we'll have to hurry – they'll find a way to hide their tracks before too long.'

Thane cast another quick glance at Knox's body before he leapt out of the window. 'Fuck!' he spluttered as he landed badly. He righted himself and inhaled, searching for the killer's scent, while I clambered carefully out of the first-floor window then dropped onto the ground beside him. A sprained ankle would not have been helpful.

'Have you got it?' I asked.

Thane pointed. 'This way.'

He took off down the alleyway and I sprinted after him, calculating how much of a head start the killer had and which streets they'd be likely to take. An amateur's instincts would tell them to head for somewhere busy where they could lose themselves in crowds; that had its merits – and its dangers.

You could never account for what members of the public might do if you were pointed out to them as a fleeing criminal, and the blood would be hard to hide even on dark clothes. If I'd been the killer, I'd have run somewhere quiet where I could hide, clean myself off, then turn the tables on my pursuers by taking them out for good – or at least identify who was on my trail. I'd learn a great deal about whoever had murdered Knox Thunderstick by the choices they made and the direction they took.

Thane paused when he reached the end of the alley and I caught up with him. He swung his head from left to right to establish which way the blood-covered killer had gone. When he turned to the left, my eyes narrowed a fraction. Interesting: the killer had chosen the crowds, most likely opting for the chaos of Hirsel Street. They might even pass Pork Pies. I sighed. Poor Harriet.

'The scent of blood is still incredibly strong,' Thane said. 'Our killer will attract attention – and not just from us.'

Good point. I glanced up at the sky. It was only four o'clock in the afternoon but this was Scotland in mid-winter; the sun would set in less than thirty minutes and the vampires would come out to play, making the most of the long nights before the long days of summer began. There wasn't a vamp in Coldstream who wouldn't be drawn to that amount of blood. Surely the killer, whoever they were, realised that and knew that time was not on their side.

We sprinted towards Hirsel Street. Although my sense of smell was nothing compared to Thane's, I fancied I could also smell the iron-rich tang of Knox Thunderstick's blood. For obvious reasons I was reasonably inured to death, but the druid drummer had been tortured and that made me sick to my stomach.

Our feet pounded the cobblestones, our speed and determined expressions causing consternation on the faces of passersby as we reached the busier streets. We swung right and then left. I'd expected Thane's nose to lead us onto Hirsel Street itself, but instead he bypassed that junction and ran on. Maybe the killer was making a beeline for their home; if that were the case, we'd have them cornered.

But then Thane's feet came to a stuttering halt.

'What is it?' I asked.

'The scent has gone,' he growled. He backtracked five metres to the crossroads then looked left and right. 'They were here.' He frowned. 'Shit! They circled around this entire area.' He waved a frustrated hand at the tightly packed shops and business premises. 'They could have gone into any of these buildings.'

I looked around: a barber's shop, a coffee shop, a quiet-looking pub, a witchery store and... I stared at the red and white flag positioned above the awning of an old stone building on the corner. 'There.' I pointed. 'They've gone in there.'

Thane followed my finger. 'Turkish baths,' he breathed. 'A hammam. They've gone to clean themselves up.'

I nodded. 'And steal some clothes left lying around in a locker room.' I smiled. 'Let's go.'

We marched grimly towards the building. When Thane pushed open the front door, I was assailed by heady smells of essential oils: jasmine, musk, orris. It would be difficult even for a werewolf to distinguish the scent of blood amid such strong perfumes, but Thane's eyes flicked to mine, confirming that we were in the right place.

There was nobody behind the marble-topped front desk and I had the horrible thought that our killer was continuing their deadly work and the hammam staff had also been murdered. Then a narrow door to the left of the desk opened and a woman strolled out carrying a steaming mug of tea. When she saw us, she blinked in surprise. 'Oh! I'm sorry!' She hastily put down the mug and plastered on a warm, professional smile. 'Have you been waiting long?'

Thane opened his mouth to speak but I knew that questions from a stressed werewolf would probably startle her into silence. Smiling brightly, I broke in. 'Not too long! Have you been taking a well-deserved break?'

I sensed Thane bristle at my side but I knew what I was doing. We needed the staff on our side if we were going to locate our target.

A trace of guilt crossed the woman's face. 'Yes. I shouldn't abandon the desk but I was desperate for a brew.'

That meant she could have been away from her position for up to ten minutes, more than enough time for someone to slip in unnoticed. 'I completely understand,' I said warmly. 'I'm a tea jenny myself.'

The woman relaxed slightly and pointed to a small silver object on the desk. 'There's a bell,' she said helpfully. 'Next time you can ring if there's nobody here.'

'We'll be sure to do that.'

Thane was hopping from foot to foot; his impatience was getting the better of him. 'Why don't you go through,' I suggested to him. 'I'll sort out everything here.'

He moved before I finished my sentence and walked quickly to the door marked with the universal symbol for men.

'I'm Kit,' I said, continuing my attempt to keep the woman engaged.

'Alara,' she said.

'That must make you a water fairy,' I said. 'From Lake Baikal.' Fairy, as opposed to fae; there was a distinct difference.

She looked surprised. 'Yes, my family came from that region. Not many people here know of it.'

I smiled serenely. 'I'm well-travelled – though I've never visited a hammam before.'

'Oh, you'll love it. We use some specially formulated oils that we buy from a Turkish witchery in Istanbul. They make all the difference. It's a very relaxing experience.'

Maybe it was under normal circumstances but I doubted

this visit would be relaxing. 'Your changing rooms,' I said. 'Just women and men? Nothing gender neutral?'

'Unfortunately not,' she said. 'Our baths are gender neutral, but not the changing rooms. However, if you have specific requirements, I can...'

'No, no. I just wondered.' It was good to know that our killer's routes were limited. I leaned forward. 'And is there a back door?' Alara stared at me. 'I have a fear of being trapped in a building,' I said. 'It's an old phobia that I can't seem to shake.'

She nodded as if she'd heard far stranger things. 'Then you'll be fine here. We have three separate fire exits, all located on this floor.'

Three? Damn. 'Great,' I said cheerfully. I took out my wallet and handed her some money to cover both my and Thane's entry into the hammam. I'd learned all I needed to know.

'If you wait a moment or two, I'll get your change,' Alara said.

'That won't be necessary.' I beamed. 'Use it to buy more teabags.' And then, before she could say anything else, I darted towards the women's changing rooms.

There were only two people inside, both in a state of undress, and they paid me no attention. From their casual chatter, they knew each other and weren't murderers on the run. I double-checked the cubicles and headed through the opposite door that led towards the interior of the hammam.

I spotted Thane immediately. His expression was stony. 'Anything?' I asked.

He shook his head. 'Not even any abandoned bloodied clothing – but he'd been in there. I could smell Knox's blood.'

Well, at least we could assume our killer was male given that he'd chosen the men's changing rooms. It also meant, however, that our murderous bastard was taking his clothes with him. It was a smart move, what I would have done if the clothes could somehow have been traced to me. I wondered if that meant something about his clothes could identify him.

I glanced down the marble corridor where there were several marked doors. I doubted our target would be spending any time in a hot room. 'There,' I said softly. 'Showers.'

We exchanged glances and moved towards the room. It was immediately obvious that it was empty. Then Thane stiffened and pointed. 'Look. Blood.'

I looked down at the wet floor. He was right: there was a faint trickle of watery blood dribbling towards a drain in the corner. The killer had been here and made fast work of washing himself. There was another door out of the shower room. 'Come on,' I said. 'He must be this way.'

We burst through and I ran for the nearest fire exit, pushed it open and gazed outside. Nothing. At my irritated hiss, Thane barrelled further down the hallway towards another brightly marked exit sign. The third fire exit had to be somewhere else in the building. 'No sign of him,' he said.

Shit. 'You go out and circle round,' I said. 'See if you can pick up any scent. I'll check that he's not doubled back.' I didn't pause for confirmation, simply returned the way I'd come.

Nothing was out of the ordinary and nothing had changed – until I reached the reception area where an annoyed druid was bellowing at Alara. 'Somebody's nicked my clothes! Some bloody thief has taken everything I was wearing when I walked in here!'

I ran out of the front door praying that Thane had had more luck, but when I found him at the western side of the building his expression told me everything. 'Fuck,' I muttered.

He gazed at me bleakly. 'Yeah.'

FOURTEEN

N o matter how hard I tried, I couldn't connect the dots and work out what Rory Taggert and Knox Thunderstick had to do with each other. However, I knew that Knox's surreptitious jaunt to the mortuary and then his subsequent murder couldn't be a coincidence.

'Shall I come in with you?' Thane asked quietly when we finally reached Pork Pies' glass door.

The interior was brightly lit and welcoming, which only made me feel worse. 'You've been banned.'

He ran a hand across his short copper hair. 'I expect Knox Thunderstick's sister will make an exception under the circumstances.'

It would be easier with him by my side, but unfortunately there would probably be a confrontation before I could even start to tell Harriet what had happened. 'It's better if I speak to her alone,' I said with a heavy heart.

Thane expelled a long breath. 'Very well. I'll wait out here.'

Reluctantly, I walked into the café. Harriet was behind the counter, a clipboard in one hand and a pen in the other as she marked off stock. She started to smile in greeting when she saw me, but her grin faded when she registered my expression. 'You found Knox.' It wasn't a question.

'Can we talk in the back?' I asked. This would be better without an audience and there were several customers.

Harriet had turned deathly pale. 'No. Tell me here. Tell me where he is.'

'Harriet—'

Her hands clenched into tight fists. 'Tell me!'

Shit. I half-closed my eyes then opened them again; she deserved my full gaze.

This was an aspect of death that I'd never experienced. I'd never had to be this person before and I didn't want to be this person now. 'We went to his house. We knocked on his door and then we heard a gunshot.'

Harriet didn't make a sound.

I swallowed. 'We broke in. Knox's bedroom door was barricaded by a wardrobe. It took a bit of time to shove it open. When we did...'

She was already reaching for her coat. 'He's dead, then.' Her voice was flat.

'Yes. I'm sorry. Somebody killed him.'

'Did you see who did it?'

'No. We tried to find him but he'd gone.'

'The werewolf couldn't track his scent?'

I sucked in a breath. 'For a short distance, but not far enough to catch up with him.' There seemed little point in telling her about the hammam. It was information she didn't need, not right now.

Harriet pushed past me and headed for the door. I grabbed her arm. 'No, don't go.'

'I have to see him for myself.'

'No,' I said. 'You don't.'

Anguish dulled her eyes. 'It's bad?' she whispered. I

managed a nod. She stared at me for a long moment. 'I still have to see him.'

It was a terrible idea but at the end of the day it was her choice. I couldn't physically hold her back. 'Then let us come with you,' I offered.

'Do whatever the fuck you want.' Harriet pulled away from me and marched out of the café.

HARRIET RESOLUTELY IGNORED us both as she ran at high speed, still wearing an apron branded with the Pork Pies logo underneath her coat. Knox Thunderstick's house was lit up like a beacon by the time we reached it. There were uniformed MET officers, several hovering Redcaps, and three very stern-looking tattooed officials who were doubtless from the druids' board of governors.

I wasn't surprised; even if Knox's neighbours hadn't heard the gunshot, someone passing would have seen the broken window and checked on him; it was that sort of neighbourhood and we already knew that he was held in high esteem. That was good, I decided. These were the sort of people who would be equipped to deal with Harriet's grief in a way that I wasn't.

One of the druids crooked his finger towards the Redcaps and told them they could remove the body. Harriet ran towards them. 'Where is he?' she shrieked, her high-pitched cry reverberating through me with its uncontained pain. 'Where is my brother?'

The druid official frowned. 'You're not one of us,' he said, his powers of observation at her lack of tattoos leading him to state the bloody obvious.

'He's my foster brother,' Harriet snarled. 'Let me through. I want to see him!'

There were several mutters and dubious glances then another voice cut in from slightly further away. 'She's telling the truth. They grew up together – they're siblings in everything but blood.'

I glanced across and saw the singer from the Blue Tattoos; he must have come to the house in search of Knox. I hoped for his sake that he hadn't gone inside and seen his friend's body. He was a young druid and that sort of image could scar him for life.

The druids nodded, then approached Harriet and spoke to her quietly before taking her into the house. I flinched involuntarily and Thane shuddered. 'We have to make this right,' he said. 'For her sake.'

'I'm not convinced anything will make this right,' I replied. With heavy footsteps, I approached the singer. 'I'm so sorry about your friend.'

He stared at me. 'You were at Pork Pies earlier,' he said numbly. 'You brought Harriet here?'

'Yeah.' I indicated Thane who had joined us. 'We came looking for Knox and...' My voice trailed off. What could I say? That we'd found his dead, tortured body? That we'd chased after his killer and let them get away? I sighed. 'I'm sorry,' I repeated lamely.

'He didn't deserve this,' the druid said.

I still had no idea what to say; I'd have made a terrible grief counsellor. Thankfully Thane wasn't as witless as I was. 'I heard you mention at Pork Pies that Knox hadn't turned up for your rehearsal yesterday,' he said.

'Huh? Oh, that was because of some stupid witch. I caught up with him last night. He must have been killed today,' he said, misunderstanding Thane's reason for the comment. 'We were together last night.'

He'd caught my attention. 'A witch?' I asked.

'Some daft idiot from the council asking questions about one of Knox's old mates. He spent all morning interrogating Knox, wouldn't let him leave.' He shrugged, unable to muster up much interest in what had happened the previous day given the events of today.

Shivers were already running down my spine. 'Who?'

'Dunno. He wanted to know about someone Knox used to knock about with at school. Knox didn't tell me who.'

I didn't take my eyes away from the singer. 'Who was the witch? Who was asking all those questions?'

He shrugged again. 'Knox told me his name but...' His nose wrinkled. 'Nah, can't remember it.'

My skin prickled as my thoughts raced.

I heard a vaguely familiar voice. 'That's them. That's the couple who stopped by Knox's house a couple of hours ago.' It was the troll, the one who lived opposite Knox. He was pointing at us and frowning.

Two burly MET officers marched forward. 'Hands in the air!' one of them yelled.

'Stay where you are!' shouted the other. 'You're under arrest!'

Seriously? 'We didn't kill him,' Thane protested. 'We *found* him.'

'Are you the ones who made the anonymous report about his body?'

Thane's eyes narrowed. 'Anonymous report? What anonymous report?'

Both MET officers glared. 'If you didn't make the report then you must have killed him.'

What kind of screwed-up logic was that? 'If we killed him,' I said, irritated, 'why would we come back to the scene of the crime?'

'That's what killers do,' the first MET idiot said.

Not the professional ones or the ones with an ounce of sense. 'You've been reading too many crime novels.'

'I'm a trained officer,' he sniffed. 'I've done all the courses.'

Yeah, yeah.

The second MET man scratched his chin. 'She doesn't look like a killer.'

'Thank you,' I said.

His colleague rolled his eyes. 'Anyone can be a killer. Besides,' he gestured to Thane, 'the wolf might have done it.' He looked at me. 'Has he coerced you into joining him on a killing spree?'

For fuck's sake. This was ridiculous.

The man pursed his lips. 'We'll find out more when we interrogate you down at the station.' He snapped a pair of handcuffs on Thane's wrists then did the same to me. I smarted with embarrassment; in all my years as an assassin I had never been arrested. *Never*. And yet now I was being dragged away when I'd not actually done anything.

The druid singer snapped his fingers. 'Wait!' We all looked at him. 'I remember his name now,' he said. 'It was Jackson. That was the witch who questioned Knox yesterday. Daniel Jackson.'

My stomach dropped. I was still staring at the druid when the MET officers hauled both Thane and me down the street.

I HOPED that we'd be interviewed as soon as we arrived at the MET lock-up; I wanted to clear my name as quickly as possible so I could get out and find Fetch Jackson. I'd known the bastard witch was suspicious, but the fact that he'd tracked down Knox Thunderstick a full day before he'd identified Rory Taggert's body made him suspect numero uno. He had questions to answer. Hard questions. There was every likelihood that he'd killed Knox. I couldn't imagine why, but I couldn't shake the thought now that it had been planted.

Instead of being taken to an interview room, Thane and I were shoved unceremoniously into a cold cell. 'Hey!' I protested. 'This isn't right! Just interview us and let us go!'

Thane added his voice to my complaints. 'We've done nothing wrong. The faster you clear us, the faster you can get out there and find the real killer.'

'We've contacted Captain Montgomery,' the MET officer said. 'He's been selected as lead investigator for this case. When he arrives, he will question you.'

'When will that be?' I demanded.

The answer was annoyingly smug. 'When he gets here.'

'I'm a single parent,' I yelled through the bars. 'I've got a family to feed!' I pointed to Thane. 'He's the same! Our kids will be hungry!'

'You should have thought of that before you murdered an innocent druid.' The officer spun on his heel and stalked off. So much for innocent until proven guilty.

Thane's brow creased with worry. 'Tiddles is little more than a kitten. I can't stay out all night. She needs me.'

'Exactly.' I growled and thumped my fist against the bars in frustration. I didn't have time for this shit.

I sighed deeply, marched to a corner of the small cell and sat down on the edge of the bed. I hadn't expected to be in any sort of danger today so I hadn't left my usual letter on Dave's doorstep with instructions for if I didn't return. I crossed my fingers and hoped that he'd notice that I wasn't there and he'd take care of the cats. There wasn't much I could do about Tiddles, though.

'We've met Montgomery before,' I said. 'He takes his job seriously. We won't be kept here for long.'

A languid voice echoed towards us from another cell. 'You wanna bet? You're not the only ones in here waiting to be questioned. We're all waiting for Captain Montgomery. The turnkey told us he's on the other side of Coldstream.'

My shoulders slumped. Thane looked furious. This could be a very long evening.

The first hour passed slowly, punctuated only by the arrival of trays of beige and brown slop that I supposed was meant to pass as food. Thane and I spoke little, aware that not only were the other detainees listening but quite possibly the MET were too.

While Wilberforce Montgomery hadn't struck me as a bad sort when we'd met late last year, the MET weren't known for either their intelligence or their integrity. I wasn't willing to yield any information to them until I knew exactly who I was dealing with, and what they were planning to do with it. We certainly couldn't risk anyone alerting the witches' council about Daniel Jackson; they'd close ranks in a heartbeat and we'd never find the truth. The smart thing to do was stay quiet.

About three hours after we'd been brought in, we heard a door open and heavy footsteps began treading in our direction. I brightened: that hadn't been so bad.

I got to my feet but it wasn't Captain Montgomery's face who appeared in front of the bars, it was the damned MET officer who'd brought us our poor excuse for food. 'We need to get out of here,' I pleaded.

He shrugged. 'Not my call. You can't go until Captain M says so. And Captain M ain't here.'

Goddamnit.

'Why are you here bothering us, then?' Thane asked.

He pointed at me. 'You've got a visitor.' He motioned towards someone who was standing out of our sight. 'You've got five minutes.'

'I only require two,' said an unfamiliar voice with an oddly stilted accent.

A remarkably thin figure wearing a bright-green velvet suit appeared. I blinked at his mottled skin and yellow eyes: a spriggan. Typically their kind worked for the Fae, who rarely made an appearance in Coldstream. What the hell was one doing here?

'Boris,' Thane said. 'I should have guessed.'

I stared at him. 'You know this guy?'

'Oh yes. He works for Mallory.' Thane grinned. 'When I say "works", I mean he owes her a very large favour and is working it off. How long do you have left in her service?'

'Two years, five months and twelve days,' Boris said. 'Barely any time at all.'

When you were practically Fae, that was probably true, though it wasn't the sort of long indenture I fancied. Thank goodness Mallory had placed a twelve-month limit on what I owed her.

'I have your blood contract,' the spriggan said to me, holding up a rolled-up parchment. 'I need you to sign it before Mallory can proceed. I would have been here earlier but,' his grin was coldly amused, 'it took some time to track you down.'

That was fair. I took the parchment from him, unsealed the wax and opened it. It was standard fare and contained no surprises. Thane glanced at it over my shoulder then said, in a low voice, 'You can still change your mind. You can back out until you sign it, Kit.'

I was well aware of that. However, matters had progressed since I'd spoken to Mallory that afternoon and I still wanted to know what the witches' council were up to. For one thing, that would tell me whether Fetch Jackson was working on his own behalf or as an official council representative. Besides, a verbal agreement was as good for me as one sealed in blood and I'd already agreed to this. I had plenty of faults but I liked to think I was honourable.

'It's fine,' I said.

The MET officer had patted me down and taken my lovely curved dagger when I'd been arrested but it appeared that Boris had come prepared. He dug into his pocket and pulled out a small knife. 'You can't give her that!' the officer barked. 'She's a prisoner!'

'I have to draw blood,' I said patiently.

The officer was unmoved. I considered and then, against my better judgment, stuck out my hand so the spriggan could make the cut for me. 'You'd better clean that blade,' I warned.

He tutted. 'I have no interest in the likes of you.' He sliced expertly across my finger so only a bead of crimson blood oozed forth. I marked the contract while Boris made a show of wiping the blade.

'If you are still in custody tomorrow night,' he said, 'Mallory will come and find you to fulfil the terms of the contract. Otherwise she will stick to the original plan and meet you at the restaurant.'

'I will *not* be in custody.'

The MET officer barked a laugh. 'We'll see.'

I glared at him. 'Where is Captain Montgomery? He should be here by now.'

'He's a busy man. He's scheduled your interrogation for tomorrow morning. The two of you are here for the night.'

What?

'You can't do that!' Thane glared, unable to disguise his anger.

'Can't I? Oh, I'll let you go then,' the officer said sarcastically.

'Our families—'

'Yeah, yeah. You need to feed your kids. You'll have to make alternative arrangements for them.'

Thane's green eyes spat fury. 'How are we supposed to do that from here?'

I glanced at the spriggan. I didn't want to owe any more favours, not if I could help it.

'Ask your lawyer,' the officer suggested.

'Huh?'

Boris went out, only to be replaced by a second figure.

'Good evening. Quite a mess you two have got yourselves into, isn't it?'

My shoulders dropped. 'Hi, Trilby.'

They grinned. 'Hi, Kit.'

FIFTEEN

Either Trilby actually possessed real legal credentials or they were extraordinarily good at lying because the officer allowed them into our cell then departed so that we could talk without being overheard.

I was certain that someone was still eavesdropping but Trilby was prepared for that. They took out a small glass vial and scattered the liquid contents in a circle on the cell floor before beckoning Thane and I inside it. As soon as I stepped across the liquid line, I knew what they'd done: the sound inside the circle was different to outside, as if we were underwater.

'A noise nullifying spell?' Thane asked. 'Impressive.'

Trilby waved an airy hand. 'Every good lawyer comes prepared.'

I tilted my head. 'Are you a lawyer?' They only smiled. 'How did you know we were here?' Again, Trilby's response was a grin. 'You,' I said, 'are most definitely an enigma.'

They swept a bow. 'Thank you.'

I tried a different tack. 'Why are you here, Trilby?'

This time, they nodded approvingly. 'It appeared that you

might require some help. The stall is closed for the day and I wasn't doing anything else noteworthy, so I thought I'd pop along. I detoured via your house on my way here. I hope you don't mind but I went inside and gave some food to your feline friends.'

There weren't many people who I would feel comfortable allowing into my house when I wasn't home, but I had no problem with Trilby going in – and at least I knew the cats were fed and watered. Trilby had no visible scratches so presumably my furry family had been content with the arrangement, too.

Thane opened his mouth but Trilby forestalled him. 'Yes,' they said. 'I went by your place too.'

'How do you know where I'm staying?'

I knew before he finished his sentence that was one of the many questions that Trilby wouldn't answer. 'I fed your young demon kitty,' they said instead. 'And then, because she's only a baby, I thought I ought to go one better.'

Trilby unbuttoned their long coat and revealed Tiddles' tiny snoring form nestled in a harness against their chest. 'It's amazing,' they said with an odd emphasis, 'what one can conceal when concealment is required.'

Indeed. I beamed. 'Your help is greatly appreciated.'

'I thought it might be.' They gently lifted the little ginger cat and passed her to Thane. 'My work here is done.' Trilby tipped their hat, dusted off their palms, then stepped out of the circle and called for the MET officer.

'Wait,' Thane said to me. 'Did they bring Tiddles so that you can...?'

'Hide her,' I hissed, interrupting him as I scuffed away the liquid.

An instant later, the officer appeared. 'That was fast,' he said to Trilby.

They shrugged. 'I have done all I can. Bye, kiddies.'

The officer mirrored Trilby's shrug and opened the cell door. They walked out without a backward glance.

Thane, who had hidden Tiddles behind his back in a move that would have fooled very few people, gave me a long look. 'What exactly is Trilby?' he asked.

It was a good question. 'I have absolutely no idea.' I stared beyond the bars of the cell. 'Perhaps we're not meant to know.'

'I'm glad they're on our side,' he said. 'I'd hate to make an enemy of them.'

I nodded fervently. 'Come on then,' I said. 'Let's get this over and done with.'

'Kit—'

'We have to find out the truth about Fetch Daniel Jackson,' I said. 'If we hesitate, the witches' council will bundle him away and we'll be sent down for Knox Thunderstick's murder.'

Thane was still reluctant. 'What if it hurts her?'

'It won't.'

'But—'

I smiled gently. 'Thane, do you think I'd ever do anything that would hurt a cat?'

'No, but—' His voice trailed off.

'She'll stay here throughout. You'll be able to see for yourself that she's unaffected.'

He frowned. 'You have to be close to the original cat for the magic to work effectively. Fetch Jackson could be anywhere in the city.'

'True,' I conceded. 'But the witches' council headquarters are not far from here. The magic should stretch far enough for me to gain access.'

'You'll never get into their inner sanctum, no matter what body you're wearing.'

'I don't need to. I only need to find Fetch Jackson.' I splayed my hands. 'It's better than staying here all night doing nothing.

Trilby brought Tiddles for a reason.' I'd have preferred one of my own cats but beggars couldn't be choosers.

In the end, it was Tiddles herself who made the decision. She emitted a tiny squeak of a miaow from behind Thane's back, wriggled free, jumped down and scampered over to my feet.

'Very well,' he sighed.

'She'll be fine,' I reiterated. I bent down, scratched her ears, thanked her and plucked a small tuft of soft ginger fur from her side. Tiddles purred loudly in response.

I met Thane's eyes, silently conveying that this was the right move. He blinked slowly in agreement. With that part out of the way, I tipped my head back and swallowed the fur.

I'd never used a cat as young as Tiddles for my transformation so I had no idea what to expect. Usually the pain was agonising, and I was prepared for a similar experience now; instead, even though my body went rigid and started to shake, I felt only a flicker of discomfort. Huh. Maybe that was because of Tiddles' age. Or maybe it was because she held a closer relationship with the demon netherworld from where all cats originated.

Either way, the spasms were easier to handle and, when I rose up in the air and began to spin as my body chemistry altered, I felt both surprise and gratitude. Within seconds I was on all fours and testing out my new form.

A cat sith wasn't like a werewolf. Wolves like Thane only transformed during the full moon and they had no choice. Alexander MacTire was something of a different beast and had proved that he could change at least part of himself regardless of the lunar calendar, but he was definitely the exception to the rule. And every werewolf, no matter who they were, always took the same lupine form.

I was different. For one thing, barely any cat siths existed and nobody ever suspected that the moggy that wandered past them would be anything other than a cat. Plus, the body I transformed into and the characteristics I assumed depended on the cat whose fur I'd swallowed, so it was different every time. On this occasion, I was imbued with an adolescent's sense of fun and fizzing energy. I could already predict that it would be difficult to maintain focus.

Concentrate, I told my feline self sternly. A lot is riding on this.

I padded somewhat unsteadily towards Tiddles who raised her paw and batted at me playfully. I resisted the urge to return the action. I had to be serious. I twitched my ears to indicate my thanks and glanced up at the now-gigantic form of Thane.

'I have to admit you're kind of cute,' he said.

There was no *kind of* about it. I was gorgeous and I knew it. I nudged his ankle with my head before twisting around and slinking away, escaping easily between the cell bars. Time to find a murderous witch.

I might have looked like a beautiful teenage cat but I still wasn't supposed to be there and I didn't want any of the MET officers to spot me. I wound my way down the cold hallway to the doorway at the end; it was securely closed and I had no way of opening it. Fortunately a slight breeze rippled my fur so I back-tracked slightly. There was an open window to my left that would do perfectly. I purred, bunched my muscles and sprang upwards.

It wasn't a high jump – even my old girl, She Who Loves Sunbeams, could have made it. But not me: somehow I misjudged the leap and smacked into the side of the wall instead of landing on the windowsill. Oops. Being a young cat was harder than I'd realised. My spatial awareness clearly wasn't fully developed.

I shook myself off and took a moment to regroup, grooming

my fur in an instinctive need to pretend I wasn't embarrassed even though nobody had witnessed my failure. Then, when I was ready, I tried again and nailed it. I would have to be careful in future; this youthful body was still learning and I had to remember that.

I gazed out at the street. It was fully dark now, which benefited me because not only would my vision be enhanced but I'd be less likely to be noticed.

I was on the ground floor so it was only a short drop but, mindful of my adolescent clumsiness, I took my time. I skittered head first down the wall like a lizard until gravity took over and I was forced to jump the last metre. My landing certainly wasn't elegant but it was good enough.

I sniffed, turned right and moved quickly towards the headquarters of the witches' council. I was coming for Fetch Jackson, whether he liked it or not.

EVEN IN THE wealthier parts of Coldstream most buildings were tightly packed; although there was plenty of empty land in the borders of Scotland, magical land such as this was far less abundant. Occasionally a bid was made to extend the boundaries and allow more construction for the ever-growing population of Preternaturals, but it was both difficult and expensive to achieve. The further you strayed from the border between Scotland and England, the less ancient magic was bound into the land.

Most Coldstream residents ended up in far smaller spaces than they felt they deserved. If you wanted a big property, the compromise usually involved living in an area where there was less natural magic and therefore fewer benefits to be gained from it – but there were exceptions, and naturally the bureaucratic witches' council was one of those.

Their headquarters were not only astonishingly large but also boasted elaborate gardens. The council claimed they required the space for their hedge witches and that the special herbs and plants that were grown there required special conditions, but on the few occasions I'd visited I'd seen little evidence of that. There was little more than variegated rose bushes and carefully manicured lawns.

It seemed wasteful not only to me but to many Coldstream residents that so much space was available in the centre of the city and could only be used by a fraction of its citizens. The witches would tell me to know my place; they'd been the first to settle here generations ago – and they believed they deserved greater privileges as a result.

But it wasn't politics that brought me padding towards the wall that surrounded the witches' home; I was on a mission and this was the only place I could think of where I might find Daniel Jackson, or at least learn his whereabouts.

The layers of security grew more complex and impregnable as you made your way inside. Nobody but a council witch could access the inner rooms where they met to discuss their agendas, which was why I'd asked for Mallory's help in finding out what they were currently focusing on – and why I remained dubious that she'd be able to find out.

The outer section, however, wouldn't be too difficult to navigate because the barrier there was as much a psychological one as a real one. Unless you were a cat.

I didn't need to scale the walls because I was small enough to slip through a narrow gap in the gates. As far as I could tell, they were made out of iron on one side and silver on the other, so either the witches wanted to keep both erratic werewolves and tricksy Fae off their property or they were showing off. Nothing worked as a natural adherent for witches unless it was magically enhanced first – and they were stupidly proud of the fact.

I wandered up the gravelled path to the building's ornate front door. Despite the late hour it was wide open and I padded straight inside, my tiny claws clicking on the marble floor. Barrier magic brushed against my fur as I crossed the threshold, but no alarms sounded and my entrance was unimpeded. Little cats weren't counted as immediate foes; I reckoned I could get around at least three more layers of security before I could go no further into the witches' stronghold. They weren't always as smart as they liked to think they were.

I'd been inside this building a few times before during the course of my old job so I was reasonably familiar with the layout. I'd never actually killed anyone here – that would have been far too risky a manoeuvre for any assassin – but I'd come here to complete basic reconnaissance on four different targets and I knew the best vantage points. There was a dining room on the first floor that would be a good bet for picking up any gossipy titbits about Fetch Jackson's current whereabouts. It was as good a place to start as any.

I sauntered past the bored-looking witch at the front desk who was engrossed in the papers in front of her. From past experience I knew that the best way to stay under the radar in a place like this was to act as much like a real cat as possible. Somebody would spot me sooner or later, but as long as they believed I was a cat I'd be okay. If I slunk around the shadows, they'd be suspicious.

The woman didn't look up. It was almost insulting, given how cute I looked.

I didn't pause when I reached the foot of stairs; instead, I launched myself upwards, my paws barely touching each step. As soon as I was on the landing, I swung to my right. I could already hear the buzz of chatter and smell the heady aroma of decent food. Perhaps I'd get a chance to nab a few tasty scraps. I purred: anything would beat the horror of the food the MET had served us earlier. There was no reason why I couldn't multi-task.

Although it was after 9pm, the dining hall was still busy and most tables were occupied. Doubtless there was a hierarchy that determined who sat where. I wanted to avoid the lower-level witches and find the council members because they'd be more likely to mention Fetch Jackson in conversation. He might even be in the room, chomping on a steak.

I looked around, but my low vantage point made it difficult to see the whole room. My whiskers bristled with annoyance: finding the right witches would be harder than I'd expected. Unwilling to waste any more time, I made a beeline for the nearest table, figuring that I could skulk around the witches' feet beneath the long white tablecloths until I found someone useful.

It was surprising how much you could tell about a person from their shoes. The first pair I passed were scuffed, suggesting that their owners spent a lot of time pounding the streets of Coldstream. It looked as if the witches at this table were grunts who delivered messages and performed scutwork. That was confirmed when I caught a snippet of their conversation.

'If I have to spend another three hours tramping around Danksville tomorrow,' a female voice said, 'I will kill someone.'

I'd like to see her try. We Danksville residents were tough.

I smirked and wound through table legs until I reached the next group. Their shoes were in better condition, though they certainly weren't expensive. And one of the witches had recently stepped in dog excrement. I recoiled. There was no need to eavesdrop on this conversation; besides, if I lingered I'd pass out from the smell.

I headed to the next table then the one after that. It was only when I reached a larger table, whose occupants wore handmade footwear that showed evidence of re-soling and smelled of pricey leather, that I reckoned I might be getting somewhere.

'This is ridiculous,' said an irritated man wearing stacked brogues. 'How long does it take to brew a cup of damned coffee?'

I rolled my eyes and stepped over his feet.

'I told Madeleine that she needs to get the contract signed as soon as possible before the Hightowers change their mind,' murmured a stiletto-wearing woman.

I paused. I still hadn't entirely discounted Quentin Hightower from these bloody events.

'They'll get to it,' her companion replied. 'They're only distracted because their son and heir tripped, fell into the Tweed and caught a cold.'

There was a loud snicker. 'That man is such a fucking idiot.'

'Thank goodness he's not on the council,' came the rejoinder. 'Birthright only gets you so far.'

'Head first into a shitty river, if you're Quentin Hightower.'

I picked up my paws and kept moving. There was nothing to be learned here.

'You know we only have a small sample,' a man wearing tan-brown loafers said.

The woman next to him, in kitten heels and skin-tone tights, sniffed. 'All the more reason to give me some so I can try to propagate some seedlings.'

'Brockensworth has already tried to do that and failed. The leaves alone aren't enough. We need the seeds.'

I veered around his feet. There was a pair of shiny black boots ahead that I had a good feeling about.

'Hasn't Jackson come up with the goods yet?' said Kitten Heels, with a definite whine.

I froze.

'Apparently not. It's probably why he's not shown up to dinner tonight. He's too afraid to face us with his incompetence.'

'The man has to eat.'

'He lives off chicken noodles. You've smelled his office, right?'

I gave an involuntary purr, far louder than I should have done, but thankfully it appeared to go unnoticed. Bingo.

SIXTEEN

I left the dining hall far more quickly than I'd entered it. I might not know where Fetch Jackson was but now I knew what to look for – or rather what to *smell* for. My stomach grumbled. Bring on the chicken chow mein.

The witches' offices were on the third floor where the magical security would be far stronger, but I refused to believe I couldn't access them. I'd come this far; I couldn't give up now.

I returned to the main landing and headed for the next set of stairs. Shit: a trio of witches was descending and there was no way I could avoid them. It was too late to hide, so I'd have to play cat and brazen it out. I swallowed hard and started to climb. *Nothing to see here*, I projected. *Just a little cat out for a walk in the scary witches' council headquarters. Miaow.*

It was the young witch in the middle who spotted me first. 'Hello, kitty!'

Her companions turned. 'What's that moggy doing here?' the one on the left asked suspiciously. Damn it: she clearly possessed several thousand more brain cells than the other witches I'd encountered so far.

'I'm allergic to fucking cats,' complained the male witch on the right.

Excellent. I swerved and headed straight for his ankles.

'Shit!' he exploded, jumping backwards.

I couldn't let him get away that easily. I leapt upwards and wrapped myself around his lower legs, purring loudly. He kicked out, but I was canny and jumped up another step to avoid his foot. Then, because he'd annoyed me, I launched myself upwards and dug my claws into the fabric of his cloak so I could scramble onto his shoulder.

'Get off!' he shrieked. 'Get off me!'

His two companions were laughing hysterically. 'It's ... just ... a ... cat ... James!' said the first one.

I rubbed my head against his ear. He howled as if I'd bitten him and started to hop from foot to foot. 'Get it off me! Get it fucking off me!' He reached up to grab me. Sensing that this time he'd succeed, I extended my claws and scraped them against the soft flesh of his cheek, then I bounded off his shoulder and sprinted up the stairs and away.

'I'll skin you alive and eat you for breakfast!'

Yeah, yeah. He'd have to catch me first. I ran along the second-floor landing to the next set of stairs. I could still hear his complaints – and his companions' sniggers – when I reached the third floor. Doubtless he'd soon be making an official complaint to someone, so my time was limited.

That wouldn't have been a problem if it weren't for the buzz of the magical ward I could sense right in front of me. I didn't need to throw myself at it to know that it was too strong for me. I'd never get past it without some canny thinking or a clever detour.

I drew as close as I dared, my skin tingling beneath my fur. I sniffed and caught the metallic tang of powerful enchantments. Hmm: that wasn't good, not good at all. I'd hoped that any wards wouldn't reach the floor and I could duck underneath them, but whoever had set this one in place had been particularly diligent.

I glanced to my right and then my left. The gleaming wooden banister that hugged the staircase continued in both directions, framing the open hallway. Could I leap onto it and walk it like a tightrope in the hope that there was a gap in the ward further up? I'd have to be mindful of my youthful clumsiness – the last thing I wanted was to plunge three storeys to the ground floor. In this body I'd probably survive the fall, but it wasn't a given.

I gazed warily at the polished wood. My claws were sharp but I doubted they'd be much use on that slippery surface. Damn. I had to give it a go. I had to *try*. Bunching my muscles, I focused on the narrow banister. I could do this; I just had to concentrate. I would jump on a count of three.

One.

Two.

Two and a half.

Three.

I stayed where I was.

This was stupid. I was in the wrong body and I wasn't foolishly reckless. Even if there was a weak point in the wards and I didn't plunge to my death before I found it, I had no plan about what to do once I found Fetch Daniel Jackson. How would I get him to talk to me without raising the alarm? How would I escape after I'd interrogated him? I'd be risking my life for absolutely nothing.

I stared at the banister for another long moment then turned tail and slunk down the stairs with a lot less speed and attitude than I'd ascended them. I tried not to think about the look in Thane's eyes when I told him my trip had been a waste of time. Damn. Double damn.

When I reached the first-floor landing, it was apparent that the meal was over. Streams of well-fed, rosy-cheeked witches filed past, and more than a few eyes widened in my direction. I huffed. I wasn't in the mood to be kicked again by any whining idiots with allergies but neither did I feel like rushing out of the council headquarters.

I avoided the occasional coaxing hand that reached out to me and darted behind a heavy looking pedestal and statue in a dark corner. Hunkering down, I waited for everyone to pass. It seemed to take an incredibly long time.

When they'd all disappeared, white-coated members of staff appeared. They were witches too, though considerably less talented and with less impressive lineages than those who'd sat down for dinner. The bustle of important people was replaced by the hustle of employees keen to get their jobs done so they could get home as soon as possible.

Clinking trolleys filled with dirty crockery and cutlery passed by, halting briefly near the stairs where levitational magic was applied and the crockery floated downwards, presumably to the kitchen. A dumb waiter would have been far easier, I decided, as several stained tablecloths descended. Witches often chose the most complicated system simply because they could. The more powerful they were, the less common sense they seemed to have and the lazier they were.

I followed the floating tablecloths with disinterested eyes – then I watched them more closely. The linen wasn't taking the same path as the crockery: it turned right instead of left before disappearing. I hesitated, then slid out from my hiding spot.

It was much quieter now, so it was easy to slip unobtrusively down the final staircase after the departing laundry. A group of witches was standing nearby, one of whom was wearing familiar kitten heels. I felt a brush of tension as I nipped past her, but she was engrossed in her conversation and neither Kitten Heels nor her companions seemed to notice me.

I stayed in the shadows where I wouldn't be spotted. The clump of tablecloths travelled fifty metres before another white-coated staff member plucked them from the air and threw them into a large, wheeled trolley. She looked down the hallway to check if there were any more then, with a bored sigh, pushed the trolley through a wide door. I slipped through it before it closed in my whiskered face.

I'd expected the laundry room to be busy and I was prepared to work hard to stay out of sight, but I needn't have worried. There were only two people inside – the woman I'd already seen and a younger man who was little more than a teenager. Both of them were engrossed in their mundane task; even if they'd spotted the small ginger cat who'd come into the room, I doubted they'd have cared.

Magic buzzed at the far side of the room where sheets, towels, tablecloths and clothes were being dried; enchanted bursts of warm air were a boon to anyone with loads of washing to dry, though I knew from my own experience that the actual process of washing was more effective if it was done in a machine with real water. Spells could be useful on stubborn stains but clothes washed magically never felt truly clean or fresh. That was why the staff were separating the piles of dirty clothes into colours and types, bundling them into vast washing machines then taking them out for magically enhanced drying.

I eyed the different piles and focused on some small tin tubs that appeared to contain dark clothing. There were scribbled notes attached to each container, doubtless to identify who the contents belonged to. A lot of the council witches used the service here for their personal laundry; witches who were too lazy to carry their plates down a flight of stairs were also too lazy to do their own washing.

Giving the two busy workers a wide berth, I edged around the perimeter of the room, padded to the tubs and squinted at the labels. At least they were neatly printed and easy to read.

S. Lawrence. F. Austin. E. Saunders. H. Risbridger.

A few of the names were vaguely familiar but nothing specific came to mind. I kept going.

N. Bradley. K. Hammer. M. Sijugo.

I bared my teeth. This was likely a wild-goose chase.

B. Hausman. R. Mitt.

I sighed. I ought to give up. It was hot, and I was tired and hungry.

S. Bernhope. M. Patel.

Thane was locked up in the MET cell with Tiddles and probably getting worried.

X. Smith. V. Thomson. G. McDonald.

The longer I stayed away from the jail, the more chance that my disappearance would be noticed.

S. Pickover. D. Jackson. H. Puttman.

I stopped then gazed again at the metal tub inscribed D. Jackson. A pile of dark clothing lay inside that looked similar to what the Fetch had been wearing at the mortuary that morning, though I couldn't be certain. He'd struck me as the kind of man who always wore dark clothes like most of the council witches; bright orange and spangly purple didn't suggest you were a serious person capable of great things.

When I shoved my head inside the tub, my nose twitched and I immediately recoiled. Bloody hell: his aftershave was brutal. I sneezed three times but the musky, unpleasant scent still clung to my nostrils. I'd certainly not smelled anything like that on Fetch Jackson that morning.

I willed myself to stick my head into the bucket again and

examine the clothes more closely. Several areas of the material looked stiff and unyielding, suggesting something had been spilled onto it and then dried: something dark and sticky like syrup. Or blood.

I swallowed hard. Suddenly my suspicion had hardened into near certainty. It *had* been him. Fetch Daniel Jackson had gone after Knox Thunderstick, tortured him and killed him.

I was stunned enough to rock back for a moment – and that was almost my undoing. A pair of hands appeared and the tub rose up. The female member of staff was taking the clothes to one of the machines where all the evidence would be washed away.

I gave a screeching miaow of protest and the woman peered over the tub. 'There's a cat!' she exclaimed. 'Somebody let a cat in here!'

'Probably escaped from one of those bastards upstairs,' the young man said. 'Check if it's got a collar.'

'You check,' she said. 'I've got my hands full.' She turned towards the machine and tossed the contents of the tub inside. No, I couldn't let her do it.

I sprang forward, leapt and landed inside the tub. My paws sank onto the last few blood-encrusted items.

'Hey!' the woman protested and her face contorted into a spasm that I couldn't interpret. Either she thought I was the cutest thing since the city-wide invasion of blue-haired sprites at the turn of the millennium, or she was about to throw the tub in the air and send my little ginger cat body flying towards the ceiling.

I didn't wait to find out. I dropped my head, snatched the first thing I could with my teeth and launched myself out of the tub, then I was off and running. I smacked into the door with such force that I managed to push it open.

I had my prize. I was out of there as quickly as my four legs could take me.

SEVENTEEN

I didn't pause during my return journey, not even to check what I'd nabbed from the laundry tub. It was small and I suddenly had the horrible thought that I was carrying Fetch Jackson's underwear in my mouth, even though the material felt unusual for that sort of thing.

There were only a few lights on inside the MET building, which was a good sign; if anyone had noticed my absence, there would have been far more activity. The ball of tension inside me dissolved when I saw that the window was still open. I bounded up to the sill, this time nailing the jump with the ease that I usually displayed: better late than never.

I hopped onto the floor and slid through the gap in the cell bars. Home sweet home.

Thane sat bolt upright and stared at me through the gloom. Tiddles' eyes were shining at me from the pillow beside him. 'You're back,' he breathed. 'Thank goodness.'

I purred in response and spat out the piece of clothing. It was time to find out what I'd been carrying. I breathed a sigh of relief when I saw that it was a glove and not a skid-marked pair of underpants.

I moved back to avoid touching it and hawked up my usual hairball. While I jerked and twitched my way back into my human body, Thane crouched down and sniffed the glove, taking care not to touch it and contaminate it. 'That's blood,' he muttered. 'Knox Thunderstick's blood.' He raised his eyebrows, then waited until I was able to speak.

As soon as I'd regained control of my vocal chords, I told him what had transpired. He listened carefully. 'You're a wonder, Kit McCafferty,' he murmured when I'd finished. 'It had occurred to me that Jackson could have been the killer, but it didn't seem possible. You not only believed it was possible but you found the evidence to prove it.'

I'd only found that evidence because I'd been stymied by the witches' security and I hadn't wanted to face Thane without something to show for Tiddles' sacrifice. The laundry had been a long shot; I'd thought that if Daniel Jackson was the culprit, he'd be arrogant and lazy enough to drop off his bloodied clothes for someone else to clean. He'd used that godawful aftershave to disguise the scent of blood and assumed that would be enough.

'I got lucky,' I said.

Thane disagreed. 'If I've learnt one thing about you, it's that you make your own luck.' As he picked up Tiddles and cradled her against his chest, a zippy kick of unexpected lust tightened in the pit of my belly. Men and kittens, that was all it took for me. The fact that he was a ginger man with a ginger kitten somehow added to the allure.

I wet my lips. Not the time, Kit, I told myself. And definitely not the place.

'Of course,' Thane mused, 'we still don't know Jackson's motive.'

I dragged my eyes back to his face. He was right: what on earth did a highly placed witch like Daniel Jackson want with the likes of a grungy druid like Knox Thunderstick – or with Rory Taggert, for that matter? There were still a lot of unanswered questions.

I pointed to the glove. 'He was wearing that in the mortuary this morning. Between that and the blood, there should be more than enough to make sure he's arrested.'

'We'll have to wait until morning when Montgomery finally drags his arse here. I wouldn't trust any of these other MET goons with that glove.' He glanced at the bed. 'You look done in, Kit. We should get some sleep. There's room on that thing, even if it's not exactly a feather mattress. We can both fit on it if we snuggle together.'

It would be a tight snuggle. My mouth was suddenly dry in a way it hadn't been for years.

'You can rest easy,' he said gently. 'You'll be able to sleep well now you know that Harriet will have the closure she deserves. Her brother's killer is about to be brought to justice.'

Uh-huh: if only that had been what I was thinking. 'Small mercies,' I whispered. My stomach tightened with guilt and Harriet's grief-ravaged face flashed into my head.

I unlaced my boots and kicked them off while Thane lay down. He scooted back against the wall leaving me more than enough space, and placed Tiddles carefully beside him. As soon as I tried to lay down, the little ginger cat hissed at me. 'Tiddles! Stop that!' he admonished.

I smiled. 'I guess she's jealous.' The demon cat had no problem offering up her fur so I could affect a transformation, but sharing Thane was a different matter. I didn't blame her. 'Don't worry,' I said to her softly. 'We're only going to sleep. You're still number one.'

Tiddles growled faintly. I blinked at her slowly and, after a huffy moment or two, she blinked back at me. It was an agreement of sorts. I lay down, far more aware of Thane's body against mine than the thin mattress or Tiddles' irritation.

'Relax,' Thane murmured in my ear and pulled me closer until we were spooning. I was enveloped by his hard body and his heady vetiver scent. 'She won't bite.'

What Tiddles might or might not do was the furthest thing from my mind but I took his advice. I was desperately tired. I closed my eyes, regulated my breathing and passed into a deep sleep within seconds.

∼

Captain Wilberforce Montgomery gazed impassively at the glove which was still on the floor of the cell, untouched since I'd dropped it from my feline jaws. 'Where did it come from?' he asked. 'Did it materialise out of thin air?'

'In a manner of speaking,' I said.

He folded his arms. 'You'll have to do better than that, Ms McCafferty.'

The fewer people who knew what I was, the better. I had no reason not to trust Montgomery – but neither did I have any reason to trust him. 'All I can say is that I have some special skills that enabled me to bring it here,' I replied.

'You used some form of enchantment,' he said flatly.

'Yes.'

'But you won't tell me what enchantment it was.'

'No.'

'Then how can I trust it?'

Thane stepped forward. 'Test it. You won't find my fingerprints on it, or Kit's. That glove is covered in Knox Thunderstick's blood, and the last person who wore it was Fetch Daniel Jackson. What more do you need?'

Montgomery gave him a long, irritated look. 'Before I bring

a Fetch in for questioning?' he asked. 'Goodness, I can't begin to imagine what other information I might require.'

He had a point; even if he could prove that Jackson had tortured and killed Knox Thunderstick, the witches' council would swoop in and take control. It would be out of the MET's hands before Montgomery could say, 'You're under arrest.'

'This is all linked to the John Doe who was pulled out of the Tweed yesterday,' I said. 'Fetch Jackson identified him as Rory Taggert but...' My voice faltered when I saw Montgomery's face. 'You don't know anything about him, do you?'

'I know Quentin Hightower fell into the Tweed. As far as I'm aware, there was nobody else in the river that day.'

Somehow Daniel Jackson had hushed it up. 'You need to talk to Jackson sooner rather than later,' I said.

Montgomery lifted his eyes heavenward. 'You seem to be under the impression that I have power here. I do not.' He pointed at the glove. 'You also seem to think that item will be enough for me to let you both waltz out of here.'

Thane spoke calmly. 'You don't have to arrest Jackson. Just bring him in for a few questions.'

'Or I could charge you both with murder.' Montgomery bared his teeth. 'It'd be cleaner and easier. Less paperwork.'

I dropped my head and affected my meek cat-lady routine. 'All we've done is try to be good citizens. We're only trying to help you.' I sneaked a look at him. 'But of course, we should have realised that you're capable enough without our help. You're a busy man but we thought we could be of service. Why don't you check the timeline, then you'll see that we couldn't possibly have killed Mr Thunderstick.' I shuddered delicately and placed my hands on my cheeks as if I were horrified. 'The idea is abhorrent.'

Unfortunately Captain Montgomery still looked sceptical; very sceptical.

I sucked in a shaky breath. 'We went to check on Knox Thunderstick. He's a lovely young man and we wanted to make sure he was alright. We arrived at his door fifteen minutes after we left Pork Pies café – lots of witnesses saw us leave and Knox's neighbour saw us arrive at his house. We only broke in when we heard a gunshot. We found Knox dead and set off in pursuit of the killer.'

'I'm a werewolf,' Thane offered, though it was obvious to anyone with eyes that he possessed lupine powers. 'I followed his scent. It led us to a Turkish bath where we believe the killer cleaned himself up and stole a fresh set of clothes. More witnesses saw us at the baths. There is nothing to suggest we're responsible for what happened to Knox. We didn't do this.'

Montgomery flicked his eyes between us.

'Don't you want to solve the murder, captain, instead of running around Coldstream investigating petty crime? Don't you want to be proud of yourself for once?' My prim, cat-lady voice held a hint of admonishment.

'Don't try and manipulate me, Ms McCafferty.'

He was getting smarter. I met his gaze. 'Then please,' I wheedled with what I hoped combined innocent haughtiness and well-meaning desperation, 'do your job.'

Tiddles miaowed from behind Thane. I appreciated her support but this wasn't a good time for her to make her presence known.

Montgomery stared. 'Is that a cat?'

There wasn't much point in denying it. 'Emotional support cat,' Thane said smoothly.

I nudged him. 'Kitten, really. She's barely five months' old.'

He nodded. 'Kitten. I hate being confined in small spaces and I needed some help to stay calm.'

Montgomery sighed heavily. 'How did she get in here?' Neither of us said anything. 'I suppose,' he continued sarcastically, 'that she's the one who found the glove.' He was closer to the truth than he realised.

The captain looked exasperated. 'Since when did werewolves like cats?'

'Oh, I love cats,' Thane responded. 'Always have. Always will.'

There was a deep answering warmth in my belly. 'Please, captain,' I said, 'speak to Fetch Jackson. See what he has to say for himself.'

He shook his head, but it was in resignation rather than refusal. He jabbed his finger at us. 'Don't go anywhere.'

'How could we?' I asked, my eyes wide. 'We're locked in.'

Montgomery harrumphed – then he ordered one of the other officers to stand in front of our cell and watch our every movement.

EIGHTEEN

I didn't expect Daniel Jackson to agree to be questioned. A MET officer couldn't stroll into the witches' council and demand a formal interview without a very good reason; the council would easily block such an approach. Despite there being only circumstantial evidence, it wouldn't have surprised me if Montgomery had returned and charged Thane and me with Knox Thunderstick's murder.

Consequently, two hours later when I was gazing gloomily at the congealed breakfast that I couldn't imagine a starving feral moggy trying to eat, I was shocked that he reappeared and opened the cell door. 'The two of you are free to go,' he said.

'You've arrested Fetch Jackson?'

'Don't be silly. I've checked the timeline you gave me and confirmed your stories. There is nothing to suggest you had anything to do with Mr Thunderstick's death.'

He must have spoken to Harriet at the café and Alara at the hammam. While I was glad to have my name cleared, I wasn't yet ready to leave. 'What are you doing about Jackson?'

'That is not your concern, Ms McCafferty.' Montgomery gestured to the empty corridor. 'Please leave.'

I stayed where I was and folded my arms. Thane moved next to me and did the same. Montgomery stared at us. 'This isn't helping,' he sighed.

We waited.

'Fetch Jackson has a regular outreach meeting scheduled at a community centre in Bankton in an hour. I'll meet him there.'

Something about his tone made me smile. Montgomery was planning to surprise Jackson and bring him in for questioning before the witches' council could stop him. It was what I would have done – but it was more than I'd expected from a MET detective.

'And?' Thane asked, not yet understanding. 'You'll meet him and do what exactly?'

Montgomery adjusted his starched cuffs. 'I'll see what he has to say for himself.' He jabbed his stubby fingers at us. 'If I see either of you at the community centre, the *meeting,*' he emphasised the word, 'will not occur.'

Because a forewarned Fetch was a Fetch who'd find a way to avoid it. Montgomery's warning confirmed his unvoiced plan to me. 'Thank you,' I said quietly.

'If I lose my job over this, I'll be coming for you.'

I kept my expression blank. 'You're doing the right thing,' I said. I dropped into a half-curtsey, grabbed Thane's elbow and marched him out of the cell.

THERE WAS no question about where we had to go first. I'd been out all night and I had a furry family to look after. We jumped on the first tram we could and high-tailed it back to Danksville.

I saw She Without An Ear as soon as I turned onto my street. She was sitting in the centre of the cobbled road and staring at us. I was touched that she'd been worried enough to keep an eye out for my return, but when I approached her she hissed dramatically.

'Don't be like that,' I told her. 'It wasn't my fault. I'm here now.' Her eyes narrowed. 'I know Trilby fed you and checked on you last night. Did they come back this morning? Or did Dave give you breakfast?'

Her whiskers quivered with indignation. 'I'll get you some treats,' I promised. She turned her head away. 'That dried herring you like?'

She miaowed and I sensed that she was softening. Unfortunately, that was when Tiddles chose to pop her head out from underneath Thane's coat. She Without An Ear hissed again, glared at me then turned and stalked towards the house.

'She's only coming to visit!' I called. 'She's not going to stay with us forever!'

The ginger cat didn't look back and I grimaced. That could have gone better.

'Is there a problem?' Thane asked, hugging Tiddles closer.

'No.'

He looked at me and I pulled a face. 'Maybe.' I'd have to do some grovelling, that was all.

By the time we'd opened my gate and walked into the garden, She Without An Ear had vanished. He Who Crunches Bird Bones, He Who Must Sleep and She Who Loves Sunbeams were gazing at me from the front step.

'I'm sorry.' I splayed my fingers and dropped my head to add weight to my apology. 'I would've been here last night if I could have been. You guys know that.'

She Who Loves Sunbeams stared at me without blinking before padding forward and winding around my ankles. She was always the first to forgive.

I exhaled. 'This is Tiddles,' I said. 'She'll be hanging around here today while Thane and I go out again on business.'

He Who Crunches Bird Bones stiffened. 'I'm trying to solve a double murder,' I pleaded. 'I'll be back with you all tonight.'

He Who Must Sleep miaowed softly.

'I didn't name her Tiddles,' I said quickly. 'It's only a temporary name until she comes up with her own.'

Thane frowned, but he was smart enough not to argue in front of the cats.

'Where is He Who Roams Wide?' I asked. All three cats gazed at me blankly. 'Is he inside?' Again there was no response and my stomach tightened. It wasn't like the adventurous black cat to hold a grudge because I'd stayed out all night – he did that often enough himself.

Dave's front door opened and he ambled out, peering at us from beneath the hood of his terry-cloth dressing gown. 'You're back then,' he grunted. 'Did you enjoy gallivanting around town?'

'We weren't gallivanting,' I said. 'We were in jail.'

He raised an eyebrow before turning to Thane. 'Don't let her lead you astray.' He wagged a finger in warning. 'She's more dangerous than she looks.'

'Ain't that the truth,' Thane agreed.

'I am *not* dangerous!' I said, visibly bristling. At the very least Dave wasn't supposed to know that I was dangerous anyway.

He rubbed his chin. 'Mmm.'

It wasn't wise to protest too much. 'Have you seen He Who Roams Wide?' I asked.

'Am I supposed to know which bloody moggy of yours that is?' he grumped. 'I don't know their daft names. There's far too many of them to keep track of – but I did feed them all this morning.' He bared his teeth. 'You're welcome.'

'Was my black male cat there?' I asked. 'Did he eat?'

'*You're welcome,*' Dave repeated.

I breathed. 'Thank you for feeding them.'

He scowled. 'Finally. Manners cost nothing, you know.' He waved a hand towards the gate. 'Yes, the black cat was there. Yes, he ate, then he went off but I didn't see where.'

I relaxed. That was okay; He Who Roams Wide was only living up to his name. 'Thank you,' I said again.

Dave scowled harder. 'You're welcome.'

AFTER HELPING Tiddles settle in and ensuring there was more than enough food and water for all the cats, I took a quick shower and changed into clean clothes. Thane also washed and I found a clean T-shirt in a pile of old clothes that I reckoned would fit him.

'We can go via your place if you want,' I said. 'It won't take long to make a detour first.'

'I don't smell that bad, do I?'

He smelled great.

He pulled off his old shirt, exposing his taut, muscled chest, then yanked on the T-shirt. It was a snug fit, especially around his shoulders, but it covered his modesty. More's the pity. 'Were you eyeing me up, Kit?' he asked archly.

I shrugged. 'It's not every day I have a half-naked werewolf lolling around my house.'

'Lolling? This isn't lolling.' He offered a crooked smile that contained a hint of cheeky promise. 'I can show you real lolling, if you want.'

I was genuinely tempted. 'We have a lot to do. You can show me later.'

'I bet Alexander MacTire doesn't do lolling.'

On that count, I suspected he was correct.

We headed first to Pork Pies. In the wake of Knox's murder,

the café wasn't open for business though there were people inside and I could see the familiar shape of Harriet's head through the frosted glass. Feeling uncharacteristically nervous, I licked my lips then rapped on the window.

It was the waiter from our first visit who opened the door. 'We're closed today,' he said firmly.

'It's Kit and Thane,' I said. 'We want a quick word with Harriet and the Blue Tattoos.'

He recognised belatedly that we were the couple who'd spoken to him about hiring the Blue Tattoos. 'You'll have to get another band for your wedding. The Blue Tattoos are no longer available.'

I winced. 'That's not why we're here.'

Fortunately, Harriet had heard me and came over. Her pale, strained face displayed every inch of her grief. The waiter, sensing this was a private conversation, slipped back inside.

'What is it?' Harriet asked. 'Have they found the bastard who killed my brother?'

Thane obviously didn't want to give her false hope until we knew more. 'Progress is being made,' he hedged.

'The MET guy said you two had been arrested.'

'It wasn't us,' I responded quickly. 'We didn't kill Knox.'

Harriet gave me a tired look. 'I know *that*,' she said with a trace of irritation. 'Has anyone else been arrested?'

There was no way of knowing whether Fetch Jackson was in custody yet or not, so I decided not to say anything to Harriet yet. Her grief was too raw. 'I still think that Knox's murder and Rory Taggert's death are linked,' I said, avoiding both her question – and her Truth-Seeking skills. 'Last night, the Blue Tattoos' singer said that there was a Fetch who wanted to know about an old schoolfriend of Knox's.'

'You think that friend might be this Rory Taggert? I know

most of Knox's friends and it isn't a name I recognise. I already told you that.'

'Maybe Knox never mentioned him.'

Harriet stared at me with dull eyes for a long moment then turned her head and called over her shoulder. 'Cyril!'

The Blue Tattoos' singer shuffled to the doorway. 'Oh,' he said, looking at me. 'It's you again.'

'I need to know more about the schoolfriend that the Fetch was questioning Knox about,' I said.

He shrugged. 'I don't know the guy.'

'There must be something, some detail that Knox mentioned,' Thane said. 'Where this old friend lives? Who he works for? Anything will help.'

Cyril pursed his lips as he thought, but it was Harriet who answered. 'Honestly, there are only a couple of people from school who Knox stayed in touch with. A troll called Ian...'

I shook my head.

'The nymph,' Cyril said to her. 'I've forgotten her name.'

'Adrienne,' Harriet replied. 'Adrienne McDonald.'

No.

'And then there's Simon,' Cyril added.

Damn it. I persisted. 'Definitely nobody called Rory?'

'Not that I've heard of.'

Disappointment flooded me even though it had been a worth a try.

'That's quite an eclectic group of friends,' Thane said, trying to soften the blow.

Harriet smiled faintly. 'Yeah. Knox liked most people and he didn't care who or what they were. He met up quite regularly with his friends from school. They got a few odd looks whenever all four of them came here together.'

'I'm not surprised,' Cyril said. 'A druid, a troll, a nymph and a witch? That's pretty unusual.'

Both Thane and I stiffened. 'A witch?' I asked.

'Yeah. Simon is a witch,' Harriet said. 'Is that relevant?'

Thane leaned forward. 'What does he look like?'

She shrugged. 'Blondish hair. About the same height as Cyril – oh, and he has a scar on his chin. He could conjure up a spell to heal it properly but he likes it. He thinks it makes him look more interesting.' She paused. 'It doesn't.' She sighed. 'I'll have to get in touch with him and let him know what's happened.'

I doubted she could do that since the body in the Mathers Street mortuary that Fetch Jackson had identified as Rory Taggert had a conspicuous scar on its chin. 'What's Simon's last name?' I asked. 'Where does he live?'

Harriet finally registered something was wrong and her eyes narrowed. 'Campbell. Simon Campbell. He lives towards the edge of the city. I've got his address somewhere if you need it.'

I kept my gaze steady. 'We need it.'

'What was Knox mixed up in?' Harriet whispered.

'I don't know,' I told her honestly. 'But we'll do everything we can to find out.'

NINETEEN

Simon Campbell lived in a modern tenement building in the far reaches of Coldstream. The location said a lot; although it was a well-kept building, and several passersby smiled at Thane and me, it wasn't the sort of place where anyone with great magical or financial endowments would choose to live. The natural ground enchantments were so weak that I could barely detect them. Whoever Simon Campbell was, he hadn't possessed much power.

We clomped up the stone stairs to Simon's third-floor flat. His name was neatly printed on the front door beneath the doorbell. Thane stepped forward and rang it; unsurprisingly, nobody answered.

I flipped over the doormat, but there was no spare key handily hidden underneath. I stepped back and glanced around on the off-chance Simon Campbell might have used another spot. I could easily pick the lock but there was no point in doing that if there was a simpler way to get inside.

'Stand back.' Thane braced his body. 'I've got this.'

I stared at him. 'What are you doing?'

'Kicking the door down.' He grinned at me. 'I'm stronger than I look.'

'I don't care how strong you are. We just spent the night in a cell, so I'm not about to do anything that will get us arrested again. Break down that door and every person in this building will hear us and call the MET!'

He frowned. 'You used to be an assassin, Kit. Since when did you have respect for the law?'

'I was an assassin who never got caught,' I told him haughtily. I took my keys from my pocket, unscrewed the fob and produced my very small, very trusty lockpick.

Understanding dawned. 'You're saying there's more than one way to skin a cat.'

'I hate that idiom,' I hissed. It should hardly have been a surprise that I wasn't a fan of feline taxidermy.

'Fair enough.' Thane paused. 'How about "there's more than one way to seduce a werewolf"?'

I gave him a long look and he winked.

Hunkering down, I squinted. My brass lockpick had been charmed by a skilled witch to work with many different types of locks. It wasn't perfect – for one thing, it wasn't indestructible and its magic wasn't eternal, so it would only function for a certain number of lockpicking attempts – but it was an old tool of my trade and I was fond of it. It didn't work on warded doors or magically enhanced keyholes, but there was no sign of those even though Simon Campbell had been a witch.

I hesitated, listening for any sound that suggested a neighbour might be approaching. When I was sure the coast was clear, I inserted the pick and wiggled it. It only took a moment before there was a satisfying click and the door swung open. I gave Thane a triumphant glance but he wasn't watching me and admiring my prowess. He was staring open-mouthed at the interior of Simon Campbell's flat.

The place was a mess. Not the sort of 'I can't be bothered to clean up after myself mess', but more of a 'stampeding ogres had a riot in my home when they were on a mission to break everything I own' mess. It had been ransacked.

Thane let out a low whistle. 'Fuck. If Simon Campbell is our Rory Taggert, his killer must have come here afterwards.'

I nodded. 'There were no keys found on the body and that lock hadn't been tampered with. Somebody was searching for something – they probably killed Campbell, took his keys and came here to find it.'

We both gazed at the devastation. 'Daniel fucking Jackson,' Thane muttered.

I nodded. There was a nasty taste in my mouth that I did my best to swallow.

We didn't spend long looking around; if there'd been anything here to find, there was little chance that it was still around. I picked up a smashed photo frame and turned it over to reveal a picture of four smiling faces.

I immediately recognised Knox Thunderstick. Next to him was a smirking troll and a nymph, probably Ian and Adrienne, his other two friends. My gaze slid past them with disinterest because I was certain that the figure at the end had to be Simon Campbell. He was grinning, his right hand resting protectively on the gold buckle of his belt, his left hand slung around the nymph's shoulders. His features matched those of the body recovered from the River Tweed. Yeah, this was my John Doe.

Rory Taggert had probably never existed; Fetch Jackson must have created a character using Simon Campbell's photos to stop the likes of me from delving too deeply into the case.

I held the photo out to Thane. 'It's definitely John Doe.'

He nodded slowly, unsurprised. 'I think we might have a motive of sorts as well. Look at this place.' He picked up a small gold box from the floor. 'A garden-variety burglar would have stolen this, and there are other valuables still lying around. Whoever created this mess wasn't interested in thieving, they were searching for something specific. I reckon Simon Campbell had something that Daniel Jackson wanted. The Fetch killed him, then came here to get it.' His eyes narrowed in speculation. 'From the way he's turned over every inch of this flat, it doesn't look like he found it.'

'Maybe that's why Knox was tortured,' I said quietly. 'Perhaps Jackson thought that Simon Campbell had given it to his friend to look after.'

'What could be so valuable that a respectable council witch would murder two people?'

'Financial gain is a common motive for murder,' I mused. 'But you're right – a double murder of this sort would have to bring an enormous reward. The payoff would need to be worth the risk, and I can't imagine what Knox or Campbell could have owned that would justify this. Neither of them were wealthy or particularly powerful.'

Thane tapped the photo, indicating the frozen smiles of Adrienne the nymph and Ian the troll. 'If we can locate these two, we might find out. Let's hope that Jackson is in custody by now and he hasn't already paid them a visit.'

I glanced again at the photo – and my jaw dropped. Oh shit. Thane immediately registered my expression. 'What?' he asked. 'What is it?'

I didn't look up: my gaze was fixed on the troll and his drooping moustache. It didn't suit him, but that wasn't what was bothering me. 'The troll, Ian,' I whispered. 'I've seen him before.'

'Where?'

I swallowed. 'He's in one of the lockers at the Mathers Street mortuary. He's dead, too.'

We were both sweating and breathing heavily by the time we got back to Pork Pies. There were no signs of life behind the frosted glass. I rattled the doorknob but it was locked, and a sign stuck to the door stated that the café was closed for the foreseeable future.

'Where would Harriet have gone?' Thane asked.

I shook my head. 'I don't know.'

'Do you know where she lives?'

'No.'

'We have to find Adrienne. If the nymph isn't already dead, she could be in real trouble.'

I gritted my teeth. 'I know.'

'If Montgomery hasn't arrested Daniel Jackson, he could be on his way to kill her.'

For fuck's sake. '*I know.*' I looked at Thane; his nostrils were flared and his body was tense. 'Don't panic.' I spoke the words aloud for myself as much as for him. 'We have to stay calm and think logically.'

He grimaced. 'You're right.'

I looked at the deserted café. 'Go back to the MET, find Montgomery and see if he's found Jackson. And ask if he can help track down Adrienne.'

'What are you going to do?'

I pointed through the glass. 'There's someone else in there who might be able to help. I'll catch you up. I won't be more than ten minutes behind.'

'Kit...'

'Do you trust me?' I asked.

He didn't hesitate. 'Always.'

I gave him a little nudge. 'Then go.'

As Thane took off, sprinting down the street in the direction of the MET, I dug out my lockpick for a second time. A couple were strolling towards me, hand in hand, but I didn't wait until they'd passed by – I simply picked the lock in full view. I was no longer in the mood for trying to hide my actions now there were lives at stake.

My only attempt at fooling them was to give them a dotty cat-lady glance and mutter about losing my keys. My old boss would have been horrified; if I'd had time to stop and think, I'd have been horrified, too.

I burst into the café and the door banged behind me. No alarm squealed and there was no magic to prevent my entry; with a Cursed Portrait in residence, there wasn't any need for them. Lady Augusta had already begun to shriek. 'Alert! Alert!' Her cut-glass voice was incredibly piercing. 'Intruder alert!'

I careened into the back room. 'Stop yelling. I need you to be quiet and focus. This is important. Knox's friend, the nymph called Adrienne – do you know where she is?'

'Intruder! Thief! Fire! Help!'

I marched up to the portrait and braced my hands on either side of the picture frame. Lady Augusta's eyes widened and genuine fear flashed across her painted features. Good: I needed her to be scared.

'I've already told you to be quiet.' I didn't raise my voice: words spoken quietly were often far, far scarier than the most screechy of shouts. 'I'm not here to hurt you – I don't care about you. I'm trying to help Harriet and stop anyone else from getting killed. The nymph, Adrienne.' I held up the photo that I'd nabbed from Simon Campbell's flat. 'Where can I find her?'

Lady Augusta pouted sulkily but her eyes swung to the photo. 'I have never seen that girl before.'

Damn it. 'Are you sure?'

'Yes.' She tossed her head. 'I don't like nymphs. They're too airy-fairy.'

This was Coldstream: half the city was airy-fairy. Lady Augusta, however, had no reason to lie. I'd have to find Adrienne by other means. 'What about Harriet?' I asked. 'Where has she gone?'

This time Lady Augusta only stared at me. I stared back then allowed a beat to pass before I softened my voice and tried again. 'She trusts me, you know that. You need to trust me, too. I'm on Harriet's side. Tell me where she is. Please.'

Lady Augusta blinked then sighed, and I knew I had her. 'Apparently somebody has been arrested for Knox's murder. She has gone to the Magical Enforcement Team to find out who.'

I was already half out of the door. Thank goodness Thane was already on his way there. 'That's it?' Lady Augusta yelled after me. 'You're just going to run off again?'

Dave's scowling face flashed into my head and I came to a stuttering halt. 'Thank you,' I called. 'Thank you for your help.'

As I left, I heard a final mutter from the Cursed Portrait. 'You're fucking welcome.'

TWENTY

The MET building looked normal. There was a ray of sunshine casting a glow on its grey façade, but beyond that its appearance was the same as it had been a few hours ago when Thane and I had left after our night in the cell.

Unfortunately the building didn't *sound* normal. In fact, the shouts drifting through the open windows were loud enough to have given Lady Augusta a run for her money. Perhaps I ought to have brought her along.

Several curious passersby had stopped to listen, though the words were indistinct even if the fury wasn't. I skirted around a group of young women. 'We should go in and see what's happening,' a brown-haired druid whispered, as if she were afraid of being overheard.

'Don't be silly, Tabitha. It could be dangerous,' one of her companions told her. 'Curiosity killed the cat.'

Yeah – but satisfaction brought it back.

As I moved away from them towards the front door I heard another voice say, 'I'm sure those were council witches storming in there. Those guys are scary.'

I stiffened, then marched into the building a little bit faster.

I was expecting a scene of carnage but it was still a shock when I saw what was going on. Lady Augusta had been correct: from the collection of furious people in the small front room, Daniel Jackson was being held in one of the MET cells. At least on one level that meant that, unless he'd already gotten to her, Adrienne was safe for now.

Some of the people inside the poorly titled Welcome Room at the front of the MET offices were hiding their anger better than others. Harriet wasn't doing a particularly good job of concealing her emotions: her cheeks were bright red, her hair was askew and her eyes were wild. At least she had good reason for her fury.

'I want to talk to him!' she yelled. 'I want to talk to the bastard witch who killed my brother!'

Theoretically that wasn't a bad idea; as a Truth Seeker she'd could easily tell if he was lying. But the uncontrolled rage in her face, while wholly understandable, made her unpredictable – especially if she wanted to keep her ability hidden. It would be better if she waited until she was calmer, though if the four council witches had any say in the matter she would never get to speak to Daniel Jackson.

They stood in a line as if they were barricading access to the cells, their mouths tight and their spines ramrod stiff. None of them had removed their pointed black hats and none of them were shouting, but their blistering rage still filled the room.

'Our colleague is not a killer.'

'He is an upstanding member of the Coldstream community.'

'There is no reason to hold him here.'

'We shall investigate the druid's death and find the real culprit.' The lines slid out of their mouths with the too-smooth delivery of the over-rehearsed.

'Lies!' Harriet shrieked. 'All lies!' She stepped forward and instantly three MET officers moved towards her as if they were afraid of what she might do.

Thane, who was beside her, put up his hands to warn them off. 'Back away,' he growled. 'Don't touch her.'

Two burly druids appeared from behind him. I didn't recognise them but I knew their type: these weren't the sort of laid-back fellows who formed folksy bands like the Blue Tattoos. The intricacy of the tattoos on their faces suggested that they were as close to the druidic board of governors as it was possible to get.

That was curious. Knox Thunderstick hadn't been an important member of their community. The only reason for their involvement that sprang to mind was that this was an opportunity for them to piss off the witches.

'A member of the witches' council has brutally murdered an innocent young druid,' said the nearest one. 'Fetch Daniel Jackson must be held to account for his crimes.'

'*Alleged* crimes!' snarled a witch. 'And he falls into our jurisdiction. We will question him and investigate what has happened.'

'That is unacceptable,' the second druid stated. 'Particularly since Fetch Jackson is a council member. You witches cannot be trusted in this.'

'How dare you question our integrity in this manner!'

I gazed from one irate face to another then glanced at Thane. Our eyes met. This situation was seconds away from descending into an all-out brawl. Even in the worst circumstances, the druids and the witches usually managed to remain cordial, so this aggression was unprecedented. It was also inexplicable, given that neither group usually put much effort into helping lower-status members of their communities.

I wondered what would happen if the troll leaders learned

about Ian's death. Would they also be as desperate to wrest control of the situation?

There was a rush of cold air as the outside door opened again. I glanced over my shoulder and paused when I saw who had entered. Well now: this was suddenly very interesting.

'Good day,' Quentin Hightower said, nodding at the small angry crowd. 'I came as quickly as I could when I heard what was happening.'

The last time I'd seen Hightower, he'd been soaked to the skin and daubed in gloopy mud. He cut an entirely different figure now: his clothes were dry, clean and free from river gunk – and both expensive and ridiculous. His suit was some sort of bizarre lilac and yellow checked pattern; although I had nothing against those colours per se, they did nothing for his tanned skin. Together with his perfectly tied cravat, matching handkerchief and shiny brogues, he looked less like a wealthy eccentric than a pantomime dame.

I examined him more closely. His hair deserved particular attention: it was no longer flattened into droopy, wet rats' tails but was coiffed into a bouffant of extraordinary proportions. Bloody hell. He looked like a cross between Tintin and Pepe La Pew.

I turned back to the others and registered the four council witches rolling their eyes. The druids were also smirking. I felt an odd rush of pity for Hightower. It didn't last long.

'This is a very serious situation,' he said. 'Do not worry. I shall get to the bottom of it and discern the truth. I have a knack for sorting out truth from fiction.'

That was quite a statement when you were in the presence of an actual Truth Seeker – not that Hightower knew that. Harriet stared hard at him and her mouth tightened. I suspected I knew the reason why. If Quentin Hightower believed in himself to the extent that he said, he wouldn't know whether his own words were truths or lies – and that meant she wouldn't know either.

'I shall question Fetch Jackson,' Hightower went on. '*I* will be the independent investigator this terrible situation calls for.'

'You're a witch,' one of the druids snarled. 'You're far from independent.'

'And we do not require your intervention,' a council witch said. 'You're not needed here.'

'I beg to differ,' Hightower replied as he rolled up his sleeves. 'Now, what about the vampires?'

Huh? 'What do you mean?' Harriet asked. 'What vampires?'

'All vampires,' Hightower replied without missing a beat. 'We have a dead body covered in blood. Vampires like blood. We should question them immediately.'

'*All* of them?' Thane enquired.

'A man is dead!' Hightower cried. 'This is not the time to cut corners! Yes, of course we should question them all!' He glared around the room, apparently expecting us to jump to his bidding even though there wasn't a scrap of evidence that tied a vampire to any of these crimes.

'Idiot,' a druid muttered. 'We don't have time for this shit. We reserve the right to question Fetch Jackson immediately.'

'Fuck off,' replied two of the witches in unison.

Hightower sniffed. 'Swearing is terribly uncouth, my dear fellow.'

The momentary lull in tension caused by Hightower's appearance was over. I glanced around the small room and tried to calculate the smartest move. The priority had to be keeping Harriet safe. If the witches and druids wanted to kill each other, I wouldn't get in their way – and from Thane's expression, neither would he.

The door to the prisoner holding area opened and Captain Montgomery emerged. He was the only other person who appeared calm. Unfortunately, his impassive demeanour didn't dent the others' anger.

'You have to release Fetch Jackson into our custody immediately!' Spittle flew from the witch's mouth as he shouted into the MET detective's face. That certainly wasn't the way to win Captain Montgomery's heart.

The taller of the two druids didn't miss a beat. 'Absolutely not! He killed a druid in cold blood. We should question him first. He might have killed others. We need to interrogate him without interruption so we can discover the full magnitude of his crimes.'

'Preposterous!' the witch screamed.

Hightower stepped forward. 'I shall take charge of this situation, detective. I know what I'm doing.'

The druid raised his fists. 'You're taking charge of nothing, you plank!'

Despite Thane's efforts to keep Harriet calm, she got in on the act. 'Daniel Jackson murdered my brother. Let me talk to him! Let me see what he has to say for himself!' Her voice rose higher with every word, pain in each syllable. My heart went out to her but none of this was helping the situation.

I hoped that Thane had thought to check her for weapons; while I'd fully understand – and silently applaud – Harriet attacking anyone who held her back, I knew that she wasn't a violent person at heart and she'd regret hurting anyone.

Montgomery cleared his throat; an odd glint in his eye suggesting he was enjoying the drama. That didn't make him a bad person; his work days were probably spent clearing up the aftermath of petty crimes and filling in paperwork so this fiasco would be an interesting break from routine. However, it also meant that I couldn't predict how he would react or what he would say.

I prepared for the worst. If I had to take my dagger out and use it to help Harriet, I would. It would damn me in the process but it would be worth it.

'I understand that tempers are high,' Montgomery began. 'But let's all take a beat and calm down.'

'Try telling that to my dead brother!' Harriet snarled.

'Exactly!' shouted one of the druids. 'Knox Thunderstick was tortured and killed because of that man.'

Three of the witches snorted and the fourth one smirked. 'Knox Thunderstick? What kind of fucking name is that?'

I started to move forward before Harriet hit him and ended up being charged herself, but thankfully Thane was already there and doing his best to hold her back.

I checked the witch's face; by the looks of things, he'd been hoping that Harriet would punch him so she'd be arrested and shoved out of his way. A council witch like him knew how to deal with druid officials and mysterious dead bodies, but angry grieving relatives who weren't part of the witch community were another matter.

I gave him a narrow, dead-eyed look and moved forward to flank Harriet on her other side. Try to manipulate her again, I promised him silently, and you'll live to regret it.

Captain Montgomery frowned at the three MET officers who were still in attendance but proving to be as much use as a cat flap on a submarine, then he cleared his throat again. 'This is an unusual situation,' he intoned. 'Under normal circumstances, Fetch Jackson would be under the jurisdiction of the witches' council.'

'Exactly!' called one of the witches. 'Finally somebody is speaking sense. You should never have arrested him in the first place and he should never have been brought here. This is a council matter.'

Montgomery turned to her. 'Ma'am,' he said. 'Right now you are under *my* jurisdiction. This is my building. Interrupt me again and you will be thrown out.' He raised his eyebrows meaningfully at his hapless colleagues who, in a surprising display of energy, moved towards her. The witch, sensing she was losing the argument, held up her hands in temporary submission.

'My dear fellow,' Quentin Hightower interjected. 'I shall—'

Montgomery glared at him. 'You'll shut up. I am in charge here.' Now he really seemed to be enjoying himself. This was probably the only opportunity he'd ever had to put both a snotty witch from the council and a high-placed witch like Hightower into their place. I applauded silently. Bravo.

'Let us not forget that the victim here is Knox Thunderstick,' the captain continued, 'He is dead, and his murder deserves our full attention. I have spoken to Fetch Daniel Jackson. He is aware of the evidence against him. but he maintains that he is innocent of all charges and wishes to clear his name.'

Suspicion curled deep in my belly. I wondered if Jackson had a trick up his sleeve to absolve himself.

'I have spoken to my superiors,' Montgomery went on, 'and it has been decided that under the circumstances a special team will be convened to take Fetch Jackson's formal statement and interview him. One witch of your choosing,' he nodded towards the council members, 'one druid of your choosing,' he gestured at the two tattooed officials, 'and me.

'In order to give everyone a chance to prepare and examine the evidence, this session will start here at 9am tomorrow. Once the interview is completed in accordance with Coldstream law, Fetch Jackson will either be released or passed to the witches' council for trial and sentencing. That will depend on any evidence or alibi that he brings forth to confirm or deny his innocence.'

By the look of things, nobody was happy with that outcome. Hightower opened his mouth to complain then looked at Montgomery's face and thought better of it. His mouth closed once more. Good.

It was a smart move on Montgomery's part; he was giving every invested party a chance to be part of the questioning process, at least to begin with. It would also make it harder for the witches' council to avoid taking action if Jackson's guilt was confirmed, and it would give the druids the chance to represent Knox's interests.

I glanced at Harriet. She needed to look Jackson in the eye and hear him speak for himself. 'If I may, captain?' I said.

'Yes?'

The witches nudged each other. 'Who is that?' one of them asked. The druids looked equally baffled.

I ignored them. 'As Knox's closest family member, his foster sister should be allowed to attend as well.'

'We don't allow family members to question suspects, Ms McCafferty,' Montgomery replied. 'With good reason.'

'You can put a spell of silence on me,' Harriet said quickly. 'I won't say anything. I just want to be there.' Her gaze dropped. 'For Knox.'

The captain gave her a long, assessing look. 'Very well,' he said finally. 'Those terms are reasonable.'

Especially given Harriet's Truth-Seeking skills. Regardless of what happened to Fetch Jackson, she would at least learn the truth about what had happened to Knox. She might even learn why he'd been killed, though I doubted that Jones would offer an actual explanation.

I felt Thane's eyes on me once more and I nodded. 'One more thing,' he said, speaking loudly.

'*You* cannot come to the interrogation,' Montgomery said.

'I should think not!' Hightower blustered for no reason whatsoever.

'That's not what I was going to say.' Thane smiled, though

it didn't reach his eyes. 'There are two more victims that we believe Fetch Jackson has killed.' You could have heard a pin drop. 'Simon Campbell, a young witch who was a friend of Knox's, and Ian...' He looked at me again and I shrugged. 'We don't know his last name. Ian the troll. Both their bodies are at the Mathers Street mortuary.'

'Ravensheart,' Harriet whispered, her face pale. 'Ian Ravensheart.' She stared at Thane. 'What about Adrienne? She's the fourth member of their friendship group.'

'Tell us where she lives,' I said. 'We'll check on her as soon as we can.'

She nodded dumbly as everyone else in the room, Captain Montgomery included, stared at Thane and I in shock. Look at us, I thought. We're the good guys. I, Kit McCafferty, had hunted down an evildoer with the help of my trusty werewolf partner – and not even killed anyone in the process.

'Well,' Thane murmured, with another sidelong look at me, 'it looks like our work here is done.'

TWENTY-ONE

'**W**as it a good idea to persuade the MET to let Harriet sit in on the interview?' Thane enquired, as we walked quickly towards Adrienne McDonald's home. 'She's very upset, Kit. She might take it upon herself to attack Fetch Jackson and land herself in deep shit. The council witches won't care about her grief, they'll demand she's locked up.'

I couldn't tell him that Harriet was a Truth Seeker. 'Harriet is a strong woman. She deserves to be there – she's one of the few people in Knox's life who truly cared for him. She should be able to look her brother's attacker in the face and hear what he has to say for himself.' I sighed. 'And this might be her only chance.'

He was silent for a moment before he said, 'I hope that the witches' council mete out appropriate justice. He's murdered three people.'

And we had no idea why. I reached for his hand and squeezed his fingers. He gave me a tight smile in return.

Unlike her friends, Adrienne lived in a prosperous part of town. I knew the neighbourhood; I'd been there on my own murderous business more than once. It was diverse in terms of Preternaturals, if not in wealth: witches, druids, trolls, dryads, vampires – anyone with a bulging bank balance lived there.

Her street was filled with grand townhouses, and I knew without checking that they'd all have magical security systems in place. Perhaps that was why she hadn't turned up dead like her schoolfriends. It gave me hope that she was still alright.

We found her house easily, a pretty sandstone affair draped in enchanted lilac wisteria. 'I wonder if Knox was responsible for this,' Thane said as he fingered one of the perfect blooms. Most of the other buildings were plant-free, so it was entirely possible.

He stepped up to the door and knocked, using the heavy gold-coloured ring bolted to the glossy moss-green façade. I moved to the window and peered inside. Heavy brocade curtains had been pulled back and tied with golden ropes, and I could see the furniture beyond. The room was tidy and, more importantly, undisturbed. Nobody had broken in here and ransacked the room.

Thane and I stiffened when there was a sharp clunk but this was no echoing gunshot, merely Adrienne's neighbour, peering out of her own front door to frown at us. 'Who are you?' she demanded suspiciously. 'What do you want?'

It might be a well-to-do area but it wasn't friendly. I plastered on my best cat-lady smile. 'Good afternoon,' I beamed. 'Isn't it a lovely day for this time of year?' It was already dark but it was the sentiment rather than the accuracy that was important.

The woman folded her arms and glared, not prepared to soften an inch.

'Hello, ma'am,' Thane drawled, with a twinkle in his emerald eyes. 'We're here to see Adrienne. We shouldn't have turned up unannounced but we were in the neighbourhood and thought we'd drop by.' He held out his hand. 'I'm Thane. This is my friend, Kit.'

Something about his gentlemanly demeanour did the trick because she unfolded her arms and a blush rose up her cheeks. 'Oh, that's alright then. Adrienne isn't in – you just missed her. She left for work about fifteen minutes ago. I saw her go past the window.'

Thane clicked his tongue. 'She always did work too hard. I suppose she won't be back until late?'

'Probably not. She works nights.'

So Adrienne was probably employed by one of the Coldstream grottos like most nymphs were. She'd be unavailable until morning, which was good for her and bad for us.

The woman touched her hair absently, smoothing down a non-existent wayward curl. I glanced from her to Thane and back again. Huh.

'If you come back late tomorrow morning,' she said, 'you should catch her.'

'Thank you,' Thane murmured. 'Thank you so much.'

The woman giggled. I stared. When she returned to her house and closed her door, Thane turned to me and lifted an eyebrow. 'You're right,' he said.

'About what?'

'Talking about the weather. There are far better ways to initiate conversation. It didn't work for me in the bar the other night and now it didn't work for you.'

'Well, thank goodness you were here to flirt with her instead!'

Thane swept a bow. 'I exist only to please,' he purred. He leaned towards me. 'But if you think that counts as flirting, Kit, you have a lot to learn.'

Yeah, yeah.

His eyes glinted and he tilted his head, although the effect was lost given that his hair was shorn close to his skull and there were no lustrous locks to fall artlessly across his forehead. His tongue darted out and he slowly wet his lips.

'Do you need a Chapstick?' I enquired.

'Your mouth is all the ChapStick I require,' he said huskily.

I gave him a long look.

'I like that outfit,' Thane continued, oblivious to my amused irritation. 'Did you buy it at a discount? Because it will be one hundred percent off at my house.'

I folded my arms. 'Seriously?'

His mouth crooked up. 'Alright, I admit I'm cheesy. But something about being in your presence makes my thoughts turn to mush.'

'Is that because you know I could kill you in a heartbeat?'

He clasped his heart. 'You've already killed me. I've died and gone to heaven.'

I covered his hand with both of mine. 'That's a shame. I've always preferred devils to angels.'

His face relaxed into a grin. 'I think both our approaches could do with some work.'

As his familiar vetiver scent enveloped me, I was suddenly very aware of the heat of his skin beneath my fingers. 'I wasn't the one trying to flirt. When I do,' I whispered, 'you'll know about it.'

'When?' he whispered back. 'Not if?'

My mouth was painfully dry. A light flicked on in the front window of the neighbour's house and the woman peered out at us. If we continued to linger, her suspicions would return. 'That's enough messing around.' I pulled back, hoping I didn't look too flustered. 'At least we know Adrienne is okay.'

He sobered, too. 'Yes – and with Fetch Jackson locked up for the night, she'll be safe at work. We'll have to tell her what's happened to her friends, but I guess that'll wait until tomorrow.' He grimaced. 'There's no rush for bad news.'

No, there wasn't. Poor Adrienne.

'Let's head back to yours,' he said. 'I'll pick up Tiddles and leave you to get ready.'

I gazed at him, confused. 'Get ready?'

'It's Friday night, Kit. You've got a date with Alexander MacTire.'

Oh. I'd forgotten all about that. Shit.

I HAD ABSOLUTELY no idea what to wear for dinner with one of the most powerful werewolf alphas in one of Coldstream's most exclusive restaurants. My wardrobe wasn't exactly packed with glitzy evening wear but I managed to find a slinky dark-red cocktail dress. I'd worn it when I'd been contracted to slip poison into the drink of a high-powered faun who had a habit of cheating his clients out of the contents of their bank accounts. It had looked good on me then and had helped me gain access to the exclusive party where he was holding court. Unfortunately that had been some years ago; while the dress was glamorous enough to pass the test of fashion time, I wasn't quite the lean assassin that I used to be. I enjoyed my new curves because they made me look softer and feel sexier, but they didn't quite fit into the dress even when I sucked in my stomach.

She Without An Ear miaowed at me from the door. 'Alright,' I muttered. 'There's no need for that sort of language.' I peeled off the red dress, thrilled to be able to breathe normally again. Black trousers and a bland top then. If MacTire was disappointed by my outfit then we'd both know that this 'date' was a terrible idea.

He Who Roams Wide had returned without giving any indication of where he'd been. Not that I could pass judgment, given my own roaming recently. I gave him a long cuddle then spent time with each of the other cats in turn, promising that I'd be home before midnight.

I was already running late when I darted out of the door towards the middle of Coldstream. Perhaps I'd enjoy myself; perhaps this would become the true romance I'd been missing out on all these years. Stranger things had happened. Then I thought of Thane and grimaced.

The scene was set before I crossed the threshold of Vallese. Red roses framed the doorway, filling half the street with their perfume; tiny candles lit the red carpet that led to the front door. A violinist wearing a tuxedo was playing in the guests; the poor guy must have been freezing his balls off, even with thermal long johns and a sprinkling of magical heat to keep his fingers moving.

I turned to the maître'd who was greeting me. 'This is still January, right? I've not fallen asleep and woken up on Valentine's Day?'

He smiled with such professional suaveness that I felt like the most important customer in the world. 'No, ma'am, alas this is still January.' He tapped the side of his nose with a white-gloved finger. 'Although at Vallese we like to think of every day as Valentine's Day.'

I returned his smile sweetly. 'I think I just threw up a little in my mouth.'

The maître'd didn't miss a beat as he rolled his eyes and whispered, 'Try working here every day.'

'Oh, you're good.'

He winked. 'Let me show you to your table, Ms McCafferty. Mr MacTire is waiting for you.'

Jeez. The maître'd knew my name. MacTire had probably

told him so he could do this performance. That was why I preferred cafes like Pork Pies: I was far more comfortable cloaked in anonymity.

Alexander MacTire was sitting in a dark, intimate corner wearing a navy suit and a pink shirt that was open at the collar. The colours suited him; he looked as if he'd put far more effort into dressing for the evening than I had. I swallowed and walked towards him, feeling even more uncomfortable when he stood up to pull out my chair. 'Kit,' he murmured. 'You came.'

'I said that I would.' Realising I might have sounded slightly defensive, I smiled to soften my words. 'I like to keep my promises.'

'Something that I already know about you.' He kissed my cheek and his designer stubble brushed against my skin. We both sat down. 'I trust you've not been for any more cold water dips lately?' he went on.

I snorted. 'I've been avoiding swimming sessions.'

'I'm glad to hear it.' His eyes danced and, not for the first time, I realised just how good looking he was. 'I thought I'd wait before I ordered drinks. Would red wine suit you?'

'Sure.'

'They do a wonderful Tuscan merlot here if you like something full bodied. It has notes of fig and blackcurrant.'

'Does the bottle have a pretty label?' I asked.

MacTire blinked. 'Huh?'

'That's how I judge my wines,' I explained. 'The aesthetic appeal of the label.'

His brow furrowed faintly then he flashed a white-toothed grin and managed a laugh. 'I'm sure it's a beautiful label.' He raised a finger. In an instant, a waiter was by our side.

Unsurprisingly the wine was delicious, even though the label was shockingly ordinary. The food menu was confidently short and we both ordered a starter and main course. Once the waiter had gone, MacTire leaned back in his chair. 'What have you been up to the last few days?'

'I've been … busy.' I pulled a face. 'To be honest, I don't want to talk about it. It's not been much fun and I'd like to have a few hours thinking about something else.'

He shrugged. 'Fair enough.'

I eyed him. 'What have *you* been up to?'

'Paperwork, mostly. People seem to think it's glamorous being head of a werewolf pack, but there's a lot of bureaucracy and form-filling and not much adventure.'

'You should do something about that.'

'Perhaps I should. Nicholas is always telling me that I lead a very boring life.'

I smiled. He smiled. It was all very pleasant and polite.

I looked away and gazed at the other diners. There was an interesting collection of well-heeled people, and I wondered if Fetch Jackson had ever dined at Vallese. Probably: it seemed the sort of place he'd appreciate.

'How are the cats?' MacTire asked, when the starters arrived.

Between mouthfuls of a stuffed courgette flower I regaled him with a tale about He Who Crunches Bird Bones, who'd recently started trying to befriend one of the chubby ponies who lived in one of my neighbours' gardens. My cat had decided that the best way to win the little horse's heart was to bring him gifts in the form of odd socks stolen from houses up and down the street.

MacTire pursed his mouth. 'Oh.' He paused. 'Cute.'

Once the plates had been cleared away, he told me a complicated story involving money laundering and another werewolf pack. I listened and nodded all the way through – *most* of the way through. I lost concentration at one point when

MacTire tried to explain the intricacies of lupine inheritance laws.

'Hmm,' I told him, displaying the full extent to which I cared.

He nodded. 'Indeed.'

When the pasta arrived, MacTire forked a swirl of spaghetti and chewed thoughtfully before swallowing. Finally he said, 'It's been nice weather lately. For January.'

I looked at him and he looked at me, then I burst out laughing. MacTire stared at me stony-faced before he also cracked a grin. 'This isn't working, is it?'

'I like you,' I said. 'And you're definitely the most handsome man I've ever met.' MacTire nodded, accepting his due. 'But it turns out that I'm not attracted to you at all.'

'I like you too, Kit. You're fun and clever and capable.'

I noted sardonically that he didn't say I was the most beautiful woman he'd ever met.

'However, I have to say that this evening has proved that I'm not attracted to you either. The element of danger that you bring with you intrigued me enough to suggest otherwise but...' He shrugged. 'I was wrong. This isn't meant to be.'

I felt a sense of overwhelming relief and raised my glass of wine. 'I'll drink to that.' MacTire matched my action and we both took a long gulp.

The waiter suddenly reappeared. 'I'm sorry to interrupt your meal,' he said, 'but there's a woman here who says she needs to talk to you, Ms McCafferty. I'm afraid she won't take no for an answer.'

My eyes widened. Mallory. 'I'm sorry,' I said to MacTire. 'I need to speak to her. I'll step outside. It won't take long – a minute or two at best.'

He waved a hand. 'Bring her in here. I'll go to the restroom and leave you to talk for a few moments.'

I watched him go. Alexander MacTire was definitely a gentleman but he would never be *my* gentleman. And that was no bad thing.

'Hey, Kit!' Mallory arrived, slightly breathless and red-cheeked. She sat down on the chair that MacTire had just vacated. 'Sorry I'm late – it took longer than I thought to get the information you needed. The witches' council has been in disarray all day.' She raised an eyebrow. 'Something about one of their own getting arrested for murder, which I believe you know about?'

'You're well-informed.'

She smiled. 'That's my job. Anyway, I'll knock a month off your waiting period because of the delay. If I don't come to you for the return favour within the next eleven months, you are released from further obligations. Is that okay with you?'

More than okay. Mallory was little more than an hour late and, frankly, her interruption had been welcome. 'Sure.'

She grabbed a hunk of crusty bread from the basket and started ripping at it with her teeth. 'So,' she said, getting down to business. 'You wanted to know what was top of the council agenda this week. Despite the spanner in the works with the arrest, there's only one topic that has been consuming the witches.' She swallowed a mouthful. 'This is great bread.' She took a swig from MacTire's glass. 'Good wine, too,' she commented. 'A Tuscan merlot?'

'So I've been told.'

She smacked her lips. 'Tasty. Very full-bodied. I like the notes of fig.'

'The council?' I prompted. I didn't give two figs about the wine – or any figs, for that matter.

'Oh yes. They're preoccupied with silphium.'

I frowned. What?

'In fact, the witch who's been arrested for murder – Fetch

Daniel Jackson? – had been tasked with retrieving it. Interesting, wouldn't you say?'

'What the hell is silphium?'

A shadow fell between us: Alexander MacTire was back. 'Silphium is the most desirable, most potent, most magical herb that has ever existed,' he offered.

Mallory waved up at him. 'What he said.'

'It's also been extinct for the last two thousand years,' he added.

She winked. 'Supposedly. Although perhaps "dormant" would be a better word. Whatever, it's priceless. If it existed today, Preternaturals would kill not just for its power but for the money a tiny silphium cutting could potentially command.'

'Kill for it?' I asked through gritted teeth.

'Oh yes, I'm quite certain,' Mallory said. 'Rivers of blood would run through the streets of Coldstream if somebody possessed silphium.' She took another sip of the wine and leaned back in MacTire's chair. 'This really is an exquisite merlot.'

I only stared.

TWENTY-TWO

The silence would have continued far longer if not for Alexander MacTire. He crossed his arms and gazed down at Mallory. 'That's my wine.'

She drained his glass. 'Did you choose it? It's delicious!'

That clearly wasn't the response he'd been expecting. 'That's also my chair.'

'Oh.' Her messy curls shivered as she looked around for another one. 'You'd think an upmarket place like this could afford more seating.' She caught the nearest waiter's eye and gestured for help. He looked at MacTire for approval.

The werewolf alpha frowned. 'Five more minutes,' I said to him. 'I want to find out more about this silphium stuff.'

Mallory glanced between MacTire and me. 'Oh no!' She clamped a hand to her mouth. 'Are you on a date? Have I gate-crashed? I'm so sorry. I'd hate to interrupt a budding romance.'

MacTire nodded at the waiter to bring a third chair. 'On that count you're safe.'

'Ah.' Mallory nodded wisely. 'Your hunt continues, then.'

'What do you mean?' he growled.

'Your search for the perfect mate. You've not found her yet.'

His eyes narrowed and I hastily raised my hands. 'Don't look at me – I didn't tell Mallory I was having dinner with you. She had no idea who I'd be here with. In fact I've never mentioned you to her.'

She was oblivious to his scowl. 'Kit is right,' she said cheerfully. 'I figured it out all by myself. Go me!'

The waiter arrived with the chair and MacTire sat down, unappeased. 'And who *are* you?'

'Mallory Nash,' she said. 'And you are Alexander MacTire.' She raised her empty glass towards the waiter. 'Could we get another bottle here?'

When the waiter looked at MacTire again, he nodded reluctantly. I smirked; this was more fun than I could have imagined, though from Alexander MacTire's expression he didn't seem to agree. I jumped in to explain. 'Mallory is a broker,' I said. 'Of sorts.'

'Secrets and favours,' she added. 'Not stocks and shares.'

'I asked her to find out what the witches' council is worried about this week in return for an as-yet unspecified favour.'

MacTire's eyes flicked to me. 'Risky.'

'There are caveats as to what Kit will do for me in return,' Mallory assured him. 'There are always caveats.'

As he leaned back and gazed at her, it was difficult to tell whether he was fascinated or horrified. Perhaps both. 'How do you know about me?' he asked. His voice was low and silky but it held an edge of danger. Alexander MacTire was alpha of one of the most powerful werewolf packs in Coldstream for a reason; he wasn't a cuddly puppy, he was a predator. I hoped Mallory realised that.

Oblivious, she went on. 'Let's say that a potential client came to me not too long ago and asked for a favour – she not only wanted you to notice her but also consider her seriously for the position of First Mate. I'm only telling you because I declined the opportunity for reasons we won't go into.'

She looked at me. 'My real clients' business is sacrosanct and I'm not in the habit of gossiping. I won't go blabbing about your request to anyone, Kit.' I believed her.

MacTire wasn't mollified. 'Who?' he demanded. 'Who asked you to do this?'

She waved an airy hand. 'I'm not going to tell you that.'

His eyes glittered with annoyance. 'You declined because you couldn't help her. Right?'

'Wrong.' She eyed him over her empty glass. 'I knew exactly how to achieve what she wanted, I just didn't want to do it.'

'How?' he demanded. 'How would you have done it?'

This conversation was veering in directions that didn't interest me. 'If we could get back to the matter of this silphium...'

Neither of them looked at me. The sommelier appeared, smiled at us all and started refilling our glasses. I said thank you; Mallory and MacTire didn't even glance at him.

'It's the annual Wolf Ball next month,' Mallory said.

'So?'

'You're attending the ball with your beta wolf, Samantha, as your date,' she told him.

Wow. How did she know that? I sneaked a peek at MacTire. His expression was controlled but I reckoned he was as surprised as I was at her insider information.

'When you arrive at the steps of the Grand Hotel, it would be an easy matter to distract Samantha. While she's busy, my potential client would appear dressed in blue because it's your favourite colour. I'd also advise her to wear a natural perfume based on roses because that would grab your attention. Then she'd make her approach. I didn't iron out all the details because I didn't take her on as a client, but I expect it would have been something along the lines of a little drama where she helped an elderly guest in front of you so she appeared both strong and compassionate.' She shrugged. 'But I'm only conjecturing.'

'It wouldn't have worked,' MacTire said.

Mallory grinned. 'I beg to differ. It definitely would have worked – up to a point, at least. Even my wiliest machinations can only go so far.' She took another sip of wine. 'There would at least have been consensual sexual congress. Beyond that, I can't say.'

Alexander MacTire was open-mouthed, and so was I. The only difference between us was that I believed Mallory could have pulled it off whereas MacTire remained more sceptical.

'Okay-dokey,' I said, more loudly than I'd intended. 'About that silphium…'

Mallory shook herself and gave a small tinkling laugh. 'Yes, of course. Sorry, Kit. We can go elsewhere to discuss it privately, if you wish?'

MacTire had already heard most of it, plus he clearly knew more about silphium than I did. He could stay. He might even be able to add something to the conversation – if he could shake off his preoccupation with Mallory's revelations.

'It's fine,' I said. 'Go on.'

'Alright. Silphium is also called laserwort. It was well known in Roman times and was originally grown in the North African city of Cyrene, which is in modern-day Libya – although it's nothing more now than a collection of archaeological ruins.'

'I've never heard of it,' I said.

'Julius Caesar and Pliny the Younger both mentioned silphium,' MacTire said. At my look, his lip curled. 'I was forced to learn Latin when I was a kid. My father told me it would be useful, but this is the first time I've ever found that to be true.'

'I feel the same way about algebra,' Mallory told him. She was probably well aware that Alexander MacTire's father had been a brutal, violent bastard. 'What else do you know about it?'

He toyed with the stem of his wine glass. 'Not much. It was potent and was believed to be literally worth its weight in gold, but it was over-harvested and became extinct two thousand years ago.'

Mallory nodded. 'According to historical reports, the last stalk was given to Emperor Nero around AD54.' She turned to me. 'It was a remedy for both mental illness and physical complaints, an effective aphrodisiac and a seasoning for food. It was also used as a perfume. In its potent form, its resin could be a magical enhancement but nobody knows for sure how powerful it was. It's not been seen for two millennia.'

'Then why is it a hot topic for the witches' council?'

'Because,' Mallory said in a low voice, 'ten days ago a witch passed them a sample of some fresh silphium leaves.'

I sucked in a breath. 'This witch. Was he called Simon Campbell, by any chance?'

'Yes,' she answered, her cool, clever eyes watching me. 'That was indeed his name.'

WE FINISHED the bottle of wine and declined dessert, although from Mallory's expression she would happily have ordered every sweet on the menu then asked for second helpings.

'All this silphium stuff is serious business,' I said. 'At least three people may have been murdered because of it – and although the killer has been caught, he's a highly placed witch who sits on the council.'

'A Fetch?' MacTire was astonished.

'Yes. The council knows about silphium and it seems likely that the druids' board of governors are aware of it too, given how enthusiastic they were about questioning that particular Fetch.'

MacTire gave a low whistle. 'If one of those groups obtained genuine silphium, they'd embargo it for everyone else in Coldstream so they could control its distribution, and they'd grow their own magic and wealth in the process. It would shift the balance of power across the entire city – hell, maybe across the world.'

'I don't know if silphium exists, or if it's in Coldstream,' I said. 'If it is, I certainly don't know where it might be. But I need your word that you won't speak about this to anyone else unless its existence is proven and it becomes public knowledge.'

MacTire eyed me. 'You ask a lot. There are plenty of werewolf packs that would be just as interested in obtaining silphium as the witches and druids. We could write our own cheques for generations to come if we became its sole suppliers.'

I snorted. 'Your life is complicated enough.'

He grinned. 'True. Even if I wasn't already in your debt, I have no interest in starting a war over a plant. The money would be nice, though.'

'You're already rich.'

MacTire's white-toothed grin stretched wider. 'Nobody will hear about silphium from me.' I waited, keeping my gaze on him. 'You can trust me, Kit.'

'All the same, I'd like your word,' I returned. And because I was prepared to play hard ball, I added, 'You told me when I rescued your nephew that you'd do anything I wished to repay the debt.'

His smile disappeared at my heavy-handed approach. 'Fine. You have my word that I won't mention it to anyone.' He gestured to Mallory. 'Your turn.'

Mallory laughed easily. 'You have my word, Kit – of course you do. For one thing I'm a squib, so silphium's magical properties are no use to me.' Alexander MacTire stared at her. 'And I don't need money. It doesn't interest me.'

He looked sceptical. 'Really,' he said in a flat tone of voice.

She smiled serenely. 'Really.'

I believed her even if he didn't. 'Thank you, both of you.' I caught the waiter's eye. 'Please allow me to pay for dinner.'

'Not a chance,' MacTire growled. 'I invited you here.'

'Then let me pay for Mallory's share of the wine.'

'No.'

I glared at him in mock irritation and he returned the look.

The waiter moved smoothly over to our table. 'Your evening has already been taken care of.'

We stared at him. 'What do you mean?' the werewolf alpha asked.

'Compliments of Mr Vallese himself.' He turned a half-inch and bowed to Mallory. 'He hopes you enjoyed your evening, Ms Nash, and reminds you that you are always welcome to dine here with any of your friends.' With that, he backed away.

I smothered a laugh; MacTire still looked confused. 'Wait. What?' he asked.

Mallory didn't say anything but her eyes were dancing with amusement.

I patted his hand. 'I need to get home. I promised my cats that I'd be back before midnight.'

Although my blood was fizzing with the anticipation of telling Thane what I'd learned about silphium, it was late and neither of us had slept well recently. If Thane was sensible, he'd already be curled up in bed with Tiddles snoozing beside him.

I decided to find him in the morning so we could track down Adrienne together; she was the one remaining person who might know where the silphium was. For now, I would jump on the first tram to Danksville, secure in the knowledge that there was a murderer behind bars and a motive in the bag.

TWENTY-THREE

I woke up early, luxuriating in the warmth of my bed. All five cats had clearly forgiven me for my earlier transgression in staying out all night and had snuggled around my body. She Who Loves Sunbeams had even stretched a protective paw across my cheek to guard against any escape attempt.

I had no plans to do any such thing. It was pitch dark outside and I reckoned I could snooze for a good few hours before I had to get up. This was more like the early retirement I'd anticipated; this was what I wanted.

I turned over and buried my face in my pillow.

Thump.

'What the hell was that?' I muttered and covered my ears.

Thump. Thump.

Damn it. Go away.

Thump. Thump. Thump. 'Kit! Wake up! Open the door!'

I sat bolt upright, disturbing three of the sleeping cats. I apologised to them hastily. It sounded like Trilby, but I couldn't imagine what they would be doing at my front door at that hour of the morning.

'Kit!'

Shit. It really was them. I cursed, scooted out of bed and grabbed a jumper before making my way blearily to the door. I opened it and peered out. Trilby looked bright-eyed and bushy tailed. Their clothes were uncreased, their hat was perfectly perched on their head and they looked wide awake – but they weren't smiling.

'What are you doing here?' I asked. 'It's practically the middle of the night.'

'It's 4.30 in the morning, Kit, hardly the middle of the night. Besides, you need to put on some proper clothes and get moving. You've got work to do.'

I passed a hand in front of my face. 'Trilby...'

They gazed at me grimly. 'There's an attack underway.'

Suddenly I was wide awake. 'An attack? Where?'

'On the MET building. Somebody has broken in, knocked the duty officer unconscious and gone straight for the cells.'

My stomach dropped. Instantly, I knew what – or rather whom – Trilby was alluding to. 'Fetch Jackson? Is he still there? Has he escaped?'

Trilby shook their head. 'I don't know, but you should get there as fast as you can.' They turned away and trudged back to the garden gate.

'Wait! How did you know about the attack? Who told you?'

Trilby didn't answer. I cursed then darted back inside to make myself presentable. It took me four minutes to yank on appropriate clothes, grab everything I might need and run out of my front door.

BY THE TIME I arrived at the MET building, magicked lights were illuminating its façade. There were people everywhere, and a cordon had already been set up to hold them back. I pushed my way through a group of curious vampires, then stared aghast at the scene.

The front door, which would normally have been firmly closed at that hour, was hanging off its hinges; scorch marks suggested that some sort of powerful magic spell had been used to blast it open. Four paramedics were crouched around a fallen figure dressed in a MET uniform. I felt the pulse of magic as they worked on her wounds and I swallowed hard.

The acrid stench of violent magic clung to the still air. The idea that somebody would storm this building was unprecedented; even though I could see it with my own eyes, it was difficult to believe what had happened.

A hand grabbed my arm from behind. As I spun, I instinctively reached for my would-be assailant. I jabbed them with my elbow, throwing as much force as I could into their solar plexus before I swung around.

Thane choked and doubled over, wheezing and gasping for air. 'Goddamnit,' I hissed. 'Haven't you learned by now not to creep up behind me?'

The vamps stared at me with their black eyes, their expressions blank, but at least the nearest ones stepped back to put a distance between us. 'She's stronger than she looks,' one of them muttered to his companion.

'Those self-defence classes at my local community centre are worth their weight in gold,' I replied, tossing my head as I helped Thane straighten up. He wiped away involuntary tears and managed a weak smile. I didn't return it. 'Trilby?' I asked.

Thane nodded. 'About ten minutes ago.' His voice was strained but I remained unrepentant. 'They banged on my door to wake me up although Tiddles had already done that.'

At least it had saved me from waking him.

'Jackson?' he asked.

I shook my head. 'No sign of him yet.'

He rubbed his eyes again and gazed at the building. 'There must have been an army of people involved to do this.'

Not necessarily: with the right tools and the element of surprise, a single person could be responsible. 'A pinch of enchanted trevishate to blow off the doors, followed immediately with a black-market stun grenade.' I sniffed. 'Laced with valerian, if I'm not mistaken. A child could do it – not to mention someone from the witches' council.'

I cursed silently. It had never occurred to me that anyone would be so bold as to mount a brazen attack like this, even with a potential king's ransom of silphium at stake. The lengths to which greed drove people never failed to amaze me.

'You think someone from the witches' council is responsible?' Thane asked.

'Or a power-hungry druid.' I glanced to the right where a baker's dozen of pale-faced, black-hatted witches were standing. Three metres away was a cluster of tattooed druids. Both groups were glaring at each other. I examined each face in turn.

'They look as shocked as we are, Kit,' Thane murmured.

He had a point: their reactions appeared genuine. I wasn't the only one who hadn't expected this sort of brutal, decisive action. I watched them for another moment then made a decision and ducked beneath the cordon.

I marched towards the building but I didn't get very far. A stony-faced MET officer appeared seemingly out of nowhere and blocked my path. 'Where the fuck do you think you're going?' he growled.

'Has he escaped?' I demanded. 'Has Fetch Jackson gone?'

Something odd flickered in his eyes, but before he could speak there was a sharp cry from the crowd and a figure burst forward. Harriet. Oh no.

'Somebody called me and said there was a commotion here. Where is he? What has that bastard done?' She squared up to the MET officer. 'Tell me! Where is the fuck who killed my brother?'

There was a flicker of movement beyond the shattered door. I caught a glimpse of a shaken Captain Montgomery, then four paramedics appeared carrying a stretcher. On it lay Fetch Daniel Jackson. My jaw dropped. Suddenly I realised this hadn't been an escape attempt at all: it had been an assassination.

'Out of the way!' Montgomery yelled at the crowd. 'This man needs to get to a hospital!'

Bloody hell. I stepped back and grabbed hold of Harriet to encourage her to do the same. The paramedics moved past us. Jackson's face looked pale and waxy; though his eyes were open, there was a glazed edge to his irises. As I stared at him, I realised the grim truth: Daniel Jackson was dying. It was too late for any hospital or magicked medical intervention. Nothing could help him now.

Jackson raised a hand and let out a guttering wheeze, then his body seemed to collapse in on itself. The paramedics muttered to each other with the hurried calm of experienced emergency workers and lowered the stretcher to the ground. 'Daniel,' one of them said. 'Daniel, stay with us.'

The Fetch croaked. When he turned his head, his dying gaze landed on Harriet and his lips began to move. 'I didn't do it,' he whispered. 'I didn't kill Knox. I'm sorry. It was...' His voice faltered and caught in his throat as the last of the light faded from his eyes.

The paramedics started CPR immediately but I stepped back, dull with the knowledge that it was already too late. 'Harriet, come with me,' I murmured. 'We need to give them space.' I reached for her again but she staggered away from my grasp, spun back and pushed through the crowds. Unable to do anything for Fetch Jackson, I followed her.

She made it to the other side of the street before she

stopped and braced one arm against the wall of a small witchery store, gulping in ragged breaths. This time I didn't try to touch her, I simply waited until she raised her tear-filled eyes to mine.

'He wasn't lying,' she whispered. 'He was telling the truth. That man did not kill my brother.'

∾

'IT WAS A DEATHBED CONFESSION,' I told Thane as we walked away from Harriet's house. She was safely inside with her next-door neighbour making sure she was alright. I couldn't help by staying with her. I couldn't do anything to salve her complex emotions – but that didn't mean I couldn't help in other ways.

'Deathbed confession or not, it doesn't mean what he said is true,' Thane retorted.

I still couldn't tell him that Harriet was a Truth Seeker so I prevaricated wildly. 'I've heard a lot of last words, Thane. Few people lie when they face death.' That wasn't even remotely true. Lots of people lied when they are about to die. Sometimes they even lied to themselves. I doubled down regardless. 'I know what I'm talking about. Daniel Jackson isn't the killer we're looking for.'

He sent me a sidelong look. His scepticism wasn't a surprise. He knew me too well – and I wasn't deft at twisting the truth. 'It was his glove you found soaked in Knox's blood.'

'I'm not saying I understand *how* he's not the killer,' I fumbled, 'I'm saying I believe he's not.'

'Or maybe you want to believe there's someone else behind this. You're so caught up in this investigation that you don't want it to be over.'

'But it's not over,' I pointed out. 'Somebody killed Daniel

Jackson. Somebody blasted off the front doors of the MET, invaded the building and killed him.'

'That was probably the witches' council tidying up their own mess. It's obvious they believe he's a killer, no matter what they've said to the contrary, and they don't need the bad publicity Jackson would have brought to their door.'

'If that was the case, they'd have waited until *they* had him in custody, not attacked the damned MET.' I sighed and tried again. 'Look, if we assume that the underlying motive is to get hold of this silphium stuff, Fetch Jackson wouldn't have needed to tie up Knox and torture him to find out where it is. He used a truth spell on me at the mortuary. Twice. He could have used the same magic on Knox.'

Thane wasn't giving in. Bloody hell. 'Knox Thunderstick was a druid, and a pretty good one if his green-fingered skills were anything to go by. He might have been strong enough to resist such a spell. Besides, a truth spell only forces you to speak the truth – it doesn't force you to speak.'

Perhaps not, but Knox had been badly beaten before he died. He would have been prepared to say anything. I came to a halt and Thane stopped next to me. I glanced at him. 'You said you trusted me.'

'I do.'

'Fetch Daniel Jackson didn't kill Knox Thunderstick. I can't tell you how I know, I just know. I need you to believe me so we can move on.'

His green eyes looked into mine. 'Okay, Kit.' He put his hands in his pockets and started walking again.

Wait. That was it? I stared after him then shook myself and caught up. 'You don't want to discuss it anymore?'

'You've asked me to trust you. I trust you. Jackson didn't kill Knox.'

I didn't know what to say. Hell, I didn't know what to *think*.

'Yeah, it's weird for me too,' Thane said gently and grinned. 'Come on. We need to get back to Adrienne's place.' His smile disappeared. 'Because one thing is for certain – her life is still in danger and we're not finished playing heroes yet.'

Unfortunately, I was no longer feeling heroic in the slightest. But I was even more determined to get to the bottom of all this shit.

CHAPTER
TWENTY-FOUR

I'd half-expected Adrienne's nosy neighbour to appear as soon as we passed her house but no curtains twitched and her door remained closed. Maybe we'd finally got lucky and she was out. I certainly hoped so.

Thane used the door knocker as he had the previous day and, like the previous day, there was no answer. I checked through the window: Adrienne's front room remained untouched.

'Maybe Adrienne's behind all of this,' Thane offered. 'She found out that her friends had a mystical plant worth gazillions and she killed them so she could steal it for herself.'

'And she's not been at work all night at all,' I said. 'She's been breaking into the MET and murdering a Fetch in cold blood because he was getting too close to the truth.'

He scratched his chin. 'He almost caught her at Knox's house.'

'She was in the middle of torturing Knox to find out where he'd hidden the silphium when Jackson appeared.'

'Jackson realised that nobody would believe a sweet nymph could be capable of that and he'd get the blame for it.'

HELEN HARPER

'He tried to shoot her but she escaped out of the window.'

He clicked his fingers. 'That was the gunshot we heard.'

'And to give himself time, he used a blast of kinetic magic to move the wardrobe against the door.'

'He ran in one direction, stopping at the hammam to clean himself up while she ran the other way.'

'You didn't pick up her scent or another bloody trail because...' I squinted. 'Er...'

'She'd already killed Knox and cleaned herself up when Fetch Jackson arrived.'

We gazed at each other. It was a theory, a convoluted theory but a theory nonetheless.

A small nervous voice trembled from behind me. 'Somebody has killed Knox?'

I turned. Adrienne was standing in the middle of the cold street, her luminous eyes shining in horror. Oh. She swallowed and stared at us. 'Who are you?' she whispered. 'And what the fuck has happened to my friend?'

I damned myself for being so careless. Thankfully, Thane took charge of the situation. 'My name is Thane Barrow and this is Kit McCafferty. We should talk inside, Adrienne.'

She shook her head. 'No. Tell me what happened. Tell me where Knox is.'

To be fair, I wouldn't have let the likes of us into my house either, but this wasn't the sort of conversation to have on a dark street – and it was one of those few occasions when Thane's charm wouldn't be enough.

I met Adrienne's eyes and spoke to her gently in the same way I'd have spoken to She Who Loves Sunbeams. 'Let's go in so you can sit down, then we'll tell you.'

Adrienne folded her arms, clearly determined to refuse, but despite her attempt at a tough-guy exterior tears were already brimming in her eyes. My heart lurched. Breaking bad news never got any easier.

Before I could respond, something brushed against my ankles. I glanced down and saw a sleek tabby cat. Without thinking, I crouched down to stroke him. When I straightened up, Adrienne's jaw had dropped. 'I've never seen him let a stranger touch him before.' She shook her head in amazement. 'Ever.'

The cat miaowed softly. 'He Who Guards,' I said quietly. 'Nice to meet you.' The cat purred.

Adrienne's tongue wet her lips. She looked from me to the tabby and back again. 'Okay,' she said in a strained voice. 'You can come in.'

Her hands were shaking as she unlocked the front door and they were still shaking when she sat down opposite Thane and me in her large living room. He Who Guards butted his head against me, reiterating his tacit approval of my presence in his house, then jumped onto Adrienne's lap. Good. She would need him.

'Tell me,' she whispered. 'Tell me everything.'

I got straight to the point: delaying would only prolong her misery. Not that my words would cheer her up – I suspected it would be a long time before Adrienne felt cheerful again. 'There have been three murders in the past few days. We've identified the victims as Knox Thunderstick, Simon Campbell and Ian Ravensheart.'

Adrienne didn't immediately react; in fact, my devastating words barely seemed to register. The tears that had been threatening vanished. I swallowed, wishing I had a glass of water.

'We're not the authorities, Adrienne,' Thane told her. 'We're not from the MET, and we don't have any vested interest beyond bringing the killer to justice. We believe the same

209

person has murdered all three of them. As far as we can tell, it's because...'

He didn't get the chance to finish his sentence before Adrienne interrupted him. 'Silphium,' she said flatly. 'It's because of silphium.'

I leaned forward. 'You know about it?'

'I thought it was a damned weed,' she muttered. 'But Knox was sure it was silphium. I'd never even heard of it until a few weeks ago. But when I started researching what it was ...' Her voice trailed off miserably.

He Who Guards nudged her hand and his small pink tongue darted out to lick it in sympathy.

'Where did it come from?' I asked.

'Drumelzier,' she said, her eyes vacant.

I knew immediately where she meant because I'd been there myself a couple of times. There was a spot sacred to druids to the west of Coldstream but still close to the River Tweed. Myrddin – or Merlin as he was more popularly known – was supposedly buried there. The enchantments buried into the ground were certainly strong, although whether Myrddin was actually there or not remained up for debate. If an ancient magical plant was going to show up anywhere, I guessed it would show up on the grave of the most famous Preternatural of all time.

My mind flashed back to the trail of complaints I'd overheard from the beardy druids at the bar on Hirsel Street. They'd been upset that they were banned from visiting the site by the druidic board of governors, which meant that the druid governors also knew about the existence of silphium and were hoping to find more of it for themselves. It explained their raging desire to question Fetch Jackson at the MET station. Shit.

'Is it still there?' Thane asked. 'Is there any more silphium at Drumelzier?'

She shook her head. 'There was only one tiny plant. It was small and bedraggled and looked like nothing at all. Knox dug it up and brought it back here because he said it was silphium. We all laughed at him, but he was certain. He reckoned that if he could grow more of it he'd earn a fortune.'

'Did he manage to propagate the plant?' I pressed.

She nodded. 'Not from cuttings – he found a way to extract seeds from the stalk of the original plant.' Her eyes flicked between us, then she carefully nudged He Who Guards away from her lap. She stood up, walked to the mantelpiece and retrieved a small wooden box. 'See for yourself. There are some dried silphium leaves inside.'

When I opened the lid, the effect was instantaneous: I was enveloped in a cloud of magic so strong that my eyes began to water. Thane choked as I snapped the lid closed. Bloody hell.

'Knox gave us all a free sample,' Adrienne said. 'He wanted us to test it out.'

'When you say "all of us",' I prodded, 'who do you mean exactly?'

'Me, Ian and Simon. He wanted us to show it to anyone we knew who might be interested in buying it.' She gestured to the box. 'The sample was proof that it worked, that it really was silphium.'

'Did he give any to Harriet?' I asked, worried that she might also be a target.

'His foster sister?' Adrienne's mouth twisted. 'Definitely not. She disapproved of Knox's schemes so he knew better than to tell her what he was up to.'

I put the box on the table between us; even holding it felt dangerous. 'Are there any more seeds?'

'Yes.' Her eyes shifted. 'Knox thought he was being followed so he gave them to Simon to hide until an agreement had been reached with a buyer. Before you ask, I don't know where Simon put them. He didn't tell me.'

The witch's dead body lying in the thick mud by the side of the River Tweed flashed into my head. It was quite possible he'd taken that secret to his grave. 'Have you given any of this away?' I asked, indicating the box of samples.

Adrienne shook her head. 'No. Knox handed some to a few highly placed druids. Simon gave some to a couple of witches in similarly high positions...'

'A Fetch?' Thane interrupted. 'Fetch Daniel Jackson? Was he one of them?'

She wrung her hands helplessly. 'I don't know who he gave them to. I don't know who Ian gave them to either. He said he knew someone who might be interested, but I don't know who it was.'

'A troll?'

'I don't know!' Suddenly her face crumpled. 'They're all dead? All three of them?'

'I'm so sorry, Adrienne,' I said.

'Oh God.' She scooped up He Who Guards and ran out of the room. A moment later we heard a loud, anguished sob.

Thane winced, reached for my hand and squeezed it tightly. 'Adrienne might not have given away any of her silphium but she's still a target. We found her, which means the killer can find her too. They might think she has some silphium seeds as well as dried leaves and come here.'

My mouth flattened. 'It seems a likely scenario.' I glanced around the well-appointed room then smiled coldly. 'In fact, if it happens it will be the *perfect* scenario.'

~

THANE AND ADRIENNE went out via the back door, leaving the small wooden box of dried silphium leaves in full view on the coffee table. I stayed and took several moments to acquaint myself with the layout of the house. I wanted to know the potential exit and entry points, together with any good hiding spots. I probably wouldn't use them, but it was sensible to consider all possibilities.

Once I knew my plan and had established the variables and back-ups, I returned to the living room. I felt good; it had been a long time since I'd been this prepared for different outcomes. It was almost like old times.

'You and me now, bud,' I said to He Who Guards.

Nonplussed, the tabby flopped onto his back and rolled on the burnished oak floor. I obliged by crouching down and offering him some scratches. 'It won't hurt,' I promised.

His tail flicked from side to side.

'Yes,' I said. 'I know you're strong and capable and I've noticed those beautifully sharp claws that you take such good care of. But we don't know who will come through that front door or when. It's better if I deal with them.'

He Who Guards rolled again then returned to a standing position. He blinked at me once and I blinked slowly in return. 'Thank you,' I whispered. 'When this happens – *if* this happens – it's better if you keep out of the way.' His yellow eyes narrowed a fraction. 'Please.'

He looked away.

I exhaled. 'Good.' I stroked his back then reached for his sleek haunch and plucked out a tiny tuft of fur. A second later I swallowed it.

The transformation was harder than it had been with Tiddles but that wasn't surprising because He Who Guards was an older cat who'd been more resistant to the idea than Thane's youngling. My body spasmed in familiar agony before spinning

213

in mid-air, and I was dimly aware of a muffled crash as my foot caught something. Then I was panting, four paws planted on the floor.

I flexed my claws and stretched while He Who Guards watched me with slit-eyed suspicion. He hissed and batted a paw to establish that this house remained his territory and I was only a temporary guest. I blinked at him again in whole-hearted agreement and he backed off, disappearing out of the room with a warning chirrup. That was for the best; I hoped he'd heed my warning and stay away.

I stretched my back, enjoying the flexibility of my feline body. Belatedly I realised that the crash had been a nearby vase that had toppled off a shelf as my shifting body had snagged it. It lay in pieces on the floor. Oops. I hoped it hadn't been expensive, but from what I'd seen of the house and its contents it was probably a pricey antique.

I grimaced and debated trying to clear up the shards so they were out of sight, but there were too many of them for my feline teeth and paws so in the end I left them where they were.

Padding towards the nearest chair, I jumped up and curled into a corner. The chance to have an extra snooze was a real bonus. I wrapped my tail around my body and snuggled down, but it didn't feel quite right so I stood up again and tried a different position, burrowing my head into a soft velvet cushion. That didn't quite work either.

I stood up again and tried to stretch out with my front paws dangling over the edge of the seat. Mmm. Comfortable. I sighed happily, closed my eyes and relaxed all my muscles...

Three seconds later, there was a faint snick from the front door and a waft of magic as somebody broke in. Damn it: I'd thought I'd have enough time for a proper nap.

I twitched once but otherwise didn't move. I wanted to see

exactly who I was dealing with first before I acted. I wouldn't get a second opportunity to assess my target.

Quiet footsteps sounded from the hallway. This was the nearest room so Adrienne's would-be killer would check in here first before heading upstairs to see if she was asleep in her bed after her long night shift. The silphium box ought to be enough to draw them deeper into this living room where I could see them properly.

The footsteps paused momentarily at the threshold and I heard a masculine sigh. *Come on, you greedy bastard,* I projected. *Get in here already.*

The steps continued as the intruder walked in.

I stayed where I was, nothing more than a sleepy moggy paying no attention to anything other than my snooze. Through my barely open eyes, I caught a glimpse of a tanned hand.

'Silly girl,' the man muttered as he reached for the wooden box. 'Why would she leave it out in the open like this?' I'd heard that clipped voice before.

I stretched out my paws like an awakening feline then lifted my head and gazed at the man in front of me.

Quentin Hightower. I should have fucking known.

TWENTY-FIVE

M y movement caught Hightower's attention and he raised a plucked eyebrow. 'Hello, puss cat. You're a handsome bastard.' He paused. 'Not as handsome as me, though.'

I didn't miaow or hiss, which showed remarkable restraint under the circumstances. I simply watched him, sphinx-like. A ghost of a smile crossed his mouth then his gaze drifted down to the smashed vase and he clicked his tongue. 'You're in trouble, pusskins.' He paused. 'But not as much trouble as your mistress. Death is stalking Adrienne McDonald.'

My stomach tightened but I continued to stare lazily at him. I didn't want him to have any reason to think of me as anything other than a cat.

'Is she upstairs?' he asked.

Obviously I didn't answer, just dipped my head and licked my right paw before raising it to wash my face.

'Is talking to a cat the first sign of madness – or the last?' Hightower muttered under his breath.

Disappointed by my lack of response, he sighed and returned the silphium to the coffee table before walking quietly out of the room. I stretched my legs, hopped off the chair and followed him, fighting the urge to attack his ankles with my claws and fangs.

It was galling that Hightower had managed to fool me so effectively into thinking he was an idiot. He was an extraordinarily convincing actor – and that made me want to lash out at him in a daft bid to regain the upper hand. But he'd killed three people; he'd have no qualms about killing a cat. I had to be patient.

Hightower gave a cursory glance into the downstairs rooms. Satisfied they were empty, he headed upstairs, treading lightly on the thick carpet. I waited until he'd reached the first-floor landing then backed away and hawked up the hairball so I could return to human form.

It wouldn't take Hightower long to scour the upstairs rooms so I had to be quick; in fact, my legs and arms were still twitching with involuntary spasms when I ran after him, balancing on my toes to avoid making any noise. It was only when I reached the first floor that I was in full control of my body again.

That was when I slid out my dagger from the strap between my shoulders. I'd saved Quentin Hightower before, but now I would kill him. Easy come. Easy go.

There was a particular art to assassinating witches. EEL employees agreed that it was best done from a distance because, even if you possessed magic, you were taking a risk by getting up close and personal to them. You could never know for certain what magical tricks they might have hidden up their sleeves. Any hint of suspicion on a powerful witch's part, and an assassin would more likely end up injured or dead long before the target could be killed.

At that moment, however, distance was a luxury I couldn't afford. It wasn't completely disastrous. Regardless of who Hightower was or what hidden magic and intelligence lurked beneath his silly clothes and ridiculous pronouncements, he wasn't a god. It wouldn't be too hard to creep up from behind and take him unawares. Slitting his throat would be best, and it would be a swift and relatively painless death. Given the circumstances, it was far better than he deserved.

The faint creak from one of the rooms on the right told me that Hightower was snooping around Adrienne's bedroom. He Who Guards appeared from the room opposite, his expression leaving little to the imagination. He wanted me to get a move on and deal with the intruder as quickly as possible. I gestured for him to be patient then I tiptoed into the bedroom.

Quentin Hightower's back was to me. He had opened the wide, oak wardrobe doors and was gazing at the contents. *You won't find any silphium seeds in there*, I told him silently. *And you won't find Adrienne hiding in the corner.*

I adjusted my grip on the dagger and moved forward. I was within striking distance when, unfortunately, Quentin Hightower turned his head. He stared at me in shock. I didn't waste my time but simply raised my dagger and slashed it towards his exposed neck.

The tip of the blade pierced his skin and slid into his flesh but Hightower recovered faster than I had anticipated. He reached into his pocket, drew out a pinch of powder and tossed it at me. The spell – whatever it was – wrenched the dagger from my grasp with enough force for it to fly several metres through the air. It landed on the floor somewhere behind me to my left.

Damn it. Schoolgirl error: you should never ever allow your only weapon to leave your hand.

I leapt to the left, planning to retrieve the dagger and finish what I'd started, but Hightower was ready for that. He followed up his first blast with a second, more focused burst of magical power that slammed into my chest and sent me thudding to the floor. I banged my head on the way down and pain reverberated through every inch of my body. This was getting annoying. I'd had the element of surprise on my side – it should have been over by now.

Once upon a time I could have leapt to my feet without using my hands, but I didn't even attempt that now. Instead I rolled and solved two problems in one go: I avoided Hightower's third magic attack and scooted closer to my dagger. It was underneath Adrienne's bed and I would have to stretch my fingers to grab it, but it wasn't far away. My titanium-coated darling would be back with me soon.

'You again,' Hightower whispered.

Yep. I didn't reply: I wasn't there to chat. Instead I moved to block his view of the fallen dagger. If I could curl my fingers around the hilt, I could throw it at his head. That would certainly stop him talking.

'You saved my life,' he continued.

We all made mistakes. I manoeuvred my arm behind my back and my fingertips scraped the dagger's cool metal hilt, but I wasn't close enough. I allowed my gaze to meet Hightower's dark eyes and shifted another couple of inches backwards.

'Why did you do that?' he asked softly. 'Why did you save me?'

What could I say? It had seemed like a good idea at the time, though I was certainly regretting it now.

I stretched my hand and felt a surge of satisfaction when I wrapped my fingers around the dagger's hilt. I kept my eyes on Hightower, mentally calculating the trajectory and the force I'd need to bring this to an end. As he stared back at me, I registered the furious spark in his expression. Shit. I had to—

'Rigor,' Hightower whispered, the magic of imperious command rippling through the single word.

My body was forced into an immediate response and every muscle twitched until my limbs were tense and stiff. When I tried to move, nothing happened. I tried again but I couldn't. Abruptly I realised what that witchy bastard had done: he'd trapped me inside my own body. My bones had become a cage from which I couldn't escape.

What the hell kind of spell was this? I strained, trying desperately to move; if I could fight the magic somehow, there was still hope. I managed to blink my eyes. Okay, that was something. Then my big toe pulsed, which was even better, but I couldn't feel anything else. Fuck. I couldn't *do* anything else.

A spasm of panic overtook me. Help. *HELP.*

My fear was almost my undoing. My heart was hammering against my ribcage, my throat closing up. It was like I'd forgotten how to breathe. My vision started to blur.

At least there wasn't any pain. I'd envisaged my death a million times and in a million different ways over the years, but none of those imaginings had come close to this. The flare of panic that had assaulted me faded away. Everyone dies sooner or later; it was simply my time.

It was that state of calm acceptance that changed everything. As soon as I was no longer expending my effort and energy on fighting the spell, I saw the strain on Hightower's face. His forehead was oddly shiny and he'd stopped talking. The power needed to maintain the magic was too much for him; it would be too much for anyone.

Feeling oddly detached, I watched his body sag – and suddenly I was free. It was as if a heavy weight had been removed: I could breathe, move and, most importantly, act.

I grabbed my dagger then stood up and snatched his cravat with my other hand. I swallowed and murmured slightly to test my vocal chords. I was alright. I was still here.

'That's a pretty scary spell you're pulling there, buster,' I said aloud. 'But you don't have the stamina for that sort of magic.'

He reached into his pocket for another pinch of magical powder but I batted his hand away. I felt slow and sluggish in the aftermath of the rigor spell, but Hightower had been affected too and he was suffering far more than I was. The energy he'd expended to blast that spell at me had sapped his strength.

He tried to kick me. My reaction time wasn't great but, still holding his cravat, I avoided his foot and jumped to the side. Despite my grip, Hightower twisted and tried to kick me again. Sod this. I pressed the dagger into his neck. 'Please,' he croaked.

Here we go: it was time to listen to him plead for his life. I wondered how much money he'd offer me, or if he'd tell me that his family and his coven needed him. Once you'd heard one 'don't-kill-me' plea, you'd heard them all.

A bead of blood appeared on his tanned skin; it would stain his silly suit. What a shame. 'Don't hurt the nymph,' he said. 'She's done nothing wrong.' His eyes implored me. 'She doesn't deserve to die.'

I blinked then pulled back the dagger. 'So why did you come here to kill her?'

His brow furrowed. 'I came here to *save* her. You're the one who wants to kill her.' Hightower's voice sounded weak and thready. His lips were tinged blue and he was sweating even more than before. 'Aren't you?'

I squinted at him – then his eyes rolled back and his body went limp. Huh.

CHAPTER
TWENTY-SIX

I f being attacked by a rigor spell was now on my list of things to avoid, so was hauling the body of a semi-conscious witch through the streets of Coldstream with an annoyed cat weaving in front of me.

'Stop trying to trip me up,' I hissed at He Who Guards. 'This is hard enough as it is.' The tabby cat miaowed. Loudly. 'I told you already. I want to hear what he has to say, too, but right now he's going into shock. He needs proper medical attention.'

A leprechaun stopped in the street in front of us, his gaze swinging from me to the moaning, staggering figure of Quentin Hightower and the hissing cat beside us. As he looked at us uncertainly, I lifted my head and stared, allowing my pleasant cat-lady façade to disappear and reveal the dark core beneath. His green skin paled dramatically then he scurried past us, avoiding looking in our direction. Wise choice.

He Who Guards eyed me with newfound respect. 'I know what I'm doing,' I told him. It was only partly a lie. 'Trust me.'

The cat sniffed but seemed to decide that impeding my progress wasn't helpful. He trotted beside me instead, taking care to avoid Hightower's feet as they dragged along the cobbles.

Adrienne's neighbourhood might have been upmarket but it was also wholly residential, so I had to haul Hightower down several streets before we reached anywhere useful. Finally I spotted a grocer's and a gentrified witchery store; if I dragged him inside the witchery shop they would raise the alarm and find him the help he needed. It was the fastest way to get him medical attention – and also the way in which I'd lose control of the situation. I'd probably never see the damned witch again. I was in too deep now and I couldn't let that happen. I wanted answers – hell, I *deserved* answers.

I draped Hightower's arm around my neck and gripped his waist while his head lolled on my shoulders. 'How can you be so drunk so early in the day?' I scolded loudly when two women passed on the opposite side of the street. They nudged each other and giggled but didn't comment. I knew that ploy wouldn't hold up to close scrutiny, though; I had to find somewhere to hide Hightower and get him help as quickly as possible.

The first clinic we came to was a tiny place on a corner. It wasn't an establishment I'd used before – I'd never even heard of it. The Caring Touch Institution wasn't a moniker that filled me with confidence; it sounded incredibly dodgy and it certainly wasn't an *institution*. It was about the size of an old newsagents' shop, with a shabby door covered in peeling yellow paint and a tatty notice stuck in the window proclaiming medical services on the cheap.

It wasn't the sort of place I'd normally frequent but I was desperate. For one thing, I was exhausted and, for another, Quentin Hightower was growing weaker by the second. His skin was clammy and he was shaking and shuddering with every step.

I drew in a deep breath and twisted the cold metal door-knob. As the door creaked open, we fell inside with He Who Guards at our heels. I groaned in relief; Quentin Hightower simply collapsed with a shuddering breath.

The waiting room was small, covered in vomit-green tiles and devoid of people. I eyed the desk in the corner and the closed door behind it, then marched up and shouted, 'Hey! We need some help out here!' My voice echoed so I tried again. 'Hello? Is anyone there?'

The inner door remained firmly shut. Shit.

I stalked around the desk, yanked open the door and was immediately assailed by a cloud of stale alcohol and cigar smoke. Not good.

I glanced at Hightower, assessing whether I could haul his privileged arse further through the streets of Coldstream until we found another clinic. He'd passed out again. It was here or nothing.

He Who Guards leapt onto the desk and raised a paw. Yeah, yeah. I turned and strode beyond the door into the booze-fumed hallway. I'd barely taken three steps when a yawning man appeared pulling on a stained lab coat. He looked like a witch; I wasn't sure if that was a good thing or not.

He raised bleary eyes in my direction and started. 'Oi! You're not allowed back here!'

'Your receptionist told me to come straight through.'

His brow creased. 'I don't have a receptionist.'

'You need one,' I growled.

He flicked me his middle finger. 'Listen, lady. I don't know who you are and I don't care. I didn't ask you to come. Feel free to walk straight out that door and away again.'

Quentin Hightower moaned from the waiting room behind me. I grimaced and considered my options. There were a number of different ways I could play this; eventually, I discarded scary assassin in favour of a less-intimidating approach.

'I'm sorry,' I whispered. 'But I'm desperate. That man out there – he needs your help.' I allowed my eyes to fill with tears. When one escaped and rolled down my cheek, I clasped my hands. '*I* need your help.'

The bleary doctor gave me a flat look. 'Do you think I'm that gullible? Save your crocodile tears, lady.'

Huh. I wiped my cheek. 'You're smarter than you look.'

He snorted. 'You're not.'

I wasn't sure I deserved that response but complaining about it wouldn't get me anywhere. I was nothing if not adaptable so I changed tactics. 'My name is Kit – and that man out there really does need help. He's Quentin Hightower.'

The doctor raised an eyebrow. '*The* Quentin Hightower?'

'Yep. He's rich. If you help him, I'm sure there'll be a big reward in it for you.'

'Assuming he pays up after I save his rich arse.'

He *was* smart. 'I'm sure you have ways of ensuring your invoices are paid,' I said. 'I need you to heal him and keep his presence here quiet. That's all. If he doesn't pay up then I will.' I paused. 'Are you sober enough to handle it?'

I expected a snide response but instead he simply nodded. 'Yes.'

I raised my eyebrows. The doctor scowled; despite his grumpy exterior, harsh words and unwelcoming clinic, he possessed a considerable amount of professional pride. I relaxed. Now that I was beginning to understand him, I knew I could work with him.

'Good,' I said softly. We shared a look of grudging, temporary acceptance, then I licked my lips and steeled my stomach. 'I give you my word that you will receive financial recompense for your trouble.'

'Your word? You're brave.'

I shrugged. 'I'm desperate.'

'You in love with Hightower or something?'

'Or something. I need to talk to him. I need to know what he knows.'

A smile played around the doctor's lips. 'In that case I'd better get to work.' He walked past me. 'I'm Fergus, by the way.'

'Doctor Fergus?' I asked.

'Nah,' he said. 'Just Fergus.'

He Who Guards snorted. I crossed my fingers. There wasn't much else I could do.

Fergus snapped on a pair of latex gloves, which were welcome given the state of his white coat. The fact that he'd gone to the trouble of sourcing disposable medical items that weren't readily available in a city like Coldstream suggested he knew what he was doing.

Hightower flitted back into consciousness and moaned, 'Wh – what?'

'Don't talk,' Fergus said briskly. 'This will be easier if you don't.' He crouched beside him and felt his pulse, then leaned over and inhaled. His expression gave little away and a prickle of suspicion curled through me. 'I'll need your help in getting him through to the examination room,' he said.

I was by his side in a flash, heaving Hightower to his feet. 'Lead the way.'

Fergus went back behind the desk, leaving me to drag Hightower. At least I knew that this time there wouldn't be far to go.

Although the waiting room left a lot to be desired, I was pleasantly surprised by the examination room. It was clean and tidy, with a bank of painted cupboards along one side and a medical bed on the other. Ignoring his groans, I shoved

Hightower onto the bed, lifted his feet and laid him flat on his back.

'Good,' Fergus said. 'You might not be smart but at least you're strong.'

I bit the inside of my cheek to avoid making a rude retort; I didn't need Fergus the not-doctor to be polite, I only needed him to be proficient.

'Your friend is suffering from a surge,' he said. I'd guessed as much. 'A surge is when a magic wielder over-exerts themselves. Their body can't cope with the power they've extended and it shuts down to try and protect itself. It's often seen in young witches and druids who are still learning their limits, but they tend to recover quickly. It's very unusual in older practitioners. Left untreated it can be fatal.'

His explanation was unnecessary but I appreciated the effort. 'Can you treat him?' I asked. 'Will he be alright?'

Fergus didn't seem to hear me as he leaned over Hightower again. Again he inhaled deeply and this time half-closed his eyes. Interesting. Whatever manner of magic Fergus possessed, he appeared capable of sniffing out medical conditions. That was a useful skill, and I wondered what on earth he was doing in this backwater, even if he wasn't a fully qualified doctor.

'A rigor spell,' he whispered. He opened his eyes and turned to me. 'Did this man try to use a rigor-mortis spell?'

'Yeah.'

Fergus gave a low whistle. 'Fool witch.' He stepped towards me and sniffed again. 'He used the spell on you, yet you're still alive. It's as much a miracle that you're breathing as he is. Fascinating.' He raised an index finger and prodded my cheek.

I held my temper. 'I'm not the patient.'

He grinned. 'No – but you should be dead. That spell would have killed most people within seconds. There aren't many who can withstand its effects. A rigor mortis spell isn't something that slips out by accident, and I don't know any witches who could cast that level of magic and walk away afterwards. He over-estimated his ability – and he also meant to kill you. Are you quite sure you want me to revive him?'

My expression didn't alter though He Who Guards, who had come with us, hissed and arched his back. 'Yes,' I said. 'I'm sure. I need him alive and well.' At least until I'd heard what he had to say for himself.

Fergus shrugged. 'As you wish.' He addressed the tabby cat. 'You need to wait outside. Your aura isn't helpful.' He Who Guards glared malevolently but, to my astonishment, turned tail and left.

'You have a way with cats,' I murmured.

Fergus's eyes twinkled. 'Indeed. So do you.'

He knew what I was: he knew I was a cat sith. Whatever skills this man possessed, they extended further than I'd realised.

'Don't worry,' he said. 'Hippocratic oath. Your secret's safe with me.' Except I wasn't his patient and he'd already told me he wasn't a doctor.

My mouth tightened but it was a problem for another time. 'Can you help him?'

'Of course I can help him, though it will take a few hours. Leave him with me.' He glanced at the clock on the wall. 'Come back at one o'clock. He'll be right as rain by then.'

I folded my arms. 'I'd rather wait here.'

'In case he runs away?'

'I'm very concerned about Mr Hightower's welfare.'

Fergus laughed. 'I'm sure you are. Very well, then, but you'll have to wait outside with the cat.'

There were two narrow windows in the far wall of the examination room that allowed in a fair amount of natural light, but they weren't large enough for even a child to wiggle through. 'Is there a back door to this place?' I asked. I couldn't leave anything to chance.

'No.' He smirked. 'Feel free to check.' On the bed Hightower groaned and twitched. 'Don't fret,' Fergus said. 'He'll be fine.'

As I looked at the witch's pale, clammy face, I wasn't sure if that would be a good thing or not. Only time would tell.

TWENTY-SEVEN

I had no idea what Fergus did to Quentin Hightower but several times I felt waves of strange magic pulse through the walls of the waiting room. He Who Guards raised his hackles on three separate occasions but waited by my side and didn't try to leave or suggest that he sensed anything to be truly worried about.

The clinic's front door opened twice. The first time, an elderly druid popped his head around and eyed me. He didn't say a word, just harrumphed loudly and slammed the door as he disappeared again, as if he couldn't countenance the idea of waiting. About twenty minutes later, a pixie tiptoed in looking flushed and feverish, as if she were in the throes of some nasty virus. I hoped it wasn't contagious; I didn't have time to be ill.

She hugged her arms around her thin body and shivered in the corner. She didn't seem surprised by the lack of a receptionist so I reckoned she'd been to this clinic before. I considered striking up a conversation before deciding I was already busy enough with other people's problems. Even Trilby would agree that there were limits. Besides, nothing about the pixie's manner suggested she was feeling sociable.

At exactly one minute past one, the door leading to the examination room opened and Quentin Hightower walked out. He still looked pale but he was walking unaided and his skin was no longer deathly pale. Fergus had come through.

I moved to the side to block the exit to the street; I didn't want Hightower to escape before I'd had the chance to quiz him. I shouldn't have worried because the witch offered me a half-smile and sat down heavily on a chair. 'Thank you,' he said stiffly. 'That's the second time you've saved my life.'

I tilted my head. 'And that's the first time you've sounded grateful.'

The pixie stared at me, her eyes wide. When He Who Guards sprang up and launched himself at Hightower, she looked even more shocked. 'Hey!' I said sharply. 'Stop that!'

The cat lashed out, his claws snagging the trouser material around Hightower's left calf. I didn't entirely blame him; that yellow and lilac tweed *was* offensive.

'Leave him alone,' Fergus barked from the doorway. He pointed to a faded sign on the far wall that stated that violence would not be tolerated under any circumstances. I had yet to meet a cat who could read, but He Who Guards moved away to wash his face. As far as the tabby was concerned, he'd made his point.

'Mr Hightower is under orders not to exert himself for the next forty-eight hours,' Fergus said. 'If you're planning to torture him, leave it until then or his heart might give way quicker than you'd like.'

The pixie looked as if she were about to pass out.

I crossed my arms. 'I won't torture him,' I protested.

Fergus shrugged. 'So you say. Whether you do or don't, he's paid his bill in full so you are freed from your vow to meet the costs.'

That was good. I glanced at Hightower; his eyes met mine but I couldn't tell what he was thinking.

Fergus turned to the pixie and gave her a long look. 'So what have you done this time, Pippa?' She flinched under the weight of his gaze and dropped her head when he sighed. 'I've told you not to touch magicked herbs like that,' he muttered. He pointed to the examination room. 'Come on, then.'

The skinny pixie couldn't move fast enough. She darted past me, giving He Who Guards a wide berth. Fergus started to follow her. 'Thank you!' I called after him, but if he heard me he didn't react.

Within a few seconds, the only occupants of the waiting room were me, Quentin Hightower and a grumpy tabby cat. 'Well,' I said.

Hightower sighed. 'Well.' As he stared at me, for the first time I saw a flicker of something vaguely intelligent behind his eyes. Hmm. 'Who are you?' he demanded.

My expression didn't change. 'I'm the one asking the questions.'

He folded his arms. 'I am Quentin Hightower.'

'I know that.'

'I am important. And skilled. And I am a hero,' he added with a flourish.

'A knight in shining armour?' I asked, unable to help myself.

'Yes.'

'A champion of the people?'

'Of course.'

'A crusader, saviour and superhero?'

He tapped his foot impatiently. 'Yes, yes, yes. All of those things. I am in charge here, not you.' There was no trace of irony in his responses; he truly believed in his own heroism. It was utterly bizarre but it helped me a lot because now I knew exactly how to play him.

I kept my face straight. 'I'm so honoured to be in the same room as you, to be breathing the same air. My heart is a-flutter.'

He waved a hand, accepting his due rather than assuming that I was laughing at him as most would have done. 'Many people feel that way about me but it's only natural. Do sit down if you're feeling faint.'

I played along and pressed the back of my hand to my forehead. 'That's not a bad idea.' I moved away from the door and sat next to him.

'That's better,' he said. 'You didn't have to guard the door, you know. I won't run away.' So he wasn't *entirely* stupid. 'Quentin Hightower does not run away from anything.'

Okaaaaay. I held out my hand. 'I'm Kit. And I'm beginning to suspect that we both want the same thing.'

Hightower shook my hand vigorously. 'To keep people like Adrienne McDonald safe and to make sure nobody gets their grubby hands on silphium? Yes.'

'Nobody gets hold of silphium?' I asked sceptically. 'Not even you? A great witch like you could do wonderful things with some silphium seeds.'

His answer was swift but there was a steely edge to his tone. 'I could, Kitty, I could. But I do not need silphium to do wonderful things. I am already wonderful. In truth, silphium is too dangerous for any single entity to possess – even me.'

He ran a hand through his hair, which was no longer styled in a ridiculous comedy quiff but looked bedraggled and limp. Frankly, it was an improvement. 'I cannot permit anyone to control such a dangerous product.'

I gazed at him, taking in his droopy hair and his silly clothes. I was beginning to think that there was more to Hightower than met the eye and it was only his own ego which got in his way. 'You're far more than you pretend to be, aren't you, Mr Hightower?'

He smiled slightly. 'I was born with a silver spoon in my mouth. The Hightowers have been successful over the years, and it would be easy to take advantage of my position and sit back to enjoy my wealth and privilege. I want everyone in Coldstream to be equally successful. Silphium threatens the equilibrium which we all fight to maintain.' His expression darkened. 'Enough innocent people have already died because of it.'

There actually *was* something of the hero about the man. Maybe he wasn't quite the hero any of us wanted, but I couldn't claim that position either. I'd killed far more people than I'd saved; Hightower was a much better member of civilised society than I was.

'I could put silphium to good use,' he continued. 'But it wouldn't be wise. There are many who would worry that someone like me, who is already wealthy, intelligent and powerful, could be corrupted by it. I am too pure of heart to present such a danger but silphium offers too many problems, even in my capable hands. It should be found and destroyed.'

'You're a good man, Mr Hightower.'

'I am. Probably the best man in Coldstream.'

I didn't smirk. 'And you are trying to do what is best.'

'Of course.'

'You truly are a hero.'

He smiled. I dropped my voice and spoke softly. 'That must be incredibly lonely.'

His expression dimmed. 'Yes.' He looked down. 'It is.'

There was a heavy weight behind his words. Few people took Quentin Hightower seriously except himself. There was merit in his serious attitude towards his responsibilities, despite his self-involvement.

'Tell me,' I said. 'How did you get mixed up in all this?'

Hightower watched while He Who Guards huffily took up

the position I'd vacated. From the cat's expression, neither of us were to be trusted. I didn't blame him.

'I am known as someone with a big heart and a generous soul. A few weeks ago, a young witch called Simon Campbell contacted me. He told me he was peddling a magical herb that would change the world. If I was prepared to hand over enough money, he would grant me exclusive rights to it.'

'Silphium.'

'Yes. Silphium.' He scratched his chin. 'I thought it was a scam. Silphium is the holy grail and it didn't seem credible that a lowly witch with little power had found it, but I was prepared to reserve judgment until I could see it with my own eyes. I am open-minded and clever in that way.'

'Very clever,' I murmured.

He inclined his head, accepting my praise as his due. 'I arranged to meet Campbell at the riverside market to inspect his wares. I brought along several trustworthy witches from my coven who would remain anonymous until I'd confirmed the scam. Their remit was to take Campbell into custody afterwards and hand him over to the council.'

My eyes narrowed. 'You work for the witches' council?'

He barked a humourless laugh. 'Goodness, no. They think I'm a fool. But the council has its uses and it is their job to maintain law and order among witches. Sometimes they simply need a push in the right direction from the right person.'

'And that's you?'

He shrugged. 'I am but one man, but I am capable of achieving a great deal. The Campbell matter appeared a fait accompli. He was a confidence trickster who would be brought to task.'

'Except he wasn't,' I said.

'Indeed. It appears that even I can make mistakes and I

suppose it is good to admit that I can be wrong from time to time. Nobody is infallible, not even me.'

'You're very humble,' I told him.

'Humility is the beginning of wisdom,' he intoned.

He Who Guards huffed from his position by the door. I wasn't sure why the tabby cat was so disdainful because most cats were experts in displaying superiority over others. He should have been applauding, not rolling his eyes.

'I can learn a lot from you,' I said admiringly. He Who Guards huffed again. Yeah, yeah.

Hightower patted my arm. 'It didn't take my quick brain long to realise that Campbell was being truthful. He needed my protection, not my censure or to be arrested. He came to me because I am Quentin Hightower and I had it in my power to help him. I could save him. He *needed* somebody like me.'

I strongly suspected that it was Hightower's wallet and bank account that Campbell had needed but I didn't interrupt. Quentin was on a roll.

His voice dropped. 'I am afraid that I failed. I met Campbell at the market where he gave me a sample of silphium, five dried leaves sealed into a container. Five perfect silphium specimens.'

He shook his head in amazement. 'I still find it extraordinary that he had them in his possession. He told me that he had seeds that would produce more plants but there were other bidders. I had twenty-four hours to make a sealed bid for all of the seeds. If I was successful, I would be the only person capable of growing more plants. As I was examining the sample, Simon Campbell walked away.'

He gazed into the distance as he remembered. 'When I looked up again, I couldn't see him. I started to search to tell him I'd give him whatever he wanted for all of the seeds and then...' He gestured helplessly. 'I spotted him in the water. He was in the River Tweed.'

His hands tightened in his lap. He Who Guards watched him, tail flicking. The cat would have known Simon Campbell and was probably grieving as much as Adrienne.

'You didn't fall into the river, did you?' I said. 'You jumped in. You were trying to save Simon Campbell.'

'Of course I jumped in. I'm a strong swimmer – and I almost got hold of him. I was so very, very close.' He frowned. 'I don't know what happened.'

He was swept away by the currents and was in shock from the cold; that was what happened. I touched his hand. 'You did your best. Even if you'd grabbed his body, it wouldn't have made any difference. He was already dead.'

He blinked in surprise. 'What?'

'The post-mortem showed that he was stabbed to death before he entered the Tweed. While you were checking the sample, somebody slipped alongside Simon Campbell and thrust a blade into his chest. Even if you'd seen it happen, I doubt you could have done anything. He died instantly.'

Hightower sucked in a breath. 'So I didn't fail. I was already too late.'

'There was nothing that you could have done,' I agreed.

'I almost drowned, too,' Hightower sniffed. 'After I recovered, I investigated Campbell. The silphium was real. When I learned there had been more deaths of people close to him...' He shook his head. 'I confess I assumed you and the wolf were responsible.'

It didn't help that we'd been arrested because of those suspicions.

'Dearest Kitty,' he said. 'I can only apologise. Nobody like you could be a stone-cold killer.' He pointed to He Who Guards and smiled. 'You're a cat lady, a caring person.'

The cat's ears twitched and I did my best not to let my thoughts betray me. 'Absolutely,' I murmured, glad Hightower was looking at the cat and not me. 'A caring cat lady could *never* be a killer.'

'I am deeply sorry.'

I patted his hand. 'Don't worry about it.' And then, before my poor ability to lie became obvious even to Quentin Hightower, I changed the subject. 'So after you recovered from your dip in the Tweed, you did some investigating?'

He nodded. 'I was too late to get to Ravensheart and Thunderstick. By the time I learned of their existence, they were already dead.'

'Fetch Jackson,' I began. 'I suspected him but—'

Hightower interrupted. 'Daniel Jackson? He knew about the silphium seeds and was desperate to get his hands on them on behalf of the witches' council, but it's ridiculous that anyone ever thought he was the killer.'

Mmm. 'His clothes were covered in Knox Thunderstick's blood.'

'He found Thunderstick's corpse after you and the wolf left the property. He raised the alarm anonymously because he didn't want to answer any questions. The witches' council couldn't risk any whisper of silphium's existence getting out. Jackson's clothes were covered in Thunderstick's blood after he tried to revive the man, but even a fool would have known the Fetch wasn't responsible,' Hightower said dismissively.

Shit. Thanks to Harriet I knew that Jackson wasn't the culprit, but Hightower's easy dismissal of his involvement was painful. 'He died for a reason,' I said weakly.

'He was competition. He knew a lot, and he was getting close to the silphium. Maybe he'd even worked out where the seeds were, though probably not. He was not nearly as clever as me. If I didn't know their location, I doubt that Fetch Jackson did.'

Daniel Jones's dying words to Harriet echoed in my head. *I didn't kill Knox. I'm sorry. It was...* Maybe it wasn't the silphium seeds he'd discovered; maybe it was the killer's identity and that was why the Fetch also had to die.

'My present concern is the nymph,' Hightower said. 'Adrienne McDonald is the only survivor of that group of friends who knew about the silphium. I have puzzled over the problem and my sleuthing brilliance has come up with the only possible answer: *she* will be the next target.' He eyed me. 'I know you came to the same conclusion. We were both at her house for a reason.'

'Adrienne is fine,' I told him. 'She's with my friend Thane.'

'The wolf? That's good. Does she know who is behind this?'

'No.'

'Vampires,' he muttered. 'It has to be vampires.'

'There's nothing to connect vampires to any of this,' I said gently.

He grunted, and I wasn't sure whether he believed me or not, then he went on, 'Does the nymph know where the seeds are? Those are what the killer is after and I have to stop them from getting hold of them. Once I locate the bastard who is responsible for all this, I will make them regret the day they were born. I will bring them to justice! I will avenge those who have been killed and I will save the day! The killer underestimates my brilliance.' He grinned widely. 'People usually do.'

I couldn't begin to imagine why. 'Perhaps we should join forces,' I suggested. 'We both want the same thing.' Thane would understand that Hightower had his uses. I hoped.

'Good thinking.' He gave me a paternal look. 'You're not completely useless, Kitty. You'll make an excellent sidekick.' He paused. 'With the right training from me, of course.'

I glanced at He Who Guards, who was watching me with narrowed eyes, and shrugged. If I didn't kill Quentin Hightower by the end of all this, it would be a miracle.

TWENTY-EIGHT

F our of us sat in my small kitchen. Sun was streaming in from the window, suggesting that both the outside temperature and the outlook for the future were warmer than they really were.

We were doing a great job of eliminating suspects and we were doing an even better job of finding more amateur detectives to join our ranks. What would the collective term for our little group be? A symposium of sleuths? A network of Sherlocks? An assembly of misguided fools?

The one thing of which I was certain was that combining four minds was not helping our situation. None of us had any idea who the killer was or where the silphium seeds might be hidden. None of us could agree what to do next – although we all agreed about how serious the situation was.

There wasn't just a killer to worry about. I'd gotten enough of a whiff from Adrienne's dried leaves to know that Quentin Hightower's concerns about who owned the seeds was justified. Silphium's magical power was extraordinary. Of course, that just gave us something else to fret over.

At least the cats were happy. He Who Guards had curled up

on Adrienne's lap, delighted to be reunited with her. He Who Must Sleep was nestled against Quentin Hightower's arm, and She Who Loves Sunbeams was enjoying a spot by his feet where a golden shaft of sunlight had fallen. She Without An Ear was providing some much-needed warmth and comfort to me, while He Who Crunches Bird Bones was with Thane.

'I should go and get Tiddles,' he murmured. 'She's missing all the fun.'

From what I'd already learned about Tiddles, she was probably off somewhere making some fun of her own.

'There's *another* cat?' Hightower asked, genuinely astonished.

'Technically another two,' I said. 'Thane's cat is called Tiddles and my other cat is He Who Roams Wide. I don't know where he is right now. Then there are the feral cats who arrive every day for food – three or four of them usually gather in the garden. I've offered them the chance to stay permanently but they are free spirits.'

'I like cats,' he murmured, 'but that's a lot.' He Who Must Sleep opened an eye and gazed at him. She Without An Ear growled faintly.

'There's no such thing as too many cats,' I replied serenely. Thankfully that was enough to calm both bristling moggies down again.

Thane grinned, his green eyes crinkling, then he focused on Adrienne and returned to the mystery we were unable to solve no matter how many cats we had to help us. 'What about the other two Blue Tattoos musicians? Could they have the silphium seeds?'

She shook her head. 'No. They're fun guys, but he'd never have trusted them that much. Besides, it was Simon who kept hold of the seeds and hid them somewhere. I just don't know where.'

'His flat has already been searched so I don't think they can be there,' I said.

'I've been to the place where he worked,' Hightower told us. 'There was nothing there, either. I searched the entire place. Nothing escapes my hawk-eyed notice.'

Perhaps we ought to take a second look. Just in case.

'If *you* had something that was so valuable that people would kill for it, where would you put it?' Thane asked.

Hightower answered immediately. 'My family has a warded vault in the middle of our ancestral home. It has been strengthened by a range of magic users over the generations. If you're not a Hightower, it's impregnable.'

I believed him, but his answer didn't help us. 'Most of us aren't wealthy heirs to ancient fortunes. Simon Campbell certainly wasn't so we're not looking for a hidden family vault.'

'If I had something precious, I'd keep it in a safety deposit box at the bank,' Adrienne offered. 'But Simon didn't trust institutions so he wouldn't have done that.'

'And there's no record of him opening any accounts for such boxes in the last five years,' Hightower said. At my sidelong glance, he nodded smugly. 'Yes, I checked. I'm a very thorough person.'

Uh-huh.

'I know where I'd keep it,' Thane said.

I nodded. 'I know where I'd keep it too.'

We exchanged glances. 'Who else can you trust other than yourself?' he murmured.

Adrienne and Hightower squinted at us.

'If I owned something that valuable, I'd keep it on my person at all times,' I said.

'Me too,' Thane agreed.

I tapped the corner of my mouth. 'That's what Fetch Jackson thought, too. That's why he went to the mortuary – he

242

wanted to get hold of Simon's effects because he thought the silphium seeds would be among them. I bet Knox thought the same because he went to the mortuary, too. He was sneaking around in there like me.'

Adrienne straightened. 'Then that has to be the place. We locate Simon's effects and we find the seeds.'

'Except that Simon Campbell wasn't carrying anything with him at the river market before he died other than the silphium sample box, which he gave to me,' Hightower said. 'He was holding it and he didn't have a bag. I'm not even sure he had a wallet.' He linked his hands behind his head. 'If he did, my eagle eyes would have noticed.'

The less said about Quentin Hightower's eagle eyes the better.

'When his body was brought into the mortuary, it was logged with just the clothes on his back.' I chewed on my bottom lip. 'And those clothes have disappeared.'

'The seeds could have been in his pocket,' Adrienne offered. 'Maybe his killer stole his clothes from the mortuary and already has them.'

Thane shook his head. 'I don't think so. If anyone had found the silphium seeds, we'd know about it. What are the chances the seeds went into the River Tweed with Simon Campbell? His body was pulled out but they could have been washed away and lost forever.'

For a long moment we were all silent. 'It does seem the most likely scenario,' Hightower said. 'In fact, I'd been about to say the very same thing myself.'

'Of course you were,' Thane murmured.

Quentin Hightower smiled.

'Nobody wins,' I whispered. 'Nobody gets the silphium seeds, not the killer and not us.' I smiled; that would be the best outcome by far.

'Four people are already dead.' Thane frowned at my expression. 'Ian Ravensheart. Knox Thunderstick. Simon Campbell. Daniel Jackson.'

A tear rolled down Adrienne's cheek, reminding me that she'd only just discovered what had happened to her friends. She hadn't had any time to come to terms with her loss. 'Their friends and family,' she said, choking. 'Their friends and family.' She swallowed. 'Their friends and family...'

Thane reached for her hand and clasped it. 'They have to deal with the loss of their loved ones. *You* have to deal with that loss.'

Her bottom lip trembled. Hightower put his arm around her. 'I'm so very sorry.'

I gazed at her. 'You are the only person left to kill,' I mused aloud. 'You are the only one left who the killer believes could have the seeds.'

Hightower bristled. 'Even with me here to protect her, that's a little insensitive, don't you think?'

I considered apologising but I was only stating a fact.

'And I don't have the seeds,' Adrienne said. 'I'm not lying. I don't know where they are.'

I didn't doubt her for a second; I didn't need Harriet and her Truth Seeking skills to know that Adrienne was telling the truth. Those damned seeds were probably floating down the Tweed right at this moment. 'We know that, but the killer doesn't.' I was warming to my topic. 'Our original plan was a good one. If the killer is after anyone else, it'll be Adrienne. We can still use her as bait to draw him in.'

Adrienne's tears were falling more freely now.

'That might have worked this morning but this guy is smart,' Thane countered. 'If he wasn't expecting a trap before, he'll certainly be expecting it now.'

'He's not as smart as me, but the wolf is correct,' Hightower said. 'It is too late for such a trap to work. I suspect that the best we can do is keep Adrienne safe. She can come home with me.'

'And what?' I asked. 'You'll keep her hidden in your warded vault behind your castle walls and moat for the rest of time?'

'I don't have a moat. Though my castle is impressive.' He turned to Adrienne. 'You'll like it.'

'It's only a temporary solution,' I argued.

'Can you think of a permanent one?'

'We find the killer,' I said pragmatically. Then we'd kill him, though it was safer not to say that part aloud in present company.

He Who Guards appeared to be on my side. He drew himself up to a sitting position on Adrienne's lap and yawned before sweeping his feline gaze across us all. 'You're not alone,' I said to him. 'We'll help you. We'll provide protection. Adrienne won't be hurt, not while I'm around to help keep her safe.' From the glint in He Who Guards' eyes, he didn't think he needed any help.

'What do you want to do, Adrienne?' Thane asked. 'Do you want to go with Quentin? Or do you want to go home and wait to see if the real killer shows up searching for the silphium seeds?'

Her teary gaze swept across us, and suddenly I wasn't convinced she was in the right frame of mind to make any sort of decision. She'd been working all night and now her life had been turned on its head because of a straggly plant. What the nymph needed was a damned break.

She surprised me by straightening her thin shoulders and drawing in a hiccupping breath. 'All I want is to see my friends,' she said. 'Where are their bodies?'

Hightower winced. 'Adrienne, my dear...'

'I want to see them. Then I have to get some sleep.' She

lifted her chin defiantly. 'Only then can I decide what I want to do next.'

'When the chips are down and you're mired in hell, you find out what you're made of,' I said quietly. 'And you, Adrienne, are made of steel. Are you sure about this?'

She wiped her eyes and nodded. 'Where are my friends?'

'Mathers Street mortuary,' Thane told her.

She moved He Who Guards off her lap and stood up. 'I'm going there.' She sniffed loudly. 'Now.'

'It is not a good idea,' Hightower warned.

I looked at Adrienne's face. I got it: she needed this. She needed to see her friends for herself. 'Of course it is.' I beamed. 'In fact it's a great idea, Quentin, because you'll be right beside us and ready to protect Adrienne if the killer shows up or we get into trouble along the way. You're our magnificent hero.'

He looked slightly green around the gills. 'I am your magnificent hero,' he whispered.

I clapped my hands together. 'Great.'

Thane nodded. 'Fabulous.'

Adrienne set her chin into a firm line. 'Let's go.'

CHAPTER
TWENTY-NINE

Anyone watching our little posse as we approached the Mathers Street mortuary would likely have been able to deduce a great deal about our individual personalities from the way we were walking.

Naturally Quentin Hightower took the lead, striding ahead with a long gait, not glancing back to make sure we were keeping up. He expected people to follow him without question and there was no doubt that his straight back and marching swagger were designed to prove that he was a figure of authority.

Adrienne certainly believed in him; she scurried as close to him as possible. He didn't look at her. To be fair, I didn't think that Hightower had forgotten his sweeping promises to keep her safe, he was simply distracted by other matters – such as the important act of putting one foot in front of the other and looking superior while doing so. I decided he wasn't the sort of person who could multi-task.

Although it had been her idea to visit the mortuary, now that we were on our way, I suspected that Adrienne was having second thoughts. She possessed a steely inner core and wouldn't voice her fears, but her jerky looks from side to side showed her nervousness about what might happen on the mean streets of Coldstream. She knew she was a target.

She shouldn't have worried: Thane was sticking close to her and if anyone attacked he would be there to protect her within a breath. I knew he was scanning every possible viewing point and alleyway for lurking suspects. His hands were in his pockets and he appeared casual, but a closer look revealed coiled tension. He was ready for action and, if it came to it, he'd look very good kicking arse.

I pushed away a surge of regret that Hightower and Adrienne were with us. I wasn't used to working in a team, and I certainly didn't enjoy being part of this group. Thane was the exception; somehow everything felt easier when he was around. Hightower didn't turn around because it didn't occur to him to check on us; Thane didn't turn around because he knew I was right behind him and I could take care of myself. Their movements were the same but the reasons behind them were very different.

Me? I felt relaxed. We wouldn't be attacked en route to the mortuary. The killer had no fear of public places – he'd stabbed Simon Campbell in broad daylight close to a busy market before shoving him into the river. Neither was he afraid of blood or gore; Knox Thunderstick's hideous death had proved that. Our man possessed the calm capability to force his way into a building such as the MET office to take out a Fetch – but I could still poke holes in his performance. I'd give him six out of ten for his efforts thus far, with considerable room for improvement.

I listed his errors. He'd almost allowed himself to get caught at Knox Thunderstick's house. He should have dealt with Fetch Jackson long before the MET brought the council witch in for questioning. He should have tidied up after himself at Simon Campbell's flat; by leaving the place in a mess he'd shown he was looking for something and set us on the path towards the silphium. Finally, and most importantly, he'd had the chance to kill two birds with one stone at the river market – and he'd missed.

Quentin Hightower had obviously been meeting Simon Campbell to discuss silphium. The smart move would have been to kill them both at the same time but the killer had missed his opportunity. He'd left Hightower alive, suggesting that he didn't feel confident about taking on more than one person at a time. I reckoned our group of four would be safe as long as we stayed together – and that the killer's days were numbered.

Cindy's desk was empty when we trooped into the mortuary's reception area. That was unexpected. A tickle of wariness scratched at me.

'Nobody's here,' Hightower declared, his overly loud voice bouncing around the small room. 'What a shame. We should leave.' He spun around, pushed past me and reached for the door.

'Hello? Can I help you?' A young man carrying a box of tissues appeared from the corridor to the right. His nose was red and his eyes were puffy and watering, which was not a particularly good look for someone working in a mortuary. Surely grieving relatives wanted calm professionalism, not weepy emotions.

The man sneezed and I realised it wasn't sadness making him cry but illness. I took a precautionary step backwards.

'Sorry,' he apologised. 'My allergies are playing up. It happens sometimes. People bring their dogs with them to appointments, the dogs shed fur and I sneeze.' He blew his nose. 'I'm alright really.'

I instantly knew that it was far more likely to be a cat than a dog that had triggered his allergies. One particular adventure-loving, roaming cat, in fact. 'Is Cindy here?' I asked.

'She only works Monday to Fridays.' He gave a wet sniff. 'I'm Matt – I cover weekends. How can I help?' He put down the box of tissues and clasped his hands together solemnly. 'Have you suffered a recent loss?'

Adrienne started to nod but it was Quentin who spoke up. 'You know who I am.'

Matt rubbed his eyes, making a bad situation worse and causing even more raw, red blotchy marks to appear on his face. 'Uh, no. I'm sorry. Who are you? Are you related to Mrs Wooton? Her body was brought in this morning, but I'm not sure it's ready for viewing yet.'

'I am Quentin Hightower!'

Matt scratched his head. 'Hightower?' he asked, looking confused.

'From the Hightower coven!'

'Huh?'

This was almost too entertaining. Unfortunately Thane stepped in before matters could descend further. Spoilsport. 'We're here to support Adrienne McDonald.' He pointed to the nymph. 'She wishes to see the bodies of her friends to say goodbye to them.'

On surer ground now, Matt smiled. 'Do you have an appointment?' he asked. 'And permission from the families?'

Not exactly. I stepped closer to him; inevitably he sneezed again as soon as I moved. 'Is Dr Singh here? Perhaps you should get him for us.'

Matt's teary reddened gaze travelled from the pompous witch to the confident wolf to the sad nymph and to me. 'Yeah,' he said, clearly deciding that our motley crew was above his pay grade. 'I think I'll do that.'

THE LOCKER ROOM was even colder and more sterile than I remembered. Then again, last time I'd been searching for a body with an unknown identity and this time I knew who I was looking for. Adrienne's grieving presence by my side heightened the cold, clinical atmosphere in a way that my earlier dispassionate visits had not.

Adrienne was crying, albeit silently. Thane put a comforting arm around her shoulders, which she seemed to appreciate. Hightower just looked ill.

Dr Singh held up the now-familiar clipboard. 'You'll have to sign in to view each separate body,' he said. He gave me a faint smile. 'It's procedure.'

I reached for the clipboard and pen, flipped through the pages and signed where necessary. Gavin Ravensheart and Margaret Ravensheart had signed the page for Ian the troll; doubtless they were his parents. Grimacing, I wrote my name beneath theirs. Harriet and the two remaining Blue Tattoos had been in on behalf of Knox, and I added my name to that list. On the final page, I noted that nobody had come to see Simon Campbell since Fetch Jackson and myself. 'Do I have to...?' I asked.

'Sign it again?' Dr Singh finished. 'Oh yes.'

I scrawled my name then passed the clipboard down the line.

'I heard what happened to the Fetch.' The pathologist shook his head. 'What a terrible tragedy.'

'Has his body been brought here?'

'No. The witches' council will deal with his remains. Besides, we're almost full. There have been far too many deaths lately – the Redcaps have been bringing in more bodies than usual. It happens that way sometimes. We only have so much space.'

I acknowledged his point distractedly but Hightower blanched. 'You're clearly very busy,' he muttered. 'We should come back later when things have quietened down.'

'The bodies are only held here temporarily,' I reminded him. 'This is probably Adrienne's last chance to see her friends.'

Dr Singh nodded. 'Ian Ravensheart's funeral is taking place on Monday morning. Simon Campbell and Knox Thunderstick's services are in the afternoon.' Adrienne looked even more upset.

'They've been here for a few days now,' Hightower muttered. 'Won't they smell?'

I gazed at him. He really didn't want to be confronted with the reality of a corpse, let alone three of them.

'Don't worry,' Dr Singh reassured him. 'All the bodies here are refrigerated. You don't have to worry about any unpleasant smells.' He eyed the witch; none of us wanted to deal with Quentin Hightower's vomit. 'You can go outside if you're uncomfortable. We have a very pleasant waiting room.'

Hightower puffed out his chest. 'Absolutely not. I must remain by Adrienne's side at all times. I am her protector.' Thane was doing far more to fulfil that role but none of us said that aloud.

'I can give you a senses spell,' Dr Singh suggested. 'Everyone who works regularly with the dead uses such magic sooner or later.'

My professional interest was stirred. I knew such spells existed; there had been whispers that a couple of EEL assassins who hated the sight of blood used them regularly to guard against physical reactions. I had always thought that if their reactions were so strong they should consider a different career, but we each made our own choices.

'I think that would be a good idea,' Hightower said. 'Such

magic will help Adrienne.' It wasn't Adrienne who needed the spell.

Dr Singh dipped his hand into the pocket of his lab coat and withdrew a small golden box with delicate filigree etching. He flipped the lid, revealed a collection of multi-coloured pastilles and held it out. 'Here. One will be more than enough to prevent queasiness and dull any unpleasant smells. They are an important tool of our trade. The effects last for up to seven days. They're created by Mystical Forces,' he told us, name checking one of the larger witchery stores in Coldstream.

Quentin Hightower almost snapped off the pathologist's hand. He darted forward, took one of the tiny tablets, threw it into his mouth and swallowed. Adrienne shrugged but also took one. Thane shook his head.

'Ms McCafferty?' Dr Singh enquired. 'I know you don't need one but you're welcome to take a pastille if you wish.'

'No, thank you.' I stared at the small box and its contents. 'When you say they're an important tool of your trade, are they only used by pathologists?'

'Not at all,' he replied cheerfully. 'Some doctors use them. And some undertakers.'

I licked my lips. 'What about the Redcaps?'

Dr Singh chuckled. 'I've never met a single Redcap who doesn't pop one of these beauties at least once a week. Their job can be quite gruesome. At least we have some warning about what condition bodies will be in before we see them, but the Redcaps never know what they'll find when they're called out.'

I frowned then turned to the clipboard and its collection of signed sheets. The only people who could see the bodies without noting their names were the mortuary staff and, presumably, the Redcaps. They could come and go as they pleased without question.

Thane was watching my face carefully. 'What is it, Kit?'

Probably nothing, but I felt twitchy. 'You said that you've been very busy here,' I said slowly. 'Is that the same for every mortuary in Coldstream at the moment?'

Dr Singh pursed his lips. 'I couldn't say.'

'Simon Campbell's body was brought here by the Redcaps even though other mortuaries are closer to where he died,' I persisted.

'It was an unusual situation. I believe the Redcaps who serve this establishment happened to be the first to attend the call for Mr Campbell. They probably brought his body here because this is where they work from.'

'Specific Redcaps are assigned to specific mortuaries?' I hadn't been aware of that.

'Yes. They are an independent organisation who assign groups to particular areas of the city. Each mortuary receives its own cohort of Redcaps – it's easier when we all know each other. It's not a perfect system but it mostly works.'

'Who's in charge of the Redcaps for this mortuary?'

'Each group has a team leader. Ours is an affable fellow called Fitz Williams.'

Fitz was the Redcap I'd met at the Tweed. He hadn't been affable in the slightest.

'And it would have been his call to bring Simon Campbell here?'

'I believe so.'

That wasn't what Williams had told me; he'd said that they had been *ordered* to bring Campbell's corpse here. 'Even though you were already very busy with other bodies?'

'I wasn't on duty at the time, Ms McCafferty. And anyway, the Redcaps are responsible for body retrieval and removal to mortuaries. We don't interfere with their work and they don't interfere with ours.'

Thane's clever eyes continued to watch me. 'Three victims,'

he said quietly. 'All friends but all from different parts of Cold-stream, yet they all end up in this mortuary.'

Each body had been brought here by the Redcaps; not only that, but Fitz had used a nosegay. Why would a Redcap need something to disguise the scent of death when they already had access to the magical pills that Dr Singh had offered around?

I thought of something else and turned to Hightower. 'Why did you think a vampire was involved in the murders?'

He blinked rapidly. 'Each person was killed in a different way. Whoever did this to Adrienne's poor friends understands death. Vampires are the very definition of death – they are the undead. It stands to reason that one of their bloodied ilk is involved.'

'There's nothing to indicate vampire,' Thane said, glancing at Dr Singh. 'Right?'

'Nothing on any of the bodies,' the pathologist agreed.

No, but vampires weren't the only Preternaturals who understood death. Pathologists understood death; necro-mancers understood death; assassins understood death – and so did Redcaps. I thought of Trilby and their repeated comment that I didn't ask the right questions. I'd fallen into that trap yet again.

'I'd like to talk to Fitz Williams,' I said quietly.

Adrienne had wrapped her arms around her body. Her face was pale and she looked deeply unhappy. 'Why are we talking about fucking Redcaps?' she muttered. 'We're here so I can see my friends.'

My eyes met Thane's. 'It's only circumstantial evidence,' he said.

Yep.

'We've been wrong before.'

Also yep.

'But something about this doesn't add up.'

255

Definitely yep.

'I'll track down Fitz Williams,' I said. 'You two stay here with Adrienne. Keep her safe.'

Hightower scowled. 'Who will keep you safe?'

'I'll be fine.'

He shook his head. 'No. I cannot let you leave this place on your own.' He turned his head and glanced at the rows of gleaming body lockers. Even with Dr Singh's magic pill, he didn't want to look at an array of corpses. If I left him here, he might cause problems and distract Adrienne from her own grim purpose.

I looked at Thane again and he nodded. 'I'll stay with Adrienne,' he said. 'You take Quentin. Find this Redcap and see what he has to say for himself.'

Lucky old me.

Hightower straightened his shoulders. 'Tell you what,' he said, as if Thane hadn't spoken at all. 'I'll speak to this Redcap. Kitty, you can come with me. The wolf can stay and protect Adrienne here. He's up to the job.'

I gritted my teeth. 'Sure,' I said, dredging up every ounce of remaining patience I could find. 'That's a good idea.'

He was already heading for the door. 'Come on then!'

'Don't kill Quentin Hightower, Kit,' Thane advised quietly, a faint gleam of amusement in his eyes. 'You'll only regret it later.'

I wasn't so sure about that.

CHAPTER

THIRTY

It didn't take long to establish that, like Cindy, Fitz Williams didn't work weekends, but it did take a long time to persuade Quentin Hightower that we needed to visit the Redcap ourselves. 'It makes more sense to summon Mr Williams to us,' he said several times over.

'He won't turn up to work on a Sunday, Quentin.'

'If he has any modicum of pride in his work, he will come.'

Seriously? 'Everyone is allowed time off – everyone *needs* time off. He's not at our beck and call. We have to go to him.'

He pouted. 'If you tell him that *I* am here waiting for him, he'll come. I'm Quentin Hightower, Kitty. You know that.'

Alas, I did. 'That plan might work unless he really is the perpetrator who's killed four people in quick succession,' I pointed out. 'If he's the murderer and he knows that you're on his trail, he'll be more likely to run than to come.'

'Hmmm.' He scratched his chin. 'Perhaps you're right.'

'Perhaps,' I muttered sarcastically and gave him a long look. The man was baffling. Sometimes he was capable of making clever leaps of deduction and sometimes he could be perfectly sensible; he displayed a caring nature and protective instinct towards others. Yet sometimes his brains appeared to be made from cotton wool – and it was impossible to tell from one moment to the next which version might appear. Not for the first time, I wondered what sort of man he might be if I could burst his gargantuan ego.

Sneezy Matt found Fitz's address for us: the Redcap lived less than a mile from the mortuary. As we set off, Hightower waxed lyrical about the ways in which he would get Fitz Williams to talk. 'I can be very persuasive, you know. It's always been one of my many skills.'

I didn't bother responding; Quentin Hightower wasn't interested in hearing what I had to say.

'Of course, if my sweet silver tongue isn't enough to encourage him to talk, there are other ways. We can pull off his fingernails.' He waved his hands towards me. 'You can take care of that icky stuff while I ask the questions.'

I might have possessed different morals to many other people, but I didn't agree with torture. 'This isn't the Spanish Inquisition, Quentin. We won't be doing anything of that sort.'

He rubbed his chin. 'Bribery is always an option.'

It would take an immense amount of bribery to persuade someone to cop to four murders. 'What are you suggesting?'

'My good word counts for a lot,' Hightower mused. 'I could get him onto the waiting list for the Pendle Club.' He named a famous private members' club.

'Onto the waiting list? Wow.'

He flicked me a look. 'You are mocking me. It's a highly prestigious organisation, Kitty. There is a waiting list for the waiting list.'

Thank goodness it wasn't a long walk to Fitz Williams' house. The Redcap lived in a narrow terrace that was remarkably bland considering its location. As we found the right door, I crossed my fingers and hoped that he was home.

I stepped forward, knocked loudly and we only waited a few moments before the door opened. It took me a second or two to recognise Fitz out of uniform and confirm that he was the Redcap I'd encountered at the river. Without his sombre black clothes and blood-red hat, he passed for normal.

'Hello.' He smiled genially. 'I'm afraid that I'm not buying whatever you're selling.' Then his gaze focused and he jolted as he recognised my face. When he looked at Hightower, he was even more surprised. 'You're ... you're...'

'Quentin Hightower. Yes.' The witch's chest puffed out. 'It is a pleasure to make your acquaintance, Mr Williams.'

The Redcap stepped backwards, suddenly wary. 'What can I do for you?'

'We are here,' Hightower began, 'because—'

'Because,' I interrupted hastily, 'we're investigating a series of recent deaths that have been linked to the Mathers Street mortuary. As the team leader of the Redcaps assigned there, we thought you might have some insight into them. You might have seen something that other people missed when you collected the bodies.' I wanted to play this as casually as possible. It was the only way to encourage Fitz Williams to talk to us.

'It's my day off,' he said. 'Come and find me tomorrow and I'll help you all I can.' He started to close the door.

Hightower reacted with more alacrity than I expected and shoved his foot between the door and the frame, then he used his hand to keep it open. 'We've already established that you know who I am. My coven is one of the most influential and important groups in the city, Mr Williams.'

I blinked. Hightower had spoken gently but there was an air of command in his voice. I could already see reluctant acceptance in Fitz Williams' expression. Perhaps Quentin Hightower would have his uses here after all. His massive ego and vast sense of self-importance existed for a reason.

'Fine,' the Redcap muttered. 'I suppose you'd better come in.' He moved back and we were in.

The interior of the house was as unremarkable as the street. The walls were magnolia, there was no artwork on display, and the furniture was more utilitarian than pretty. We walked past a coat stand that held three identical versions of the red cap and two long, black coats. Three pairs of shiny black boots were neatly lined up on the floor, and a long black cane was leaning on the wall next to them. Everything had a place.

It was the same when we walked into the living room: there was no dust or dirt, and no haphazard cushions or books lying around. On top of the mantelpiece a gold-coloured carriage clock was ticking away merrily.

Fitz caught me looking at it. 'It was my father's,' he muttered. 'Received in return for forty years' service to the Redcaps.'

It wasn't a lot to show for forty years but I nodded anyway. 'What a lovely memento,' I said warmly.

Fitz wrinkled his nose in silent disagreement but my relaxed manner seemed to do the trick. He gestured to the chairs. 'Please, sit.'

I perched on the edge of a chair so that I could spring up and either attack or defend as the situation called for. Quentin Hightower also sat down but he sank backwards, making himself as comfortable as he could.

'We've met before,' I said, as if Williams didn't already know that. 'Down at the river when Simon Campbell's body was recovered.'

He didn't miss a beat. 'Campbell? That was his name?'

'Yes. I didn't like the thought that he would always be John Doe so I decided to find out who he was. That's how I met Mr Hightower – he was at the river at the same time as Simon

Campbell.' I kept my eyes fixed on Williams. 'In fact, they chatted to each other.'

Hightower nodded gravely. 'Simon gave me some dried silphium leaves.'

Fitz tilted his head. 'Silphium? What's that?'

I watched him carefully as Hightower replied, 'Just an old herb.'

The Redcap's face betrayed little emotion. 'Okay.' He leaned forward. 'I suppose you're curious about why my Redcaps attended that scene instead of the closer cohorts.'

I smiled brightly. 'Yes.'

Williams bit his lip. 'It's because of the coffee. Black's serves the best coffee in Coldstream, so when we have time between jobs we head there to grab a cup. It's worth the extra distance. We were already at the river market when the body was pulled from the water so it made sense to get involved.'

He addressed Hightower. 'We were in full uniform which makes us pretty conspicuous. If we hadn't helped with retrieving the body, people would have been upset. Nobody likes to see a corpse lying around unattended.'

'Fair point,' Hightower nodded. 'Very fair. You did a good thing by getting involved.'

I cleared my throat. 'You told me that you'd been ordered to take the body to Mathers Street, but you were the one in charge so you made that call, didn't you?'

Fitz's eyes were clear. 'Yes. I lied to you because I thought you were a nosy member of public who was getting in our way. It happens more often than you think. And you *were* nosy and you *were* getting in our way.'

I couldn't argue with that.

'That sounds like our Kitty!' Hightower said cheerfully. 'Now tell me, did you notice anything about the body?'

Fitz frowned. 'That's not my job.'

'But I bet you still notice things,' I said.

He acknowledged my words with a brief smile. 'The victim hadn't been attacked by river monsters in the way I'd expected. But that was because of your colleagues, wasn't it, Mr Hightower?'

'Yes.' Hightower smiled. 'It was. They are good fellows. Loyal. And strong.'

I pressed on. 'Did you notice anything else about the body? Was Mr Campbell carrying anything? Did you find anything in his pockets?'

'I didn't check his pockets – that's not what we do. We gather up bodies and transport them from the scene. It's not our job to get involved any further.'

Hightower glanced at me, pursed his lips and nodded in an obvious fashion. 'Excellent,' he said. 'Well, thank you for your time, Mr Williams. I think we have all we need.'

Not even close. 'I believe your Redcaps also attended the scene at Knox Thunderstick's house?'

Fitz gave me a polite smile. 'Who?'

'A druid,' I explained. 'He was tied to his bed, tortured and then shot.'

The Redcap's eyes widened. 'Oh yes, we were there. That was terrible. I can't imagine who would do such an awful thing to another living being. There was a lot of blood at the scene and it wasn't easy to free the body from its position on the bed. We were there because that street falls under our jurisdiction.'

'That answers that, then.' Hightower started to struggle out of his chair.

'And you also attended the death of a troll on the other side of the city. Ian Ravensheart?' I asked.

Fitz's expression darkened. 'I'm not quite sure what you're getting at. We've collected a few dead trolls recently. If you're referring to the one I think you are, that was because the

Redcaps who serve Baller Mortuary were busy retrieving the remains from a house fire nearby. We are a close-knit organisation. Each team helps out others when it is called for.'

He had an answer for everything.

'Have you ever been to the MET building, Mr Williams?' I persisted.

'Yes, I have.' He held my gaze. 'Many times. I've been there to collect bodies and to give statements. I know Captain Wilberforce Montgomery very well – he's a good man.'

'As are you,' Hightower said loudly. 'You have answered our questions without hesitation or prevarication. Thank you so much for your time, dear Fitz.'

The Redcap smiled. 'Anything for a member of the Hightower coven.'

Hightower's eyes twinkled. 'Indeed. Tell me, have you ever considered becoming a member of the Pendle Club?'

For fuck's sake. This was getting us nowhere. I stood up. 'Thanks for your time,' I said. 'We'll leave you in peace.'

'No problem.' Fitz led us out of the living room towards the front door. 'I'm happy to have been of help and I wish I could do more, but I really don't know anything about the bodies I retrieve. All we do is collect and transport – we're not investigators.'

While the Redcap reached for the door latch, I stumbled and fell against Hightower. He, in turn, staggered clumsily and his shoulder hit the coat stand before knocking into the black cane propped against the wall. It fell to the floor with a clatter.

'I'm so sorry!' I exclaimed. 'That was all my fault.' I bent down and stretched out my hand to the cane.

'Leave it!' Fitz said sharply. 'I'll get it.'

I ignored him and picked it up. It was heavier than I'd expected. When I curled my fingers around its handle and squeezed, there was an odd clicking sound. I smiled. Fitz Williams stood stock still.

'Well, look at this, Quentin.' I held up the long stick. 'This is more than just a cane. You see? There's a thin blade hidden inside it.' The metal glinted as I pulled it free from its holder. 'How interesting.'

Fitz Williams looked at me with flat, dead eyes. A heartbeat later, all hell broke loose.

THIRTY-ONE

The Redcap lunged forward, grabbed Quentin Hightower literally by the scruff of his neck and hauled him back to use as cover. He delivered a hard punch to the side of the witch's head for good measure. 'Drop the cane or your buddy gets it,' he snarled.

As far I was concerned Hightower could look after himself, but he was pale and obviously dazed from the punch. He squeaked and kicked uselessly against Fitz Williams' hold. 'Help,' he choked. 'Help me.'

For fuck's sake. 'Use that damned rigor spell.'

Hightower's eyes widened. 'No. Not again.'

So much for his knight-in-shining-armour approach. I supposed I'd have to play hero yet again. It was becoming a nasty habit.

Williams tightened his hold around Hightower's neck but he hadn't thought through his actions. If he killed Quentin Hightower, there would be nothing stopping me from killing him in return. Hostage situations like this never worked out the way the perpetrator wanted and the Redcap would realise that in about three seconds' time.

I adjusted my grip on the cane-cum-rapier, weighed up my options at lightning speed, then flicked the blade forward and scraped its tip along Williams' bare wrist. The wound was deep enough to release plenty of bright-red blood that splattered both the wooden floor and the front of Hightower's costly suit.

'Bitch!' Williams snarled as his grip on Hightower slackened.

I side-stepped and jabbed the thin blade at him again, aiming for his exposed flank. He twisted away in the nick of time and shoved Hightower towards me. The stunned witch staggered forward and sent me off-balance while Williams spun around and threw open his front door. Oh no, you don't.

When I jumped over Hightower I landed badly, but I managed to snag the black material of Williams' trousers with one hand. There were downsides to expensive clothing: the material was tightly woven and far less likely to rip even in my tight grasp.

He hissed and kicked, his boot connecting with my face with such force that my teeth rattled. Ouch. That hurt. He shoved his hand into his pocket, drew out a bag and tossed the contents at me, but his aim was off and they hit the wall and exploded into a cloud of dark green smoke. I jerked back but my skin was scorched in several spots as a few tendrils of the magicked vapour curled against me.

I heard Hightower groan, but he muttered a word and the smoke started to dissipate. At least he had some damned uses.

I avoided yet another kick in the face and used my free hand to smash down onto Williams' right knee with enough force to make him shriek in pain. I couldn't risk him escaping. Here in his house the battle was contained but anything might happen out on the street.

I released my hold on his trousers, scrambled up and jumped over him so I could close the front door, then I returned his kicks with one of my own and booted the side of his head. I could have killed him – it was a testament to my restraint that I didn't – but at least he started moaning with pain.

Hightower had pulled himself to his feet. He strode forward until he was straddling the Redcap's fallen body. It was a stupid move because Fitz wasn't out for the count yet. Before I could warn the witch, the Redcap thrust one leg upwards and connected with Hightower's groin. It was the witch's turn to scream as he staggered backwards and clutched himself.

I twisted the blade and held it in front of Fitz's eyes. One quick thrust and it would all be over for him. 'How? How did you learn about the silphium?' I demanded.

Fitz Williams glared. 'Tell me,' I hissed, lowering the tip of the rapier until it hovered an inch from his forehead. His glare intensified. 'The troll,' he bit out. 'Ravensheart came to me, thought I might be interested. He showed me a sample of the silphium but he was too stupid to know its true worth. When I realised what it was...'

'You killed him,' I said.

'I did. I shouldn't have done it.'

'Because killing is bad,' Hightower squeaked in a high-pitched voice.

Fitz rolled his eyes. 'No, because I didn't realise until it was too late that he only had some leaves. To grow more silphium, I needed seeds and Ravensheart didn't have any.'

'So you went searching for them,' I said. 'You went after Simon Campbell.'

'I followed him to the market and watched him give a sample of silphium to that idiot.' Williams jerked his head towards Hightower, who frowned. 'I couldn't allow that stupid witch to hand out silphium like it was candy to anyone who happened by.'

'So you stabbed Simon and pushed him into the Tweed.'

'I stabbed him but I *didn't* push him into the river,' Fitz corrected. 'It was muddy – it had been raining a lot. He fell in before I could search his body.'

Everything was starting to make sense. 'So that was why you played your Redcap card. After Simon's corpse was pulled out of the river, you wanted to search him and the easiest way to do that was to call in your buddies and make it a job.'

The Redcap grunted. 'It was a waste of time. He didn't have any silphium seeds on him. I found his keys in his pocket and used them to get into his flat, but there weren't any seeds there either.'

'So you went after Knox.'

A trace of pride flickered in his eyes. 'I was smarter with him,' he said. 'I took my time. I questioned him.'

'You tortured him.'

Williams snorted. 'Much good it did me! He said that Campbell had the seeds but I knew that wasn't true. I'd already searched Campbell's flat and I knew from the mortuary that there was nothing else on his body. And then that damned Fetch started getting suspicious and came after me. He said he wouldn't say anything about the murders if I gave him the seeds.' He bunched his hands into fists. 'But I didn't have the fucking seeds. I couldn't risk it.'

'So you killed him too.' I clicked my tongue. 'Quite a little mess you've made for yourself.'

The Redcap's eyes spat pure hatred. 'Do you have them? Do *you* have the silphium seeds? They'll change the world. You have no idea about the powerful magic those seeds can conjure up. It's two thousand years since silphium existed and now it could be back. The person who controls the supply will be rich beyond their wildest dreams.'

I smiled. 'The seeds have gone.'

'Bullshit!'

When Hightower answered, his voice sounded more normal. 'Kitty is perfectly correct. Simon Campbell had the only silphium seeds in existence. They must have gone into the river with him. There is no more silphium, not anywhere.'

'You're lying,' Fitz snarled.

My voice was gentle. 'You know he's not. Unless any more silphium plants appear on top of Myrddin's grave, there are only a few dried leaves in existence and that's it. This is over for you now – it's over for all of us.'

Quentin Hightower leaned over Williams. 'You're wrong, Kitty. It's not over at all, not for this fellow. He will be locked up for a very long time.'

Damn it: if I'd been alone, Fitz Williams would have been dead. I hissed through my teeth but thankfully Hightower was too focused on his own achievement to notice.

'For Mr Williams, this is the beginning.' He beamed proudly. 'You fought well, sir, but you are no match for me.' He thumped his chest. 'In the end, good prevails.'

I wished that were always true but I managed to smile at Hightower anyway. 'Good work,' I told him. 'You were magnificent.'

'I was, wasn't I? I was right not to resort to another rigor spell.' He nodded to himself. 'You'll learn from this, Kitty. One day, you might be almost as good at taking down the bad guys as I am.'

I was outside on the street, absently plucking cat hairs from my top, when Captain Montgomery approached. 'Ms McCafferty,' he said, greeting me with a nod.

'Hello,' I replied, cheerfully.

'We've conducted an initial search of the property and uncovered some items of interest.'

'Oh yes?' I asked innocently.

'We found a gun,' he said. 'It will have to be sent away to Glasgow for ballistics, but it appears to match the calibre of the weapon that was used to shoot Knox Thunderstick.'

'My goodness.'

'The concealed blade you discovered inside Fitz Williams' cane seems to match the wound found on Simon Campbell's body, although we haven't confirmed that yet.' He paused. 'How did you know there was a lethal weapon concealed in it?'

Because it was where I would have hidden one if I'd been a Redcap. 'I stumbled against it by accident,' I said smoothly. 'It was pure chance.'

'Hmmm.' The captain eyed me; he'd once been prepared to believe I was a harmless cat lady but I doubted he did now, more's the pity. 'We also found a photograph which we believe was taken from Ian Ravensheart's property.' He held up a sealed bag.

I squinted at the photo of four disparate friends: a nymph, a troll, a druid and a witch. My gaze lingered on the image of Simon Campbell, the man who'd started me off on this entire investigation. He was wearing jeans held up with a belt and a dark, slouchy jumper. His right hand rested lightly on the large brass belt buckle.

'Do you notice the background? Do you recognise where this photo was taken?'

'I believe that's Myrddin's grave,' I said. 'Knox Thunderstick appears to be holding a plant.'

Montgomery nodded. 'He does. I don't recognise it. I wonder if it's important, Ms McCafferty.'

I shrugged.

'Hmm.' He watched me for another few seconds then

glanced over his shoulder at the MET officers trooping in and out of the house. Two members of the witches' council stood to the right, their expressions tight as they watched the action. On the left, there were two equally grim druids, presumably representing the druidic board of governors.

'We also found a small quantity of trevishate,' Montgomery said. 'And some magicked valerian.'

'Goodness me! You don't suppose those materials could have been used to blast off the doors of the MET office, do you?'

'It's possible. We'll have to test them to be sure.'

'Did you find anything else?' I asked. 'Any seeds, perhaps?'

'Funny,' Montgomery murmured. 'That's exactly what the witches and the druids asked me, too.'

'Oh?'

'The answer is no. There are no seeds but we did find a small nosegay that contains an interesting substance. Dried leaves of some sort. They appear to be quite powerful.'

'Is that so?'

'Yes, Ms McCafferty, it is.' He continued to watch me. 'It's quite extraordinary what you've achieved. You have tracked down a prolific murderer and ensured they will never kill again.'

'Me?' I placed a hand on my chest. 'Oh no, none of this was me. I was only tagging along. The real hero is Quentin Hightower – he is truly extraordinary.'

We both turned and looked at Hightower. He had gathered a small crowd around him and his arms were wide as he regaled his rapt audience with his tale. 'I discovered a lethal blade concealed inside Fitz Williams' cane. As soon as I saw it, I knew the truth. I knew he was a stone-cold killer who had to be brought to justice.'

'Extraordinary,' Montgomery agreed. 'Extraordinary indeed.'

I smiled, then I spotted a pair of emerald green eyes gazing at me from beyond where Quentin Hightower was standing. Thane doffed an imaginary cap and bowed. I curtsied. We both straightened and grinned at each other.

'I'll take my leave, Ms McCafferty,' Montgomery said. 'But I expect our paths will cross again before too long.'

Before I could respond, he turned on his heel and walked away. I didn't bother watching him go. Thane had missed all the action yet again and would want to hear what had happened, but this was about more than a mere update report. I wanted to enjoy a long, celebratory drink with my copper-haired werewolf. Suddenly nothing mattered except that.

CHAPTER
THIRTY-TWO

When I pushed open the door to the Mathers Street mortuary on Monday morning, Cindy was already at her desk. Perched next to her, licking his paws, was He Who Roams Wide. I gave my cat a long look. In return, he purred.

'You again?' Cindy asked. 'What now? I thought you were done with us and this whole palaver was over.'

I offered her a bright smile. 'Almost done,' I said cheerfully. 'There's one small matter to clear up.'

She sighed. 'I'll fetch Dr Singh,' she said reluctantly. 'He's through the back.'

'I don't need to talk to him, Cindy,' I told her. 'It's you I'd like a wee word with.'

She eyed me warily. 'What? If you're here to complain that I've stolen your cat, I can tell you that he's chosen to be here. He can leave at any time.'

'I know. I'm not worried about him – and thank you for looking after him. I'm sure he's enjoyed more of your excellent chicken.' As I glanced at him, He Who Roams Wide rolled onto his back and presented me with his belly. From his sleek fur and content expression, he'd been enjoying far more delicacies than chicken. Lucky boy.

'What then?'

'Have you had a pay rise in the last few days?' I enquired.

She started. 'How do you know about that?'

I wasn't going to diminish her pleasure by telling her that I'd suggested she deserved more money, so I simply nodded and put my hands into pockets. I wanted to look unthreatening; I wasn't here for a fight. 'Is it enough?' I asked.

'Enough for what?'

When I didn't respond, Cindy narrowed her eyes. 'It's very generous,' she said when it became clear that I wouldn't answer her question.

'Good,' I said. 'Because if you're earning enough money, you won't need to steal from the dead any longer.'

'What?' she exclaimed indignantly. 'What are you talking about?'

I pointed to the scarf around her neck, the same expensive silk scarf she'd been wearing the first time I'd come here. 'That's not yours,' I said.

She touched it. 'Of course it is!'

I shook my head. 'It doesn't match any of your other clothes. If you had the money to spend on things like silk scarves, you'd be wearing other expensive items.' I gestured to the delicate bracelet around her wrist. 'Like that piece of jewellery.'

'It was a present,' she said defensively. 'So was the scarf.'

Uh-huh. 'Who from?'

'None of your fucking business.' Her eyes darted from side to side. He Who Roams Wide stopped rolling around on his back and got to his feet. He butted his head against her hand and sat down, curling his tail around his body and watching me.

I kept my voice gentle. 'I don't particularly care. I know you've only taken items from bodies that don't have next of kin or remain unidentified. Dr Singh told me himself that's up to fifty people a year. I'm not judging your actions.'

'I'm not a thief!'

'After all,' I continued, 'it's not as if they need those things any more. They're dead so they don't need silk scarves or pretty bracelets.' I paused. 'Or belts with brass buckles to hold up their trousers. I bet nobody ever misses any of those items. In fact, I reckon nobody's even noticed they're missing.'

Cindy stared at me. I stared back. 'I'm not a bad person,' she whispered.

'You have to live with your conscience, Cindy,' I said. 'I have to live with mine. It's not for me to pass judgement.' I meant it and I liked to think she realised that.

'What will you do?' she asked.

'Nothing.' I smiled again. 'But I do need the clothes and the belt that came from Simon Campbell's body.'

Her eyes were wide and worried. 'I was planning to return them when he was formally identified. Then that Fetch came, and Dr Singh found out that they were missing...'

'And you thought that returning them might cause more problems than it would solve. I understand. Are they here?'

She bit her lip then she nodded. 'In my bag. I laundered the clothes,' she said, as if that might take the sting out of what she'd done. 'They were very wet and muddy.' She disappeared beneath her desk and rummaged around. He Who Roams Wide flicked his tail and I dipped my head in his direction to show that I understood.

After a moment Cindy re-emerged holding carefully ironed blue jeans, a shirt – and a belt. She dropped them onto the desk beside He Who Roams Wide. 'What were you planning to do with them?' I asked. 'They're not your size and they're men's clothes.'

Cindy hung her head. 'I was going to sell them,' she whispered. 'They wouldn't fetch much money but I thought the belt might be worth something.'

Poor Cindy had no idea. I picked it up and turned it over. Fitz Williams wasn't the only person with clever ways of concealing useful items.

I found the small catch on the underside of the belt buckle and flicked it. A section of the buckle fell away, revealing the tiny bag inside. Opening it, I gazed at the seeds. Seven little brown specks. A king's ransom.

'Wh – what?' Cindy goggled.

'Don't worry about it.' I returned the belt to the pile of clothing. 'You should put these in the back. Simon Campbell's family might want them.'

'But—'

'The filing system here is terrible,' I said kindly. 'I doubt anyone would be surprised if the clothes turned up unexpectedly. And I also doubt that I'll be back, so you don't have to worry about any more visits from me.' Hanging around mortuaries wasn't my idea of a good time. I raised my eyebrows at He Who Roams Wide. 'Are you coming?'

His whiskers twitched then he stood up, gave Cindy's hand a tiny lick and jumped off the desk before padding over to me.

'Thanks, buddy,' I told him. 'You did good.' I raised my hand in farewell as Cindy stared at me and my cat, her mouth wide open. 'Take care,' I told her. I glanced down. 'Your turn.'

He Who Roams Wide miaowed.

I DIDN'T NEED to say anything to Thane when I left the mortuary with He Who Roams Wide; he could already tell from the expression on my face. 'You know the smart thing would be to throw them into the Tweed?'

'And what if more silphium plants appear on Myrddin's grave when spring rolls around in a few months' time?'

He shrugged. 'We cross that bridge when we come to it.'

I considered. 'I'm not a fan of the passive approach. There are better ways to deal with this.'

'If any one group has sole control of those seeds, Kit...'

I smiled. 'They won't. There are seven seeds and that gives us room to work with.'

Thane rubbed his chin. 'One for the witches' council? Another for the druid governors?' I nodded. 'One for Harriet, one for Simon Campbell's family and one for the Ravenshearts?' I nodded again. 'Adrienne?'

'I think she deserves it,' I said. 'Don't you?'

'That still leaves one seed,' Thane mused. 'For you?'

'Nope.'

'Trilby?'

'I believe they have enough power at their fingertips already.'

'Me?'

I gave him a long look. 'You move around too much. Have you ever successfully grown a plant?'

'I used to have a cactus that I took with me every time I moved.'

'What happened to it?'

Guilt flashed across his face. 'It died.'

'You managed to kill a *cactus*?'

'I over-watered it. I guess I'm not green fingered,' he said.

'Uh-huh.' I started walking away from the mortuary

towards the south side of Mathers Street. He Who Roams Wide trotted beside me, his tail held high.

Thane caught up and fell into step beside us. 'So what happens to the seventh seed, Kit?'

'My next-door neighbour has a lot of space in his garden,' I said.

'Dave?'

'He won't pay attention to a small clump of weeds growing in the corner.' I grinned. 'It'll be a good insurance policy if anyone decides to try and control the whole supply of silphium.'

'Is that a wise idea?' Thane asked doubtfully.

'It's the best,' I said. I dropped back and allowed him to pull in front of me; it afforded me an excellent view of his very tight, very well-rounded arse. I tilted my head. 'The very best, in fact.'

'Kit, are you ogling my bottom?' he enquired.

'Yep.'

There was a beat of silence. Then Thane spoke again. 'Good.'

Author's Note

Author's note

I came across silphium when I was researching lost treasures for the *Thrill of the Hunt* books, and I was immediately fascinated. It was as Mallory describes: an unidentified plant that came from Cyrene and was so important to the city's economy that it was stamped on their coins. The theory is that the shape of its seeds inspired the love heart symbol that we are so familiar with today. Alas, silphium has been considered extinct since the second century BC, possibly as a result of desertification.

History suggests that silphium was used by the Romans as a seasoning, an aphrodisiac, a contraceptive and a medicine. If you'd like to know more, you can read about it on the Kew Gardens website: https://www.kew.org/read-and-watch/silphium-mystery

Alas, silphium has not been discovered on Myrddin's alleged grave – however, the famous magician is purportedly buried at Drumelzier in the Scottish borders ... right next to the River Tweed.

ABOUT THE AUTHOR

After teaching English literature in the UK, Japan and Malaysia, Helen Harper left behind the world of education following the worldwide success of her Blood Destiny series of books. She is a professional member of the Alliance of Independent Authors and writes full time, thanking her lucky stars every day that's she lucky enough to do so!

Helen has always been a book lover, devouring science fiction and fantasy tales when she was a child growing up in Scotland.

She currently lives in Edinburgh in the UK with far too many cats (and dogs!) – not to mention the dragons, fairies, demons, wizards and vampires that seem to keep appearing from nowhere.